This book is due for return on or before the last date shown below

novel with a good plot
Sydney Morning Herald

cursed

a werewolf's tale

David Wellington

piatkus

PIATKUS

First published in the US as *Frostbite* in 2009 by Three Rivers Press,
An imprint of the Crown Publishing Group, a division of
Random House, Inc., New York
First published in Great Britain as a paperback original in 2010 by Piatkus

A CIP catalogue record for this book
is available from the British Library.

ISBN 978-0-7499-5238-9

Typeset in Bembo by M Rules
Printed and bound in Great Britain by
Clays Ltd, St Ives plc

Papers used by Piatkus are natural, renewable and
recyclable products sourced from well-managed forests and certified
in accordance with the rules of the Forest Stewardship Council.

 Mixed Sources
Product group from well-managed
forests and other controlled sources
www.fsc.org   Cert no. SGS-COC-004081
© 1996 Forest Stewardship Council
FSC

Piatkus
An imprint of
Little, Brown Book Group
100 Victoria Embankment
London EC4Y 0DY

An Hachette UK Company
www.hachette.co.uk

www.piatkus.co.uk

For Mary

part one

the drunken forest

one

The ground shook, and pine needles fell from the surrounding trees like green rain. Chey grabbed a projecting tree root to steady herself and looked up to see a wall of water come roaring down the defile, straight toward her.

She barely had time to see it before it hit—like the shivering surface of a swimming pool stood up on end. It was white and it roared and when it smacked into her it slapped her face and hands as hard as if she'd fallen onto a concrete sidewalk. Ice cold water surged up her nose and her mouth flew open, and then water was in her mouth and choking her, water thick with leaves and pine cones that bashed off her exposed skin like bullets, water full of rocks and tiny pebbles and reeking of fresh silt. Her hand was torn away from the root and her feet went out from under her and she was flying, tumbling, unable to control her limbs. Her back twisted around awkwardly as the water picked her up and slammed her down again, picked her up and dropped her hard. She felt her foot bounce painfully off a rock she couldn't see—she couldn't see anything, couldn't hear anything but the voice of the water. She fought, desperately, to at least keep her head above the surface even as eddies and currents underneath sucked at her and tried to pull her down. She had a sense of incredible speed, as if she were being shot down the defile like a pinball hit by a plunger. She had a sickening, nauseating moment to realize that if her head hit a rock now she would just *die*—she was alone, and no one would be coming to help her—

And then she stopped, with a jerk that made her bones pop and shift inside her skin. The water poured over and around her and she heard a gurgling rasp and she was underwater, unable to breathe. Something was holding her down and she was drowning. With all the strength she had left she pushed upward, arcing her back, fighting the thing that held her. Fighting just to get her head above the water. She crested the surface with a sucking gasp and water flooded into her throat. Her body flailed and she was down again, submerged again. Somehow she fought her way back up.

White water surged and foamed around Chey's face. She could barely keep her mouth above the freezing torrent. Her hands reached around behind her, desperately trying to find what was holding her down, even as the water rose and she heard bubbles popping in her ears. Her skin burned with the cold and she knew she would be dead in seconds, that she had failed.

She had not been prepared for this. She thought flash floods were something that happened in the desert, not in the Northwest Territories of the Canadian Arctic. Summer had come to the north, however, and with the strengthening sun trillions of tons of snow had begun to melt. All that runoff had to go somewhere. Chey had been hiking up the narrow defile, trying to get up to a ridge so she could see where she was. She had climbed down into the narrow canyon to get away from a knife-sharp wind. It was rough going, climbing as much with her hands as her feet, but she'd been making good progress. Then she'd paused because she'd thought she'd heard something. It was a low whirring sound like a herd of caribou galloping through the trees. She had thought maybe it was an earthquake.

Now, stuck on something, unable to get free, she tried to look around. The current had dragged her backward across ground she'd just covered, pulling her over sharp rocks that tore her parka, smearing her face with grit. She could see nothing but silver, silver bubbles, the silver surface of the water above her.

Her hands were numb and her fingers kept curling up from the cold as she searched behind herself. Chey begged and pleaded with them to work, to move again. She felt nylon, felt a nylon strap—there—her pack was snagged on a jagged spur of rock. Fumbling, cursing herself, she slipped the nylon strap free. Instantly the current grabbed her again, pulling her again downward, down into the defile. She grabbed at the first shadow she could find, which turned out to be a willow shrub. Hugging it tight to herself, she coughed and sputtered and pulled air back into her lungs.

Eventually she had enough strength to pull herself upward, out of the water. It now ran only waist deep. With effort she could wade through it. After the first explosive rush much of the water's force had been spent and she could ford the brand new stream without being sucked under once more. On the far bank she dragged herself up onto cold mud and exposed tree roots and lay there, shivering, for a long time. She had to get dry, she knew. She had to warm herself up. She had fresh clothes and a lighter in her pack. Tinder and firewood would be easy enough to come by.

Slowly, painfully, she rolled over. She was still soaking wet and freezing. Her skin felt like clammy rubber. Once she warmed up she knew she would be in pain. She would have countless bruises to contend with and maybe even broken bones. It would be better than freezing to death, however. She pulled off her pack and reached for its flap. Unfamiliar scraps of fabric met her fingers.

The flap was torn in half. The pack itself was little more than a pile of rags. It must have been torn apart by the rocks when she'd been dragged by the current. It had protected her back from the same fate, but in the process it had come open and all of her supplies had come out. She shot her head around to look at the stream. Her gear, her dry clothes, her flashlight—her food—must be spread out over half the Territories, carried hither and yon by the water.

With shaking fingers she dug through the remains of the pack. There had to be something. Maybe the heavier objects had stayed put. She did find a couple of things. The base of her Coleman stove had been too heavy to wash away, though the fuel and the pots were lost, making it useless. Her cell phone was still sealed in its own compartment. It dribbled water as she held it up but it still chirped happily when she clicked it on.

She could call for help, she thought. Maybe things had gotten that bad.

No. She switched off the phone to conserve its battery. Not yet.

If she called for help now, it might come. She might get airlifted out to safety, to civilization. But then she would never be allowed to come back here, to try again. She would not be able to get what she'd come for. She shoved the phone in her pocket. She would need it, later, if she survived long enough.

The map she'd been given by the helicopter pilot was still there, though the water had made the ink run and she could barely read it. The rest of her stuff was gone. Her tent was lost.

Her dry clothes were lost. Her weapon was nowhere to be found.

She spent the last of the daylight searching up and down the steep bank of the new stream. Maybe, just maybe something had washed up on the shore. Just as the moon came up she spied a glint of silver bobbing against a half-submerged log and jumped back into the water to get it. Praying that it was what she thought it was, she grabbed it up with both hands and brought it up to her face. It was the foil pack full of energy bars. Trail food. She started to cry, but she was so hungry she tore one open and ate it instead.

That night she buried herself under a heap of pine needles and old decaying leaves.

two

In the morning she was itchy and damp and her skin felt like it had been scoured with a wire brush, but she knew that the second she tried to move out of her pile of needles, the real torment would begin.

She was right. When Chey did finally move her arms and legs and sit up, every muscle in her body felt like it had hardened into stone overnight and now was cracking. The stiffness hurt, really hurt, and she realized how rare it was to feel true pain when you lived in a civilized place. You might stub your toe on your coffee table, or even jam your finger in a car door. But you never felt a river pick you up and bang you against a bunch of jagged rocks until it got bored with you.

She sat curled around her knees for a while, just breathing.

Eventually she managed to get up on her feet. She had to make a decision. North, or south. South meant giving up. Turning her back on what she'd come for.

She checked her compass and headed north.

After an hour of walking the stiffness started to go away. It was replaced by searing pain that came with every step she took in her water-logged boots, but that she could wince away.

She kept walking, through the trees, until she thought she might collapse from exhaustion. The sun was still high above the green and yellow branches, but she couldn't take another step. So she sat down. She thought about crying for a while, but decided she didn't have the energy left. So instead she unwrapped one of her protein bars and ate it. When she was done she got back up and started walking again, because there was nothing else to do. Nothing that would help her.

Time didn't mean much among the trees, because everything looked the same and every step she took seemed exactly like the one before it. But eventually it got dark.

She kept walking.

Until she thought she heard something. A footfall on a crust of snow, maybe. Or just the sound of something breathing. Something that wasn't human.

Keep walking, she told herself. It's more afraid of you than—

She couldn't bring herself to finish that thought without laughing out loud. Which she really didn't want to do.

She came to a gap in the cover of branches overhead and a little moonlight leaked through, enough that she could look around her. The sky was alive with colors: the aurora borealis burning and raging overhead. She forced herself not to watch it, though—she needed to scan the shadows around her, searching for any sign of pursuit.

She peered and squinted so hard into the gloom that she almost fell, her hands wheeling out in front of her to catch herself, and then she decided she needed to keep an eye on her footing. Buckled by permafrost, the ground refused to lie flat. Instead it bunched up in wrinkles that could snag her ankle if she wasn't careful. The black trees stood up in random directions, at angles to the earth. The ground rose in sharp hillocks and sudden crevasses that hid glinting ice. Chey's feet kept catching on exposed roots and broken rocks. She could barely trust her perceptions anyway, not after what she'd been through, with nothing to eat but energy bars, no real sleep, no shelter except the fleece lining of her torn parka.

There was nothing out there, she told herself. It had just been her half-starved brain playing tricks on her. The forest was empty of life. She hadn't seen so much as a bird or a chipmunk all day. She stopped in her tracks and turned around to look behind her, just to prove to herself she wasn't being followed.

Between two of the trees a pair of yellow eyes flickered into glowing life, blazing like the reflectors of a pair of flashlights. They caught the fish-belly white moonlight and speared her with it. Froze her in place. Slowly, languorously, the eyes closed again and were gone, like embers flickering out at the bottom of a dead campfire.

"Oh, shit," she breathed, and then slammed a hand over her mouth. Underneath the parka she could feel the hair on the back of her arms standing up. Slowly she turned around in a circle. Wolf. That had been a wolf, a timber wolf. She was certain. Were there more of them? Was there a pack nearby?

She heard them howl then. She'd heard dogs howl at the moon before, but not like this. The howling went on and on and on, with new voices jumping in and following, a sound almost mournful in tone. They were talking among themselves and she figured they were telling each other where to find her.

She lacked the energy to go another step. Her face contracted in a grimace of real terror. Then she dug deeper inside of herself, deeper than she'd ever been before, and she ran.

The trees flashed by her, leaning to the left, the right. The gnarled ground tore at her feet, made her ankles ache and burn.

10

She kept her arms up in front of her—despite the half-full moon she could barely see anything, and could easily collide face first with a tree trunk and snap her neck. She knew it was foolish, knew that running was the worst thing she could do. But it was the only thing she could do.

To her left she saw flickering gold. The eyes again. Was it the same animal? She couldn't tell. The eyes floated alongside her, easily keeping up with her pace. The eyes weren't expending any effort at all. The feet that belonged to those eyes knew this rough land by instinct, could find the perfect footing without even looking. The Northwest Territories belonged to those eyes, those feet. Not to human weakness.

To her right she heard panting. More than one of them over there, too. It was a pack, a whole pack, and they were testing her. Seeing how fast she could run, how strong she was.

She was going to die here, as far from civilization as anyone could ever be. She was going to die.

No. Not quite yet.

Evolution had given her certain advantages. It had given her hands. Her distant ancestors had used those hands to climb, to escape from predators. She needed to unlearn two million years of civilization in a hurry. Ahead of her a tree stood up from the leaning forest, a big half-dead paper birch with thick limbs starting two meters off the ground. It rose five meters taller than anything around it. She steeled herself, clenched and unclenched her hands a few times, then dashed right at it, her aching feet catching on the loose bark that pulled away like sloughing skin. Her hands reached up and grabbed at thin branches that couldn't possibly hold her weight, twigs really. She shoved herself up the tree, her body, her face pressed as tightly to the trunk as she could get them, until a wave of ripped bark and crystalline snow came boiling across her face. Suddenly she was holding on to a thick

11

branch three meters above the earth. She pulled herself up onto it, grabbed it with her whole body. Looked down.

Six adult wolves stood staring back up at her. Their golden eyes were placid and content. She could almost see laughter there. Their long sleek bodies gleamed in the half-light. They had their tails up and wagging.

"Go away," she pleaded, but their leader, a big animal with a shaggy face, leaned backward, stretching out his forelimbs, and sank to lie down on the carpet of musty pine needles and old brown leaves. He wasn't going anywhere.

One of the others, slightly smaller—a female, maybe?—raked at the birch tree with its claws. The wolf's tongue hung out of its mouth as it reached higher and higher. It opened its mouth wide as if yawning and let out a devilish screech that elongated into a full-blown howl. The others added their voices until Chey vibrated on her perch, feeling as if they could shake her out of her refuge with nothing more than their yowling.

Were they—laughing at her? Mocking her distress? Or maybe they were just singing to pass the time. Waiting for dinner to fall out of the tree.

"Go away!" she screamed, but her voice was small inside the orchestra of their howls and yelps. She shouted and screamed but couldn't match their sound. She wanted to press her hands against her ears, to block it out, but then—

—the wolf calls stopped. All at once. In the silence that followed she could hear flakes of snow dropping to the forest floor from the branches over her head.

Then—from deep in the forest, another call came. Slightly different. It held the hint of a growl. A challenge. Instantly the wolves were up and looking from side to side. Their tails went down and they glanced at each other as if to ask if they had all heard it.

The new call came again. It was unlike the sad moaning of the wolves. It was more wicked, more chilling. It was hateful.

The wolves beneath Chey's branch scattered, disappearing into the darkness as silently as they'd come. The new cry came a third time then, but from much, much closer by.

three

They scrambled backward on her branch. She had an urge to be closer to the trunk of the tree, with as much solid wood around her as possible. Every time the howling roar came out of the forest her skin literally crawled, ripples of gooseflesh undulating up her arms and down her back.

There was something down there, something angry and loud. Something nasty enough that it could scare off an entire pack of timber wolves. What was it, some kind of bear? But it hadn't sounded like any bear she'd ever heard on television or in the movies.

She scanned the ground around her tree, straining her eyes in the dark, looking for any sign—any shimmer of movement, any footprints, any low branches stirred by something moving past.

But there was nothing. Not even the glint of light from a pair of eyes, or a reflection off a shiny coat as it moved stealthily through the underbrush. Nor could she hear anything. She craned all her perceptions downward, held her breath and listened to the creaking sounds of the tree, the faint groaning of the branch that supported her. She didn't hear any panting, or any near-silent footsteps. Maybe, she thought, it had gone away. Maybe it had never been interested in her—maybe it had been howling like that just because it had wanted to move the timber wolves along. Maybe it had no problem with her at all. Maybe it couldn't even hear or smell her, up in her tree.

Then she heard a crash as something big came running through the litter of the forest floor and she almost yelped in her terror. She felt a desperate urge to urinate, but she clamped her legs harder around the branch and that helped a little.

She heard the creature snuffling from not ten meters away. Nosing through the undergrowth like a snorting boar. Winkling out her scent, she was sure. She reached into her pocket and grabbed her cell phone for comfort. Maybe—maybe it was time to call for help. Maybe things had gone too far. But no, even that was pointless. Help could never come in time to save her now. She clutched the phone hard, as if it were a magical talisman that could protect her. She supposed if she had to she could throw it like a rock. It was the closest thing to a weapon she possessed.

She curled up against the side of the tree with her legs holding tight to the branch. She breathed through her nose, and tried not to panic, and didn't make a move.

It didn't matter, of course. The beast could probably smell her from kilometers away.

She could see it now. There had been no moment when it went from invisible to visible, but suddenly it was down there, moving. Far too close. It curled around the birch like a liquid shadow, like darkness poured out on the ground.

Then it stopped, its muscles coiling up under baggy skin. Chey stopped breathing. It looked up.

The horror was not very much larger than the timber wolves, perhaps two meters long from nose to tail, maybe a meter and a half tall at the shoulder. It possessed the same broad flat face as the wolves. If anything its muzzle was shorter but far more wicked-looking. The main difference in its features were its teeth. The timber wolves had lots of teeth, of course, yellow and sharp. This thing had enormous pearly white fangs. There was no other word for them but fangs. They were huge, and thick, so big they pushed aside its lips. They looked perfectly adapted to crushing bones. Big bones. Human bones.

The other big difference between this thing and the timber wolves was in the way its paws spread out across the snow, as broad as human hands, each digit ending in a long curved claw. Its coat was mottled silver and black, more striking in its coloration than the dull camouflage of the timber wolves.

She took its shape in all in an instant, but after she saw them she had trouble looking at anything but its eyes. *Those eyes*—they were not yellow, like those of the timber wolves, but an icy green, narrow and cold. Intelligence resided in those eyes as well as something else, a dreadful anger. She could read it quite plainly, as well as she could have read the eyes of a human being. This animal didn't want to eat her. It didn't consider her prey. It wanted to kill her.

Those eyes.

Memories lit up in her head like neon signs begging for her attention. Memories that had never been far below the surface. She knew those eyes. She'd crossed half a continent to find them. And now they were going to kill her.

The monster despised her so much it wanted to tear her to pieces and scatter her remains across the forest floor. It wanted to spill her blood on the ground and grind her skull to shards with its giant teeth. The weight of that look, of that evil stare, made her press even harder backward against the tree. It made her want to hide away, to do anything to escape such passionate loathing.

The beast's hackles came up and its tail went down. Its lips pulled back from its teeth and a noise like a motorcycle revving up leaked out from between its jaws. And then it leapt at her.

Pushing hard against the ground with its hind legs, it threw itself into the air. Its forepaws slashed at the space just below her dangling feet. Its mouth opened to grab her legs and crush them into paste. At the top of its leap it was only centimeters short of her feet. It fell back to earth with a snarl and panted as it scratched and clawed at the yielding bark, snarling and growling its thwarted desire. Chey just had time to adjust her hold on the tree before the wolf leapt at her again.

"No," she begged, but the beast came up at her as fast as if gravity had been reversed, as if the world had been turned upside down and it were falling up at her, its teeth snapping together in midair. She pulled back, trying desperately to get away, but one forepaw caught her in the ankle, a vicious claw sinking through skin and muscle to grate on the bone. Pain flashed through her like a red strobe light going off. For a second she heard only the blood rushing in her head, and saw nothing but the blood vessels at the backs of her eyes.

The monster fell back again, its claw pulling free of her flesh.

Next time it would get a better grip. She was sure of it. She would die in the next few seconds, she realized. She would die, a victim of this enraged creature, if she didn't do something, and right away.

She scrambled up against the trunk of the tree and lunged for a higher branch. She missed. Her leg throbbed and she gasped in pain, but she knew if she didn't get farther up the tree the beast would get her. It was just that simple. She reared up, grabbed a branch that looked like it might barely support her weight, and hauled herself up, even as she started hyperventilating and stars shot through her vision.

The beast jumped for her a third time, but she was out of its range. She tried not to look down, but that was impossible.

At the base of the tree the monster dropped down on its haunches and stared at her. Its breath huffed in and out of its lungs in thick plumes of vapor. It was willing her to fall, to let go and fall. She could feel its desire. Its wanting.

Then the impossible happened. It turned its gaze away from her, if only for a moment. It looked out through the trees to where the moon was beginning to sink toward the horizon. When it turned to look at her again its palpable hatred was tempered with bitter resentment. It smoldered up at her for a while, then twitched its shoulder around and disappeared into the dim forest as quickly and as quietly as it had come.

It had to be a trick, she thought. But the wolf was gone.

Those eyes!

four

The big wolf didn't come back.

Chey spent hours waiting for it to return, praying that it wouldn't, trying to imagine what she would do if it did. Her adrenaline kept her hyperventilating and trembling for a long time. Eventually it wore off and her body started hurting and her brain started going in circles. Every little sound startled her. Every time she thought she saw something move she jumped and nearly fell. The moon was down, below the horizon, and eventually the aurora flickered out as well, and the only light came from cold and tiny stars, and still she sat vigil, still she studied the ground around her, over and over until she had memorized every little detail, the placement of every twig and dead leaf. Exhaustion and cold seeped through her, freezing her in place.

At dawn she decided to climb down out of the tree.

It was harder than she thought it was going to be. Her body was stiff and grumpy, her nerves and muscles rebelling, disobeying her commands. Her ankle, where the wolf had snagged her, had swollen alarmingly. A crust of dried blood glued her

Timberland hiking sock to her skin. Every time she moved the ankle her entire leg started to shake uncontrollably.

Going up the tree had taken mere seconds—driven by panic and the survival instinct, she had reverted to her monkey ancestry and just done it. Getting back down took some thought and planning. First she had to get her hands to let go of the branch. Then she realized there was no good way to get down—no easy footholds, and the thin branches she'd used to climb up looked far less appealing when she reached out to put her weight on them. Finally, after long minutes of adjusting and readjusting her position, moving from one branch to another, teetering on the edge of a bad drop, she hung down by her arms and let herself fall onto her good foot. The touch of solid ground ran through her like an electric shock. It felt so good, though—to have something firm and reliable underneath her. To not be constantly terrified of falling. Tiredness surged up through her bones then. She dropped to her knees, wishing she could drop farther, that she could fall down entirely, lay down and go to sleep.

Not when the wolf might still be out there, though. She had no idea why it had left her, nor did she know when it might return. She would not sleep again until she knew she was safe.

With filthy weak hands she went through her pockets and checked the small collection of items she still possessed. Absurdly enough, she had thought often in the darkness that her things might have fallen out of her pockets as she raced up the tree. But no, she still had them. She had one last quarter of an energy bar, which she shoved in her mouth. The foil wrapper went back in her pocket—as bad as things were, Chey didn't litter. She had her phone, the battery almost dead. When the keys lit up blue for her she almost cried in gratitude. At least something still did what it was supposed to.

She didn't think she could say the same for the tiny compass attached to the zipper pull of her parka.

It pointed north for her, as it always had. She had followed it like a lifeline, held it carefully in her fingers like a jewel. It had been the thing that was going to save her, a connection to the civilized world of maps and coordinates and everything in its proper place. She had believed in it with much more faith than she'd ever placed in God. Now she had to admit that her faith might have been misplaced. Either the compass or her map were completely wrong. She should have reached the town of Echo Bay by now—it was almost perfectly due north of where she'd started—but she had seen nothing so far except the endless crazily tilted forest.

Maybe the town didn't exist. Maybe when they printed the map they'd made a mistake.

Maybe she was going to walk for weeks more, heading north like a good little Girl Guide until she ran right into the Arctic Ocean. Or maybe, long before that—yes, almost certainly before that happened—the wolf would find her again when there were no tall trees around, and it would kill her.

She closed her eyes and bit her lower lip. She was so scared her back hurt. Fear tried to bend her in two, to make her fall down and curl up and wish herself into nonexistence.

"Okay," she sighed to herself. "Okay." The sound of human words broke the spell. Hearing a voice, even her own, made her feel less alone and defenseless. She brushed off her parka as best she could—it was covered in tiny shreds of birch bark and less pleasant materials—and stood up. Her knee buckled the first time she stepped forward with her hurt ankle, and she had to stop for a second and wait for the roaring in her ears to die down. The next step hurt slightly less.

"Okay," she said. Louder. More confidently. The hard *k* sound was the part that helped. "Okay, you little idiot. You're going to be okay."

The trees swallowed her up without comment. Her slow pace made it easier, actually, to cross the rough ground. She had plenty of time to look and see where each foot should go, to avoid the potholes and the knobby tree roots. She had time to listen to the sound of pine needles squishing and crunching under her feet, to the squeak of old snow as her boots sank down through it. She could smell the forest, too, smell its pitch and its rotting wood and its musty perfume.

She walked for an hour, according to the clock display of her cell phone. Then she stopped to rest. Sitting down on a dry rock, she pulled her knees close to her chest and looked back the way she'd come. There was no trail or path there—she felt really proud for how she'd covered so much unbroken ground. Then she looked up and saw the paper birch she'd sheltered in the previous night.

It stood no more than a hundred meters behind her. In an hour that was all the distance she'd covered.

Tears exploded in her throat. Chey bit them back, sucking breath into her body. "No," she said, though she didn't know what she was rejecting, exactly. "No!"

She was lost.

She was alone.

She was wounded.

She knew how to add up those figures. She knew what the sum would be. Those three variables were what separated happy, healthy young women from corpses no one would ever find. Her body would fail her, the life drained out of it by the cold or the rain or by loss of blood or—or—or by the big wolf. It would come back and finish the job, and maybe eat part of her. As soon as it was gone smaller animals would pick at her flesh, and leave what they, in turn, didn't want. In time her bones would bleach white and then even they would decay, and no one, not her family, not her friends, not the ex-lovers she'd left behind her, would ever know where she'd gone. Maybe a million years from now, she thought, she would be a fossil, and some future paleontologist would dig her up, and wonder what she was doing there, so far from any human habitation.

"Goddamn it, no!" she shrieked. "I won't stop here! Not when I've come so far. Not right here!"

Her shout echoed around the trees. A few needles fell from a spruce that stuck up at a thirty-degree angle to the forest floor.

"I won't," she said, as if saying it aloud could make it so.

In the distance a bird called back to her with a high bell-like note she didn't recognize. It sounded almost mechanical, actually, less like an animal sound than something man-made. Maybe it hadn't been a bird at all. It sounded almost like a fork clinking on a metal plate.

She looked down at her compass. North was straight ahead, which meant the sound had come from the southwest. She closed her eyes and concentrated, and heard the clinking sound again. If she concentrated, really concentrated, she was pretty sure she could hear something else, too—the sizzle and pop of frying food.

five

They staggered through the trees, drawn by the smell of cooking. It was over—her nightmare of being lost in the woods was over. Finally she would see another human being, someone who could help her. Animals didn't cook their food. Wolves especially didn't cook their food. Her ankle hurt like hell and a bright light went off behind her eyes every time she stepped on that foot, but she didn't much care. There was someone nearby, somebody human. Someone who could help her, someone who could save her.

Her bad foot got her to the edge of a clearing and then gave up, spilling her across moss and snow. She raised herself up on her arms and looked around.

The clearing was no more than ten meters across, a raised bit of earth that ran down toward a thin stream meandering through the trees. A campfire had been built at its high point and a black iron skillet sat smoking in the coals, strips of what looked like back bacon glistening inside. It was enough to make her mouth water.

By the fire sat a man wearing a fur coat. No, that was giving the garment too much credit. It looked like a pile of ragged furs, brown and gray like the colors of the forest. The man himself was short, maybe shorter than Chey, though it was hard to tell when he was sitting down. He had his back to her and he was bent over the skillet, meticulously adjusting its contents.

"Hello," she croaked, and brushed dead leaves off her face.

There was no reaction. She realized her voice was so weak it might be mistaken for the creaking of the branches overhead. Chey pushed herself up higher and cleared her throat, then dredged up the strength to say, "Hey! You! Over here!"

The man turned and Chey let out a strangled yelp. At first his face seemed featureless and raw. Then she realized he was wearing a mask. It was painted white and it had narrow flat slots where his eyes and his mouth must be. Stripes of brown paint led upward from the eye slots.

The man reached up and pushed the mask up, onto the top of his head. Beneath it his face was wide and round and very surprised. He'd probably never expected to see another human in these woods—much less a bedraggled, wounded woman pulling herself along the ground by her arms. He rose from where he'd been sitting by the stream and came toward her, his furs swinging as he walked.

"Dzo," he said.

"I'm sorry," Chey told him, shaking her head. "I don't speak Inuit."

"Neither do I," he said, in English. "The nearest Eskimo is in Nunavut, the next territory over. The people around here are Sahtu Dene nation. That's if you want to get particular, which I normally don't, and if there were any of them actually around here, as in, within a hundred kilometers, which there aren't. Dzo."

"Dzo," she repeated, thinking it must be a traditional greeting.

25

"Yeah, that's me."

Chey squinted in frustration. Dzo must be his name, then. It sounded a little like "Joe" but just different enough to be hard for her to pronounce.

"I'm Chey," she said. "It's short for Cheyenne."

He smiled for a moment, then gave her a friendly nod. Then, without offering her a hand up, he went back to his fire and sat down. He lay food carefully in the skillet, not even looking at her.

Chey tried to think of something to say that would express her indignation but without offending him to the point where he wouldn't help her. When she failed to think of anything appropriate, she painfully rose to her feet and limped over to where he sat. She waited a while longer to be invited. When he said nothing more, she gave up and sat down on a rotten log next to his fire. The warmth it gave off was almost painful as it thawed out her frozen joints, but welcome all the same.

For a while she just sat there, hugging her knees, glad not to be walking anymore. Dzo didn't seem to mind her presence, but he didn't offer her food or ask if she was okay, either. Chey was cold and starving and as near death as she'd ever been, but even in her diminished state she could wonder at what was wrong with this guy. Didn't he see how badly she needed help?

"Wolves," she said. "They nearly got me. One kind of did. There was this pack of wolves—they followed me—"

"Wolves?" he asked. "You were attacked by wolves?" He sounded as if he was asking if she'd seen any interesting wildflowers on her way to his camp.

"Yeah. A whole pack of them," she said. "And then, this one, this big one—"

"No worries there," he told her. "A wolf will never attack a human being. Even out here, where they've never seen a human before, it just doesn't happen. You just don't look like their food.

Most likely they were just curious, or they were trying to play with you. That's all."

Her leg was proof of the opposite, she thought. But then again, it hadn't been a normal wolf that had gotten her. She thought about trying to explain what had happened, but she wasn't sure he would believe her. "I know what I saw!"

It was the best defense she could think of. It didn't seem to make much of an impression on him.

"I don't," he said. "I wasn't there."

She closed her eyes and tried to summon up some kind of calm rationality, some piece of perfect logic that would break through his surreal refusal to understand what was going on. "Look," she said, and then didn't know how to proceed. "It doesn't—it doesn't matter what I saw. I'm still lost," she said, finally.

"You'd kind of have to be," he told her. "Otherwise why would you be out here?"

She nodded, uncertain of what he meant. "I'm in trouble," she added. "I'm hurt."

Dzo looked up as if he'd just realized she was talking to him. His eyes went wide and he studied her ankle for a second. She held it up for him, let the light from the fire glisten on the dried blood that coated her pant leg. "Oh, boy," he said, finally. "Now you'll forgive me, I hope. I don't meet many new folks up here. My whatchamacallems—my social skills—are a little rusty, yeah?" He rested one fur-gloved hand on her shoulders and she almost sank into the touch, she was so glad for a little human contact after so long alone in the trees. The hand lifted away immediately, though, and then patted her shoulder two or three times. "There, there," he said, and looked away from her again.

Was he mentally handicapped, she wondered, or just unbalanced from being alone in the woods for so long? Her

27

immediate survival depended on this man. She was pretty close to despair. Struggling with her emotions, she dragged up the story, the one she'd practiced so many times she half believed it herself. She used recent real events to flesh out the bare-bones details. "I was heli-hiking out of Rae Lakes. It was a 'North of 60' adventure package, right? They take you up north, about as close to the Arctic Circle as you want to get, so you can see the real wilderness, the primeval forest and stuff. Drop you in the woods with some supplies, give you a map, and tell you where they'll come pick you up. And then when we were done they were supposed to fly us to Yellowknife for a spa day before we had to head back to civilization. For the first couple of days of hiking it was okay, I guess. I mean, I was having fun even if it was way too cold. Then out of nowhere it went to utter hell. I got separated from the rest of the group. I got lost."

She closed her eyes. Clutched herself a little harder. Went on.

"I was climbing up this valley and then there was just all this water. I was carried away and my pack was—anyway, I washed up a little way downstream with no gear and no way to contact the helicopter to come pick me up. I knew they would send helicopters to look for me, but this part of the world is just too big and too empty. They were never going to find me. If I wanted to live I had to walk out of there."

Dzo nodded, but he was watching his frying pan.

"I had to find other people, people who could get me back to safety. I had lost my good map in the river, but I still had a brochure from the heli-hiking place with a sort of map on it. It said if I walked due north I would eventually come to a place called Echo Bay."

That got his attention, though not necessarily in the way she'd hoped. Dzo let out a booming laugh. "Echo Bay? Why'd you want to go there, of all places?"

28

"It was the only town on the map," she insisted. "Here, look," she said, and pulled the crumpled, water-stained brochure out of her pocket. She smoothed it out on her thigh and showed him— the map included the roads around Yellowknife, and Echo Bay and the enormous lake beyond it, and a whole bunch of white space in between. She'd been in the white space for days now. "It's on the shore of Great Bear Lake, on the eastern shore—"

He held up a hand to stop her. "I know where it is, and I know your orienteering skills are crap, lady. You overshot your mark by a couple hundred klicks."

"What are you talking about? It was due north of my position." She grabbed the compass on her zipper pull and waved it at him. "They told us as much when they dropped us off, if we walked far enough due north we would get there. I followed this every step of the way."

"You were following that?" He started giggling. At her. "That thing points at *magnetic* north," he told her. "You wanted *true* north."

She could only stare at him as if she had no idea what he was talking about.

He sighed and held up his hands as if to say, what can you do with these southerners? "Magnetic north, that's centered on the pole of the planet's magnetic field, okay? That's where your compass is pointing, where it's always going to point. But the magnetic field doesn't line up perfect with the actual axis of the earth, the imaginary line that it rotates around. The magnetic field pole and the axis are a couple hundred kilometers away from each other. So the compass doesn't point north at all, really. Maybe down south where you come from nobody's ever heard of the difference, but up this far you always have to compensate when you're using a compass. You know that if the compass says north, you actually want to head a little bit to the west, right?"

"Okay," Chey said, not really following.

He shook his head and turned to look at his skillet again. With his bare fingers he flipped its contents over so they cooked evenly. "You keep following that compass and you'll end up in Nunavut. Which, believe it or not, is even emptier than this place. Wow, lady, it's kind of a miracle you survived this long. Considering how stupid you've got to be."

He winced when her face darkened in anger.

"Hey, hey now, I'm sorry, like I said, I'm no good with people," he told her. "Lucky for us both, I'm better with a compass." He laughed again and pulled a strip of something pale and greasy out of his skillet. "Here, eat this," he said, nearly dropping it in her lap. "I'm sure you didn't bring enough food, either."

"Thanks," she snarled, but she bit into it. It wasn't meat, whatever it was—it had barely any taste at all. "What is this?" she demanded, even as she took another bite.

"It's the inner bark of the lodgepole pine tree," he informed her. "Totally edible, I promise. Just about the only thing you can eat in this forsaken wilderness."

She'd been looking forward to back bacon, but she supposed she couldn't complain. Well, maybe a little. "You couldn't hunt for game?" she asked, as she chewed vigorously on the stringy vegetable matter.

He pulled his furs closer around himself, then smiled very wide when he said, "I'm a vegetarian."

six

Dzo let her lean on his arm as they hiked out of the clearing. It was a blessed relief not to have to put her full weight on her hurt ankle. It still throbbed like mad, though, and she was terrified it might be getting infected. She didn't want to take another step on it if she didn't have to. If he faltered, or if she lost her grip on him, it was going to hurt badly, but he didn't let that happen. He was shorter than Chey, maybe ten centimeters shorter, but his shoulder felt hard as a rock and she got the impression he could easily have carried her. Not for the first time she wondered who this guy was, and where he'd come from. She tried asking, but his answer didn't make much sense to her. "I came up from the water down there," he told her.

"No, but originally," she said, thinking she needed to be very careful to be as literal as possible when talking to him.

"Gosh," he said, and looked up at the trees as if trying to remember. "That was a long time ago. I think there was less water back then. Everything was so dry." He shrugged. "Things change, you know? Places change. Especially up here. Seems like it's different every summer."

Her leg hurt too much for her to want to quiz him further. She decided it was enough he was there, and that he could save her, and she lapsed into silence as they trudged along.

They headed along the course of the trickling stream. The water was cold and very clear. Red pine needles spun on the surface and caught on exposed tree roots and then slid past them again. Insects skimmed along the surface or walked on the water with hair-thin legs longer than their bodies. None of them were biting her, so she ignored them.

Not so very far away from the stream ran an abandoned logging road. It didn't look like much to Chey—it definitely wasn't paved, and must not have been graded in years, judging by its rough surface. Mostly it was just a winding lane, a ribbon of fallen pine needles where the trees didn't grow quite so closely together. You had to follow it carefully with your eyes to see it at all, but Dzo assured her that to the animals of the forest it was like a six-lane superhighway. "I've got a friend, now, who's only about twenty klicks from here. He can patch you up right quick," he assured her when she demanded to know where they were headed.

"Twenty kilometers?" she gasped. On her ankle she'd be lucky to get twenty more paces. He just nodded, making no attempt to reassure her that she could do it—and then led her to another clearing, where his pickup truck waited. She was so relieved to see the vehicle that tears leaked out of the corners of her eyes, dehydrated as she was.

It looked like she wasn't going to die in the woods after all.

The truck had little to recommend it other than its very existence. The body was the color of old rust, more brown than red. The bed was strewn with dirt and dead leaves and organic debris, and the passenger's side window had been replaced with yellowing plastic, held on with layer after layer of peeling invisible tape. Chey had never seen a vehicle so old and decrepit that was still capable of driving before. When Dzo turned the old screwdriver that had been jammed into the ignition lock the engine started up just fine, however, and once they were under way the truck's chained tires grabbed the snowy ground and held tight.

They rolled down the path doing no more than fifteen, Dzo keeping one easy hand on the wheel while the other drummed slowly and rhythmically on the outside of his door as if he were keeping time. The trail wound back and forth and seemed to cut back across itself. To Chey it constantly looked as if the trees would close in and cut off their forward progress altogether, but then they would chug around a corner, dead tree branches rattling and scraping at the roof, and then there was always more path ahead of them. Dzo never spoke and Chey didn't have much to say herself. Before she knew it she had put her head back and collapsed into sleep.

When the truck braked for a stop her head flew forward and she snapped back to consciousness. For a second she couldn't remember where she was, or what had happened to her, but it all flooded back when her ankle twinged and searing pain shot up all the way to her hip. She looked around and saw that the light had changed—she must have been asleep for hours. The plastic in her window warped what she could see outside, but it looked like more of the same, trees pointing up at strange angles, the ground choked with underbrush. On the other side, to the left, though, the trees had been cut back to make a neat little patch of open ground. A wood-framed house with red shutters stood in the middle of the clearing, with an outhouse to one side and a pair of low sheds to the other. Bluish smoke reefed up out of one of the sheds, dribbling out of its poorly sealed eaves, and she thought it might be on fire.

But Dzo didn't seem alarmed, so she guessed it was supposed to do that. Maybe it was a smokehouse or a sweat lodge or something.

"Is this where you live?" Chey asked.

"Nah," her savior told her. "It's my friend's place, like I told you. Mostly I sleep rough, but he's a civilized type, likes an actual bed with a pillow."

It sounded like heaven.

Dzo jumped out of the truck without a word to Chey and pulled his white mask across his face before running up to the door of the house. His furs swung back and forth as he pushed open the door and popped his head inside. He shouted "Hello" a couple of times, and then, "Hey, Monty, you around?" No answer was forthcoming. He trotted around the side of the house and was gone from view.

Chey wanted to follow—she didn't relish the prospect of being alone, even for a second longer—but she didn't dare try to walk on her hurt leg. Leaning forward to peer through the muddy windshield, she studied the roof of the house. The shingles looked immaculate, as if the roof had just been repaired. She did not find what she was looking for—satellite dishes, radio masts, shortwave antennae, anything of the kind—which made sense. If she was where she thought she was, there would be no direct connection with the outside world at all.

When Dzo didn't come back after a few minutes she decided she was going to have to make her own way over to the house. Maybe, she told herself, it would be warmer inside. Maybe it would have central heating. Or at least a wood-burning stove.

She eased her door open and then jumped down onto the packed earth of the clearing, careful to land on her good foot. She smelled wood smoke and pollen, and somewhere nearby another smell, a musky animal odor. She heard a footstep crunch on fallen pine needles and she gasped as she spun around, hopping like a spastic. There was someone behind her.

He was a slender young man dressed in a gray cotton work shirt, jeans, and a pair of undecorated cowboy boots. His hands, which she saw first, were rough and dirty, but the fingers were thin and sensitive. He had a pale face and coal black hair, cut short and combed neatly, with a part to one side. His cheeks and forehead were smooth—he couldn't be over forty, she thought—but deep cobwebs of wrinkles surrounded his eyes, as if they were much older than the rest of him. The eyes were clear and inquisitive and in color they were an icy green she had seen before. Oh, yes, she would never forget that color.

They were *those eyes.*

Gotcha, she thought to herself. She kept a tight rein on her emotions and let nothing show in her face.

seven

They smiled at the householder. "Hi. I'm Chey," she said. "Cheyenne Clark. You must be Monty," she went on, holding out her hand. He took it and shook it once, a ritual he barely had the grace to complete. His grip was firm but not crushing—the handshake of a man who had absolutely nothing to prove.

"And you must be Dzo's latest find." He looked her up and down and his eyes stopped on her hips. If he lived out here in these woods year-round (and he did, she knew, she was certain of it), she wondered how long it had been since he'd last seen a woman. "My friends call me by my Christian name, Montgomery," he told her, turning away, toward the house. He walked away from her as he spoke. His body language told her she could follow if she wanted but he didn't care one way or another. His body language was lying, and badly. She could feel his attention on her, even with his eyes turned away. "I don't know you. You can call me Mr. Powell. What's taking you so long?" he said, finally turning to look at her again. On her bad ankle she couldn't keep up with him.

He looked at her again and this time he noticed her blood-

36

stained sock and her swollen leg. "Damnation," he said, so softly she barely heard him. As softly as the noise the pine needles made when they hit the ground.

He came over to stand very close to her, close enough she could smell him. He didn't stink like a mountain man, but he wasn't wearing any deodorant or cologne or even aftershave. Mostly he smelled of wood smoke.

He bent down and started unlacing her boot. That hurt, a lot, but he didn't stop even when she whimpered and leaned back against the hood of the truck. With one quick yank he pulled off her boot, and then her sock.

She didn't want to look. She did not want to see what she'd been dreading—the angry wound, the purple suppurating flesh around it. The black-and-yellow mottling where her ankle had swollen up until the skin was ready to crack open.

"This isn't so bad," he said.

Was he humoring her? She didn't think he was the type. She risked a glance downward.

Her ankle was smeared with dried blood, but not as much of it as she'd expected. There was a scar running along the outer side of her ankle, thick with raised tissue, but . . . but it looked old. It looked like it had healed over months ago. There was no swelling, nor any sign of infection at all.

Impossible—why had it hurt so much? And how had it healed so quickly? It couldn't be that—

"Wait here," Monty growled. Without any more words he hurried off around the side of the house. She heard Dzo's voice, heard the weird little man laugh, but his mirth was cut off short. The two of them started muttering back and forth, but she couldn't hear them properly. She was pretty sure of what they were saying.

Gingerly, being very cautious, she put her injured foot back into its boot, not bothering with the sock. Then she leaned on it, just a little. It hurt to put her weight on it. It hurt a lot. But not nearly as much as she'd expected.

She could walk again. Which meant she had some options.

She limped to the front door of the house and stepped inside. She needed more information.

The little house comprised a single room and an attic, with a ladder leading up into the latter instead of stairs. It smelled of very old smoke and relatively new mildew. The sunlight coming in through the yellowed curtains gave the place a butterscotch color that was homey without being quaint. The furnishings inside, which were few in number, were mostly hewn out of raw wood. The seats of the chairs and the top of the table had been sanded down and finished, but in other places old bark still decorated the legs of a stool or the underside of a shelf. There was no television set, no radio, no sign of electricity. Well, where would it come from? There were no power plants this far north, nor any grid. It made her wonder where Dzo got fuel for his truck.

There was in fact a wood-burning stove, but it wasn't lit. A box of waterproof matches sat on top of a wood scuttle next to the stove, but there was no firewood there and she didn't see anything she could use to start a fire, so she left the stove alone. She didn't have time to get a proper fire going, anyway. Any second now the two men were going to reach a decision and come looking for her.

She searched the rest of the little house for food—she was starving, and perfectly willing to steal anything remotely edible—but turned up little of interest. Powell did all his cooking on the stove, it seemed, though there were few pots or pans in evidence. Certain he had to have food somewhere, she climbed up the ladder and investigated the cramped second

38

story. No food there either, but the upper level showed some signs of personality, at least. Powell slept on a mattress laid on the floorboards of the attic. The sheets were neatly tucked in underneath with hospital corners. A kerosene lantern stood near the pillow and was flanked by piles of books—old dog-eared paperbacks from decades past, everything from Zane Grey to spy thrillers to nurse stories. A neat stack of textbooks and technical manuals lay near the foot of the bed, mostly science stuff. Chemistry, a guide to edible plants, *Elements of Surveying and Civil Engineering.* None of the books was less than seven years old. The newest item was a well-thumbed *Old Farmer's Almanac* from 2001. At the far end of the attic she found a couple worn volumes of crossword puzzles. The puzzles had been completed in pencil, then carefully erased—stringy black bits of used eraser fell from the pages as she turned them—and then filled in once more. At the back of the pile she found a Rubik's Cube that had been partially solved, then abandoned, judging by the thick layer of dust on its uppermost face.

She climbed back down the ladder, having learned as much as she supposed she could, and poked around, still looking for food. The fried bark Dzo had given her was doing wonders for her appetite. As if it had forgotten all about the existence of food for ten days, and just now recalled it, her stomach growled and grumbled at her. She found little to satisfy her, however. Powell's cupboards were bare other than a couple of dusty cans of corn and peas that she didn't think would still be good even if she found a way to open them. The faded labels spoke of another era.

His liquor cabinet promised a little something more. She saw some half-full bottles of Scotch and considered how much she'd love to just sit and have a drink—but then she heard the two men coming around the side of the house. She couldn't quite make out what they were saying, so she crouched down under a window where she could hear better and even see them a little without being discovered herself.

"I saw her ankle," Powell said. "She got herself scratched. She's in the club, or she will be very soon."

Dzo shrugged. "Sure, that's why I brought her here."

"I imagine that made sense to you at the time," Powell said. He stopped just outside of the window, but he didn't look in. "I can't let her turn, though. She'll hurt somebody. Maybe she'll even spread this thing. I can't let her do that." He hefted something in his hands. It was an ax, the kind used to chop down trees, with a dull and rusty blade the same color as Dzo's truck. "You want to do the honors?"

"No way," Dzo said, his furs shaking in negation. She couldn't see his face behind his white mask.

"Then I will. The moon'll be up in a few minutes. If we take her head off right now I think it'll still be alright."

By the time he got to the door Chey was gone.

eight

They would have thought it was impossible to run. No matter how much it might have healed, her ankle was still sprained at the very least and all the hobbling around she'd done in the forest had left her leg stiff and sore. Yet when the option was decapitation she found she could run just fine.

Oh, it hurt. Every bone in her leg vibrated with the pain, but adrenaline or endorphins or some blessed chemical in her bloodstream kept her moving.

She dashed between the two sheds at the side of the cabin, her hand slapping the ancient wood of one of them, and caromed into the forest. The trees accepted her without comment as she weaved between their trunks, her feet digging into the carpet of pine needles. She leapt over a deadfall of gray branches as thick as her wrists and came down on the other side on top of a mass of puffballs that exploded in yellow spores. Silently she cursed herself. Any good tracker would see the broken fungi and know she had passed that way. She had reason to think Powell was an excellent tracker.

Could she outrun him? She doubted it. With every step her leg hurt less—perhaps the unwanted exercise was pumping fluid out of her swollen tissues. Still. There was no question in her mind anymore—those eyes had convinced her. He was a monster. He would be faster than her, and much, much stronger. Unless she'd misjudged the intelligence in his eyes and the way he'd watched her, he would also be sneakier. She'd already gotten a taste of that, hadn't she? She'd been on her guard when Dzo brought her to the house, ready, she had thought, for anything. Powell had crept up behind her without even trying.

She dashed around a stand of black spruce that grew so close together it looked like a palisade wall, the trunks nearly touching one another. Ducking down behind this makeshift cover, she forced herself not to make a sound. Not even to breathe too loudly. Maybe—maybe there was something she could do.

The time to use her phone had definitely come. Not that help could reach her in time, but she had to at least try.

She grabbed the cell phone out of her pocket and looked at the screen. No service, of course. Nothing new there. She popped open the battery cover, however, and flicked a tiny switch. The switch wasn't marked. It was even designed in such a way as to look like one of the prongs holding down the SIM card. A very smart person had spent time designing that switch, making it the kind of thing nobody would ever find, even if they got the phone away from her and studied it at length. The screen lit up a little brighter and displayed the message:

LOOKING FOR
SATELLITE
CONNECTION

The phone wasn't meant for this purpose, of course. She wasn't supposed to use precious battery time just to call for help in an emergency. But just then . . . she didn't have a choice.

42

"Come on, come on," she begged, forgetting she was supposed to be silent. A tiny cartoon radar dish on the screen turned back and forth. She shook the phone in her hand as if that might help.

The rusted head of the ax bit into a tree trunk near her face with a resonant *thock*. She froze in place, unable to move, unable to think. The tree vibrated with the noise and the impact. A beetle lifted into the air with an angry buzz, clearly disturbed by the shaking of the branches.

"You don't understand," Powell said, pulling his ax free from the tree trunk with a grunt. "It has to be this way."

Chey sucked breath into her lungs and stared up at him. He was still pulling the ax back, getting ready for another swing. It wouldn't take him long to recover.

Chey had been trained for this particular moment. She visualized a spot ten centimeters behind him, just as she'd been taught. Then she put every ounce of strength she had into punching that spot—her fist driving forward as if it could slam right through him. Her fist collided with his stomach and he gasped in surprise. She gasped, too. Hitting his abdominal muscles had felt like hitting a brick wall. There was no possible way she'd actually hurt him, but it looked like she'd knocked the breath out of him.

The element of surprise, she'd been taught, could mean everything. It could mean the difference between life and death.

No time to think about that, of course. She jumped up and ran again, ran without worrying what direction she was headed in or where she might end up. Her legs did what they needed to do. She was a machine. She'd been taught that line like a mantra: you are a machine, and all your parts work together. When they work together, they can achieve anything. Oxygen cycled into her lungs and carbon dioxide cycled out. She was a machine and she was functioning properly. With one hand she shoved the phone back into her pocket, knowing it couldn't help her anymore. There would be no time for help to come to her, even if she could get a clear connection. The only thing that could save her was herself.

A black-headed loon yodeled overhead and pushed into the air with broad, slow wing strokes. Chey looked up when she heard it. She imagined Powell looking up as well. It wasn't much of a diversion, but she took what she could get and swiveled on her good heel. She dashed into the woods at a ninety-degree angle to the way she'd been headed. Maybe he would keep going straight and overshoot her.

Ahead she heard water bubbling over a shelf of rock. That was good too; if she could get into the water it would carry away her scent. She had reason to believe Powell could track her by smell alone. She could follow the course of the water for a couple hundred meters, then climb back out and into the forest. It was an old trick, one foxes used instinctively when they were being chased by hounds, but she thought maybe it would work—

Powell smacked into her legs from behind, his shoulder catching the small of her back and tossing her to the ground. She hadn't heard him at all, hadn't been aware of him behind her. She tried to roll when she hit the ground and managed to get onto her back with her legs tucked up near her stomach.

"Stop now. Don't hit me again and I'll make this painless," Powell shouted at her. He sounded a little out of breath. That was all she'd managed to achieve. That was what all her training had been worth. She had winded the bastard. A little. "Look," he said, and hefted his ax. "You don't understand. I'm trying to protect you. You and other—protect other people from—"

He couldn't seem to finish his sentence. He reached up and

wiped the cuff of his shirt sleeve across his mouth. Then he looked to the side. "Blast," he finally said.

A surprisingly mild curse to come out of the mouth of an ax murderer. But he made it sound like the most profane thing he could think of.

Chey looked over as well, following his gaze, desperate to know what could be so important it would distract him in the middle of killing her. She could see the brook she'd heard before, and the gap in the trees where it had worn its path over thousands of years. A bit of actual horizon showed there, a hilltop, and a smear of silver light that graced its top. That had to be the moon, she decided. Moonrise had come.

The ax fell out of Powell's hand and thudded at her feet. No—that wasn't right. She watched it fall. She watched it fall *through* him, as if he'd suddenly turned to mist and lacked the solidity necessary to hold the ax. It had fallen through his hand. He was changing further when she looked up at him again. His skin had turned translucent and it glowed as if lit up with moonbeams. His clothes dropped off of him and fluttered to the forest floor. She could see the bones in his fingers, the twin bones in his forearm. She could see through them. He had become as insubstantial as a ghost.

Then silver light erupted behind her eyes and she didn't see anything more.

nine

When a caterpillar turns into a butterfly, it sews itself up into a cocoon just big enough to hold its body. A gossamer coffin—because it knows that in a very real sense it is dying.

Its body dissolves inside the cocoon. Other than a very few cells, the caterpillar liquefies entirely. Its eyes, its legs, its furry segmented body all disappear and are lost forever. Then it rebuilds itself. From scratch. When the butterfly emerges from the cocoon, later on, it will not resemble the original caterpillar at all. It will not remember anything of its previous life, even to the extent that butterflies are capable of remembering in the first place. It will have new powers and senses that it literally could not have conceived of before, but they will not seem strange, because the butterfly has no past experience from which to draw comparisons.

It can fly from the moment it hatches. It does not mourn its former life, any more than it mourns the quiet, liquid time in between.

Something very similar happened, but much more quickly, when the first beam of silver moonlight struck Chey from afar.

The silver light filled up her senses. It didn't so much blind her as suffuse her with light, a blossoming, cold light that passed through every cell in her body as if she were made of perfectly transparent glass. She could see it with her skin, with her heart and her bones as well as she could see it with her eyes—better, even. Beams of that light pinned her to the ground. She struggled, at first, but her struggles changed into a writhing transformation, as her body changed its shape. As her being changed.

It was not what she'd expected.

Hair did not burst out of her skin, nor did her jawbone lengthen and sprout enormous teeth. Her ears did not slide up to the top of her head and stick out in points. There was no halfway state, no hybrid creature, not even for a moment. She was a woman, and the silver light swept through her, and then—

—and then she was a wolf.

The transformation was painless. In fact, it felt good. Really good. It felt like an incredibly intense orgasm that lasted only for a split second, but afterward left her trembling with ecstasy. With a sense that this was right. Natural.

It felt like taking off a suit of uncomfortable clothes at the end of a very long and tiring day. It felt like standing under a waterfall and letting the pounding water drive all the filth and sweat off her body. It felt magical.

It did not feel as if she were a woman transforming into the shape of a wolf. It felt as if she were a wolf awakening from a long and tedious dream in which she had been forced to live in the body of a human being. The distaste she felt for such a state—for the entire state of humanity—was only matched by her relief to be back in her lupine shape, to have returned to what felt like her native skin.

When it was done she opened her eyes again and saw in a whole new way. Her eyes themselves were changed, both in shape and in function. She saw colors, but fewer than her human eyes would recognize—there was no red nor any green in this world, only shades of blue and yellow. Things in the distance were hard to focus on, while the pine needles next to her face took on a supernatural clarity. If her vision was reduced, however, her senses of smell and hearing more than compensated for the lack. She could hear martens and shrews burrowing under the ground, and the sound of a bear scratching at a tree on the far side of the valley. She could smell a whole landscape of animals and plants; she could tell how far away they were from her wholly based on the strength of their odors. It was like she had a map inside her head of the world surrounding her body out to several kilometers' distance, a map that was constantly being updated and gave her more information than she could ever possibly need. By comparison (though she did not then make the comparison, nor would she have wanted to), the awareness, the consciousness of a human being seemed pitifully limited. The woman had only been really aware of objects she could see, and even then only of objects directly in front of her. The wolf was tied in to the world around her as effortlessly and completely as if she were looking down from above with hundreds of eyes at once.

The smells—the smells—everything smelled of something. Every object in the world had a unique odor, an olfactory signature that matched up with some instinct or memory in her brain. This smell meant food. That smell meant water. A third smell meant pine needles, and it was everywhere. There was more to it, though, layers of smells on top of each other. These pine needles had been trampled on by a colony of ants. Those pine needles smelled of the urine of a rabbit—a very exciting smell, indeed. She wanted more, suddenly. She wanted to smell everything, everything in the world, and learn its secrets.

One smell predominated and kept her from fully exploring her new sensorium. It was like a solo note played against the backdrop of a grand symphony and it demanded her attention. She smelled a creature like herself. She looked up and snarled and found herself muzzle to muzzle with him. His frozen green eyes thawed a little when his gaze met hers. He looked almost sheepish.

He had tried to kill her. She couldn't remember the details, but they didn't matter. He had tried to kill her.

There was blood between them, and it had to be settled.

Every other concern in the world could wait.

With a growl back in the deepest part of her throat, she rolled onto her feet and bared her fangs.

His tail between his legs, he stepped closer and pushed his snout into her flank. He was trying to apologize, she knew. The hair between his shoulders, a saddle-shaped patch of fur, stood up and then relaxed. It was a signal and an offering.

He had tried to kill her. He would try again, unless she stopped him. Unless she killed him first. Yes, it made perfect sense. Bloodlust burned in her—a whole new sensation, but one that felt as old as time. It felt like it was etched into her bones.

Kill, kill, kill, kill him, she thought, in the rhythm of her panting breath. *Kill, kill, kill*—the thought beat in her head like a drum, panted on the back of her tongue. Her thoughts were not like human thoughts. They were simpler. More pure. There was no need to examine them, to qualify them. *Kill, kill, kill, kill him, kill.*

Her hind legs were like powerful springs. She reared up and brought her strong forelegs down on his neck, her paws smashing and tearing at the skin under all that fur. She raked her claws down between his shoulder blades and opened her mouth to snap at his throat.

Beneath her he twisted and rolled away from her attack. She bounced sideways to get in another swipe, but before she could build up the momentum he slammed into her like a freight train, all of his weight hitting her just off her center of balance. She went flying, her legs splayed, and skidded painfully across the forest floor on her back. She couldn't see where he ended up.

Her vulnerable stomach was exposed. With a snapping twist of every joint in her body, she flipped over with effortless speed. She rose to her paws, spreading her toes out to grip the soft ground. If he came at her again she wanted to be ready. She lifted her muzzle and breathed in deeply. The scents of the forest filled her brain and she caught his signature odor easily. He was running away from her, dashing through the trees, moving quickly.

She glanced back at her ankle, the one that had been injured when she was trapped in her human body. It looked strong and healthy now. Digging in with her hind legs, she leapt over a pile of dead branches and followed him.

It was the easiest thing in the world to keep track of him, even if she couldn't see him. Her eyes, barely thirty centimeters off the ground, saw little but the underbrush. He was running scared and in too much of a hurry to be silent, however, and her ears twitched back and forth as she heard him crashing through shrubs and stands of saplings.

Oh, the way the world sounded now, a great, sighing, weeping, laughing, exulting, screaming melody of objects moving through time. How she longed to just sit and listen to the planet turn, listen to all its children breathing, their hearts pounding, the air sliding noisily over their fur! But this was not the time. This was the time to *kill*.

She pushed herself to catch up with him and found herself streaking through the woods, far faster than she'd ever imagined.

The crazily tilted tree trunks all around blurred as her body rippled with speed. Her legs intuitively found the right path, her wide paws barely touching the ground and digging in before they shot her forward again. She opened her mouth and let her tongue dangle out as the ground melted away before her.

Up ahead she smelled water, muddy and stagnant. More—she smelled him. Her prey. She leapt through a copse of young larches and heard the screams of wood grouse as they startled up into the air, terrified of her. Hunger grabbed at her gut, but she put it aside and tried not to think about it. She had more important things to kill.

The trees fell away and she was on a high sandy bank overlooking a tiny lake. The sun was just going down: the tops of the trees were still brilliant green, but darkness lurked between their roots. The northern lights played over the gaudy dusk, obscured here and there by clouds. An image of the crescent moon floated on the surface of the lake like a narrow eye. She pressed her muzzle into the wind that stirred the loose guard hairs of her ruffle and felt a howl coming on. He was near, very close by, near, so near, and she was going to finish their fight. It felt good to imagine his blood in her mouth, to hear with her mind's ear the sound of his bones breaking under her attack.

She opened her mouth to let out a screeching yowl, a battle song, but before she'd even started he came at her from the side. She spun to meet his strike, but she was too late—she had misjudged his speed and ferocity. He wasted no time with feints or dominance postures, instead sinking his enormous teeth deep into the soft flesh of her haunches. With a twisting, tugging motion he tore her side wide open and her blood spattered on the ground.

Everything went black. She felt herself falling, tumbling, and then she was gone.

51

ten

They awoke with sand in her mouth, her hair matted and sticking to her face.

When she opened her eyes she saw she was still in the crazy forest, with its trees sticking up at random angles to the ground. It wasn't any part of the forest she recognized, however. She was nowhere near the little house, or the clearing by the stream, or the giant birch tree she'd sheltered in. She felt sort of as if she'd fallen asleep for a while, and sort of as if she had just blacked out. As if no time at all had passed, and she had just been transported from one place to another instantaneously.

She remembered very little, though she understood vaguely what had happened to her. She had turned into a wolf.

Oh.

Oh God.

She was just like him. When he scratched her leg—oh God. He had infected her with his curse.

The curse—

—but—she couldn't—that made her—

Her head hurt too much to put those thoughts in any kind

of proper order. She had to shelve them, as desperately as she wanted to explore them. To figure out what had gone wrong and, much more importantly, how to fix it. For the moment the demands of her body had to take precedent.

Everything hurt. Her body felt weak and ineffectual. She was freezing cold.

At least that made sense. She was naked, after all.

She pulled her knees up to her chest and hugged them hard. A strong shiver went through her and her arms shook so hard she couldn't hold them down. They rose up, away from her body, no matter how hard she tried to pull them close, to make herself small and conserve her body heat. And there was something else. She was hurt, had been hurt before she unexpectedly turned into a wolf and woke up naked at the bottom of a tall bank of ferns. She was wounded, wasn't she? The wolf had—the wolf—

She was a wolf now, too.

She shook her head, or maybe she just let the tremoring shiver run up her neck, and that helped a little. Cleared away the alarming, nasty thoughts that kept demanding to be heard.

The wolf had clawed open her ankle. The bone had been bruised, if not fractured. Running around in the woods like that must have worsened the injury, she thought. With careful fingers she probed her leg but couldn't find any tenderness. Craning forward, she looked down at her ankle. There wasn't even a scar there.

Oh God. Oh God. The wolf—Powell—the *thing* had—he had destroyed her, he had—healed her, somehow, but at what price?

There had been another injury, another grievous hurt. She could barely remember it, but, if she studied her half-glimpsed recollections, if she forced her brain to think a certain way, she could just recall flashes of light that resolved themselves into fragments of images. Though the pictures seemed half-formed and inconsequential. What came back strongest were sounds and smells. It was so hard to remember because those sounds were in frequency ranges her human ears had never heard before. And those smells—her human nose, and the part of her human brain that handled sense data from her nose, couldn't even begin to process the smells she could just about remember. But if she pieced things together, let the memories coalesce, she could get some rough idea of what had happened to her. She had transformed into a wolf. And then what? Something bad. Something violent had happened and she'd been badly hurt. She had been convinced, utterly convinced in the way only an animal can be, that she was going to die. The wolf had no ability to deny facts or obscure the obvious. The wolf had known that it was bleeding to death and that its wounds were too severe to survive. The wolf had rolled over on its side, all it could do, and waited for the end to come, waited for the moon to set, when it would transform back into the human woman. Its one simple, ugly consolation had been that the human woman it hated would die too.

Only—she hadn't.

Only now she was completely healed.

There were no scars on her body. Not even the old ones, the scars she'd gotten in nasty fights on the playground as a child, the scars that hard work had left on her hands. The scrapes, cuts, and abrasions she'd gotten while she was lost in the woods—there had been a lot of those—were all gone. What else?

Chey slowly looked down at her left breast. She'd had a tattoo there, had it done when she was sixteen. Sometimes she regretted getting it, other times she thought of it as a badge of her determination, her will. Most of the time she was barely conscious of it. It was there every time she looked in a mirror, every time she got dressed in the morning, and every time she got undressed for bed. The tattoo had become part of how she saw herself, part of her body.

It was gone. Completely gone, as if she'd never had it done.

She thought of Powell and his fresh face. Only his eyes showed his real age. Would she be like him? Would she stay young-looking forever, but with eyes crinkled in moldering rage?

Or, she thought, as a fresh shiver went through her, would she die of hypothermia on the shore of this tiny lake? She was still naked and while she sat there examining herself and digging at memories that ought to be left buried, her perfectly unblemished skin was turning blue. Her body kept shaking until she felt like she was having a seizure. The cold sand burned the soles of her feet. Her teeth chattered together so sharply that she thought they might crack. She needed to find shelter. If nothing better presented itself she could dig down into the sand, bury herself in it to trap in her body heat. And then what, she wondered? Did she hunker down and wait for the Mounties to come save her?

Oh God. Even if such nonexistent Mounties did come, would they find her in human form, or as a wolf? Would she attack them? Would they shoot her on sight, on principle? Oh God.

A truck's horn honked some way off. She jumped in surprise and shouted, "Hey, over here!," then immediately regretted it. It had to be Dzo in that truck, and he had to be honking for her. She wasn't sure she wanted to be found. He might take her back to the cabin and a warm fire. Or he might let Powell cut her head off with a rusty ax.

"Lady? That you?" Dzo's voice said, cutting through the trees. "Hey, come on, we're not going to hurt you. Not anymore."

The only people in a hundred kilometers who could help her were the same people who had tried to kill her. She could hide—or run. If she did she would either die in the frozen woods or live as—as a wolf. Too much. Too much to think about. Better just to face this, to not have to go through it alone. She stood up and waved and shouted until she heard the truck's horn again, closer this time. She ran through the woods, her arms clutched around her breasts and her pubic hair, and shouted for help. Eventually she found the truck and she pulled her arm away from her breasts to wave. She covered herself quickly again when she saw Powell in the bed of the truck glaring at her. He was wrapped in a heavy woolen blanket. Dzo drove the truck with his mask on.

Powell stood up in the bed. "Truce," he said.

"What? I'm naked and freezing. Don't play games with me," she replied.

"I want to call a truce. We stop fighting and try to get along. Okay?"

She didn't reply—but what choice did she have? He tossed her a bundle of clothing and a green blanket. He looked away just long enough for her to struggle into her pants and shirt. Dzo didn't turn away, but he didn't exactly leer at her either. She got the sense that she looked about the same to him naked or dressed. When she tried to climb up into the passenger seat, though, he shook his head and pointed at the bed with his thumb.

"Wolves in the back," he said. "I can never get the smell out of the seats."

Her face perfectly still—her soul too twisted up to let her feel anything—Chey climbed into the back. Powell stared at her openly but didn't say a word. The truck growled to life and bobbed and rolled forward along a path that had never been designed for vehicular traffic. She had to hold onto the side of the truck or be thrown around in the bed like loose cargo. She hunkered down in her blanket and tried not to look at anything. Eventually she stopped shaking so much.

eleven

They rode in silence for a while. Chey was lost deep in thoughts that didn't please her, but that she couldn't shake.

"He hurt you," Powell finally said.

Chey looked up at him with bird-fast eyes. "What?" she chirped. She was about to go into hysterics. She was about to cry. She couldn't talk to him at that moment, couldn't play the game of being a social creature. Like an injured animal hiding in its den, her personality had curled up to lick its wounds. "What?" she demanded again. "He? He who? Who hurt me?"

"He hurt you pretty badly. 'He' meaning, well, my wolf." His face was set like stone. She supposed he'd had plenty of time to get used to this. He didn't look away from her face as he spoke, didn't drop his eyes or even fidget under his blanket. Chey could read that body language from long experience. He had something uncomfortable to say to her and he was going to be a man about it, a man with a capital *M*. "I try to think of the wolf, of him, as another being, someone different from myself. That we aren't the same creature at all. That I stop existing when he appears, and vice versa."

"How's that working out for you?" Chey asked, too fast, her voice too high and too loud. She could read her own body language, too.

"It helps . . . sometimes."

Chey tried to look away from those eyes, but found she couldn't. They kept drawing her gaze back. "Okay. So . . . your wolf . . . he . . ."

"He hurt you, I think. He bit you or something. I want to say I'm sorry. I never remember what happened until later, until I'm clean again and warm and I can think straight."

"I think I'd rather not remember," Chey said.

"Fair enough."

She rubbed at her eyes with her palms. "It's going to happen again, isn't it?" she asked.

He said nothing. Maybe he thought the question was rhetorical, or maybe he didn't understand what she was asking.

"I'm going to change again. Be that wolf, again."

"Yeah," he answered.

"It's going to happen over and over. For as long as I live."

Powell finally did look away from her. It helped not to be pinned by those green eyes. "Whenever the moon rises. Every single time."

Chey shook her head and her hair bounced on her cheeks. It felt greasy and thick. "No, listen, I remember now—when you—when—when the wolf clawed me, up in that tree, the moon wasn't full. It was a half moon, at best. It wasn't full."

"They made up that guff about the full moon for the movies. Whenever even a sliver of moon is over the horizon, even when it's new, even if we can't see it, we change. We can be at the bottom of a coal mine when it comes up. We can be at the bottom of a lake and it won't matter. There's no way to stop it. Every single damned time. I've been trying to find a cure for—"

"No," she said. "Please, no more. I can't talk about the rules right now," Chey insisted. "I can't hear about this."

Powell didn't say another word for the rest of the trip.

Afternoon was well on them by the time they got back to the cabin. The men busied themselves with various tasks, picking up firewood and folding blankets. Chey stood in the middle of the yard, just outside the house. Just stood there with her arms folded and didn't move.

A curl of smoke rose from a pipe chimney sticking out of the side of the house. Inside a fire crackled and a little yellow light came through the open doorway. Was Powell waiting for her to come in on her own? Maybe he thought she just needed some space. Some time to process what had happened.

She would never get used to this, she thought. She was never going to accept it.

There was no point standing outside in the dooryard all night, though. She went inside and warmed herself by the stove.

Powell made up a bed for her, lining his rough wooden couch with blankets and pillows. It looked more like a dog bed than one meant for a human being. When he finished he took a step toward her, but she wouldn't let him come near her. He tried again, tried to touch her arm, and she recoiled as if he were a snake trying to bite her. He got the point and retired to his smokehouse. Chey followed him as far as the doorway and watched him go inside and close the door behind him. Dzo was outside refueling the truck from an enormous plastic jerry can. It was yellow with age and translucent, and she could see the shadow of the liquid sloshing back and forth inside.

"Make yourself at home, eh?" Dzo said, grinning at her.

She slammed the door shut. There was no lock, just a simple latch, but she pulled hard to make sure it caught. Then she found

60

a chair—not that nest of a bed—and threw herself down in it and had a good sulk.

A day earlier, when she had been lost in the woods, she had been certain she was going to die. It was the worst feeling she'd ever known. Now she was certain she was going to live and it was even worse.

There was no way back, no cure except death. That was what Powell had been trying to tell her. She was stuck with the wolf for the rest of her life.

What did she do next? Did she give up? There had been no room in her plans for this, for becoming a monster. How could she adjust her life to make room for a giant wolf? How could she hold a job if every twelve hours she transformed into an animal? She'd had a few boyfriends back in Edmonton. Mostly they'd been cowboy types, guys with ponytails and motorcycles. The kind of guys who might try to keep a wolf for a pet. None of them would have understood what she'd become. If she had tried to explain this to them, they might have thought it was cool. She could not agree.

She could hear her uncle's voice in her head. Telling her she was feeling sorry for herself. Bemoaning her fate instead of trying to fix it. She tried to argue with him, but even when he was actually there that had never worked. He had a bad habit of being right all the time.

"Okay," she said, finally, rubbing the bridge of her nose. "Okay. Fuck! Okay."

She rose from her chair and walked out onto the porch. As much as she didn't want to face her new circumstance, she did need answers.

The snow between the trees caught what little sunlight made it through the branches and glowed an unearthly blue. Frigid tendrils of mist snaked around the feet of the bushes. Powell was still hiding in his smokehouse, judging by the volume of aromatic fumes streaming out through the cracks around its door. Behind the house Dzo was washing out the bed of his truck with buckets of stream water.

When he saw her coming around the corner of the house he pushed up his mask and smiled at her.

"Am I a prisoner here?" she asked.

He frowned. "No," he said. "Of course not."

"So I'm free to go at any time," she tried.

He shook his head and smiled at her again. "No, sorry. We'd just have to come after you and drag you back. You might hurt somebody."

She squinted at him. "I think I have a little more self-control than that."

Dzo sighed. "A wolf—your kind of wolf—can't look at a human being without getting blood in his eyes. Normal times, he's just an animal, but you get him around people and something comes over him. He gets that taste of blood on the back of his tongue. He gets that smell, that smell in the back of his nose like suppertime has come around." Dzo shook his head. "You see a human being when you're in that state, you won't have any choice. You'll go right from zero to kill in two seconds."

"No," she said. "That's—that can't be right. What about—what about you, then?"

Dzo stared blankly at her.

"How long have you been hanging around Powell?"

Dzo laughed. "Monty? Me and Monty are old buddies. Like, a lot of years."

Chey nodded. "And have you ever been around him when he was changed? When he was a wolf, I mean." She had to remind herself how literal Dzo could be.

"Oh yeah, sure, bunches of times."

"So," Chey said, "why hasn't he killed you yet?"

"I'm special," he said, as if it were self-evident. "I'm safe. Everybody else is fair game."

"Everybody . . . You mean, anybody. Anybody who crosses his path." Her breath came faster. Her ankle pulsed with phantom pain.

"It's the main reason Monty lives up here." He spread his arms wide. "No people. It ain't for the warm weather. You're the first human being he's seen in three years. He attacked you without a thought, right?"

Chey folded her arms across her stomach. She felt suddenly quite queasy. She thought back to when she'd been up in the paper birch. She'd seen the hatred in the wolf's eyes, the need to kill. She'd seen what that madness was like, up close and personal, in a way she never wanted to repeat. "I didn't . . . I didn't know that. My god—how does something like this happen? What kind of virus does that to a person?"

Dzo threw his hands up. "You think it's some kind of disease, huh?" She nodded. "That's where you got it wrong, see. It's not any kind of virus; it's a curse. And when I say curse I don't mean some old Indian story that got handed down over the years, and when some bright fellow from McGill comes up here he's going to say, aha, it was actually a vitamin D deficiency all along. I mean a curse, a magic spell. About the biggest and baddest one ever." He hopped up onto the open bed of the truck and sat down on the tailgate. His eyes looked off into the middle distance as if he were lost in a bad memory. "See, now it happened about ten thousand years ago, and—"

Chey shook her head. She couldn't listen to his story. "I don't want to kill anyone," she breathed. She thought she might be sick. "I'd rather die myself. I'd kill myself first—but is that even possible, now?"

"Sure," he said, smiling again. "Yeah, there's ways. Bullets, poison, traps, you're pretty much good against them. But silver—"

"Silver bullets?" she asked, too quickly.

"Any kind of silver will do for you," he said. "Silver knives, silver dissolved in water you drink, silver thumbtacks if you step on 'em too hard. It's like a really bad allergy, see? You get silver in your system, you'll come down like a gored ox." He shrugged. "'Course, around here we don't keep much silver on hand for the obvious reason. I suppose you could ask Monty. Listen, if that's what you want, we can make it happen." He put a gloved hand on her shoulder. "Promise."

She shook her head. Was that really what she wanted? Maybe. But not yet.

twelve

Eventually Powell came out of his shed. Chey watched him through a window of the little house, unsure of what to think or what to do. He knew things, things she needed to learn. She couldn't bear the thought of asking him to teach her, though.

Yet when he headed out into the woods, on foot, her immediate urge was to follow him. She slipped out of the house and headed into the woods herself, trying to look casual. Trying to act as if she'd just decided to take a stroll of her own.

It didn't work. No matter how far ahead she let him get, he was always aware of her presence behind him. He would stop in the act of climbing over a moss-covered log or lifting a branch away from the path so he could climb underneath it and freeze in place for a moment, then glance back at her before continuing on his way.

When he looked at her his eyes weren't as hard as she'd remembered them. He didn't look concerned or apologetic—*but he damned well should be,* she thought—as much as sympathetic. As if he remembered his first time changing into a wolf, and knew she had to come to accepting it in her own time.

Eventually he got tired of their slow-motion game of freeze tag. He stopped in a small clearing in the woods and just waited. When she didn't follow him in after a minute he turned and stared at her. She'd thought she was perfectly concealed behind a stand of whip-thin saplings covered in shaggy needles fifty meters away, but he caught her eye as easily as if they were standing together in an otherwise empty elevator, trying not to make eye contact.

She started to come forward, a little sheepish. He nodded and called out to her, "We don't have enough time to play silly buggers."

Chey had never liked being scolded and she especially didn't like it coming from him. "Silly buggers? Who says that anymore except, like, my grandpa?" She shook her head. "Anyway, it's not like I have anything better to do."

He shook his head. "You have to start thinking differently," he told her. "You have to change the way you think about time. Time when the moon is down is precious, because it's the only time you're really yourself. Don't waste it."

Maybe he knew what she'd come to him for. She sat down on a slightly damp log and looked up at him expectantly, a pupil waiting for her teacher to start lecturing.

"You'll learn to be very conscious of moonrise and moonset. Most places that's easy but up here, in the Arctic, nothing is simple. This is the land of the midnight sun, right? And the moon cycle's crazy too. We're moving through a phase of longer moons, when the moon rises earlier each night and sets later the next day. In a couple of weeks we're going to have a very long moon—it'll stay above the horizon for five days before it sets again."

"I'll be a—I'll be that creature—for five days?" she gasped.

"No. Not the part of you that's really you," he said. "We share our bodies with them, but not our minds. They think their own animal thoughts. We don't ever completely remember what happens when we change back. I've spent a lot of time wondering why. My best guess is it's just because the wolf's memories don't make any sense when they're picked over by a human brain. It's as if you dreamed in a foreign language, and when you woke you couldn't translate what you'd said in your dream."

She'd thought something similar herself, earlier, but she kept quiet. She was learning the rules now.

"You have to understand, though, that no matter how good a person you are, you're a killer now. A savage. Come up here and look at this." Powell clambered up onto a boulder overlooking a stretch of what looked like a patchy meadow to Chey. "Even the country up here is different, and you need to be careful every time you put a foot down. This is muskeg," he told her. "Partially frozen bog land. Looks solid, right? If you try to walk on it, you'll be in for a surprise—there's plant life on top, sure, but underneath there's just water, and no way of telling how deep it might go."

"The Great White North's answer to quicksand," Chey said, and he nodded. She climbed up onto the rock next to him and had a seat.

"Our relationship with our wolves is like the muskeg, alright? We're the solid-looking surface. The trap. We can even trap ourselves, thinking we're in control. But we're not, and we'll never be. Underneath we're deadly—and we can't change that."

She sighed deeply. "Okay. So life sucks and we can't die. Great."

He shrugged. "I won't pretend I enjoy this curse. But it isn't a fate worse than death, either. The wolves aren't completely without their virtues. There are some things they do better than us. They can survive here much better because they know how to get food in ways we can't. Whenever they eat, we get the nourishment." He frowned. "I'll try to remember to teach you how to hunt tonight," he said. When the moon came up, she realized. He meant he would try to teach her how to hunt when they were wolves. She shuddered at the thought of transforming again. "This land belongs to them. For hundreds of thousands of years before people came they hunted the caribou here. You may have noticed they aren't like other wolves."

"The teeth," Chey said with a gulp of horror. When she'd been up in her tree, looking down at Powell's wolf, she'd noticed the teeth most of all.

He nodded. "The curse was cast ten thousand years ago, right at the end of the last ice age. There were timber wolves here then, but they were smaller and not so fearsome. The shamans who created this curse wanted to strike fear into the hearts of their enemies, really mess with them. So they picked an animal they knew would scare anyone—the dire wolf. They had huge teeth for crunching bones and enormous paws for walking on top of snow. That made them look like monsters to your average Paleo-Indian. Dire wolves are extinct now, but in their day they used to bring down woolly mammoths and giant sloths. They were tough sons-of-guns, see? Everything was bigger back then. And nastier."

"Dzo said a timber wolf would never attack a human being," Chey suggested. "He said we don't look like their food."

Powell nodded. "Yeah. Unless you provoke a wolf—poking it with a stick would do, I guess—it'll leave you alone. The same wasn't true of dire wolves. They were man-killers, because back then people didn't have the technology to make them afraid. There's more to it, though. The curse makes our wolves resent us. They don't like being human, any more than we like being wolves. They want to be wolves all the time—you probably felt that."

Chey nodded. She remembered exactly how good it had felt to change. It sickened her, offended her humanity. But she remembered how bad she'd felt when she changed back, too.

"They grow to hate us. I don't know if it's just natural antipathy or if the curse includes some kind of evil twist, but our kind of wolves go out of their way to destroy anything human. They would destroy us in a heartbeat if they could. There have been times when I changed back and found that I had busted all the windows out of my house because my wolf thought maybe I was sleeping inside."

"Jesus," she said. "But—"

"Yes?"

"What about Dzo? Why doesn't your wolf attack him?"

"He's gotten very good at staying out of my way, I guess," Powell told her. "Believe me, no human being wants to be nearby when the change comes."

"And there's nothing you can do to stop it?"

"You can lock yourself up when the moon is out. I've tried that and found I couldn't bear it. I couldn't take waking up in a locked room. My wolf got so hungry it went a little crazy— it spent all that night bashing itself against the walls trying to get out. It hurt itself, so much so that when I changed back I found myself in so much pain I couldn't even walk. Dzo had to bring me food. It was . . . tough. Too tough. I needed to be free."

She wondered if she could handle being locked up. It might be better than running around like an animal.

He glanced down at his watch and his face fell. "Oh, shoot. I guess I've forgotten how nice it is to have somebody new to talk to about this stuff," he told her. "The time just flew."

Chey jumped inside her skin. "You mean—"

"Brace yourself, is what I mean," he told her.

She closed her eyes and nodded. "Okay," she said. "I guess I'm as ready as I'll ever be."

He reached over and put a hand on her shoulder. As monstrous as he was, as much as he had hurt her, she didn't shrug it away, not immediately. It was some small measure of comfort, something she needed very badly. Without warning the hand got heavier and started to sink through her skin. She looked over in horror and saw it melting through her, even as her own body grew translucent. She glanced over her shoulder to see the moon—

Silver light blossomed inside her head. Her clothes fell away and her body trembled with the joy of renewal. Wolf once more.

She tasted him on the wind, felt the leathery pads of his paw on her own leg. He drew back and bounded into the forest, leaves and branches swinging wildly where he'd disappeared. She was supposed to follow him, she knew. She'd gotten as much from his smell, from the angle of his tail.

Something held her back for a moment, though. She felt something trembling under her feet as if some tiny animal were hiding down there. She looked and saw human clothes lying beneath her. Her immediate urge was to tear them apart, but instead she dug her nose into them and took a good sniff. There was something inside the clothes, something hard and round like a river-washed stone. It vibrated with a noise like bees buzzing. Once, twice. Then it stopped.

Enough. She turned toward the forest and jumped up to follow the male wolf. She still had much to learn.

thirteen

The power in her legs astounded her. Run, run, run, she could run for hours, far faster than a human, and never grow tired—it didn't feel like running at all. It felt like the world was made of rubber and she was bouncing along like a ball. Run, run, her body rippling with her panting breath, run. Her claws dug deep into the earth with every bound, absorbing the jarring impact as she touched down, then tensing to send her flying again. She ran with the rhythm of her own pulse, her heartbeat keeping time as the world flashed by around her. She opened her mouth to let the air flow in and out of her lungs, tasting its many smells as it surged back and forth. Unashamed, she let her tongue hang out of the side of her mouth, flapping between two enormous teeth like a flag in the wind.

She bounded into a narrow open space between two stands of trees that leaned away from each other. He waited for her there, his body as still as stone. The saddle of fur between his shoulders was up and she understood the signal—he wanted her quiet. She dug her claws into the lichen-covered forest floor and focused entirely on him. Her level of concentration almost scared her, it was so intense. And yet nothing had ever felt so natural. Before she had been running and the entire universe was speed and motion. Now she was crouching, waiting, and the planet itself seemed to hold its breath for her.

The male watched her carefully. He was making sure she understood what that stillness meant. What it was for.

With her stone-like immobility she proved that she did.

His ears flicked back and forth. His eyes stayed on hers. He was watching to see if she got the next step on her own. She thought she did. Silently, with the smallest motions of the flaps of skin around her nostrils, she breathed in the world around her. It was all there, all the things she'd smelled before, but back then she'd been building a map of smells in her mind, taking in the whole picture. This, she understood, was different.

He tilted his head a fraction of a degree to one side. Asking her a question. *What do you smell?* Specifically.

Enormous sections of her brain were devoted to just this activity. She ran through the vast catalog of things she could smell, trying to pick out the one he wanted. It took only milliseconds before she had it. It was as if a lover of classical music, having gone to the symphony, had been asked to pick out a single instrument's voice. It was almost laughably simple, because her brain had already flagged that particular smell, had already mapped and memorized and pinpointed it for her. The male wasn't teaching her technique or finesse here—only to accept and rely on her most basic instincts. There could be only one smell he was looking for, and she had it: an animal, a mammal, something small and defenseless. Prey.

A whole new set of thoughts, feelings, instincts lit up her mind. All of them revolving around the concept of prey—and the knowledge that she was a predator. She felt reflexively ready, felt an almost unbearable anticipation of pleasure. It was time to learn how to hunt.

Her human side flinched. She hated her human side—it was so helpless and weak and it wanted to control her, to imprison her. If she ever met her human side she would—she would—but that didn't make any sense, did it? Her brain warbled in unhappiness. It couldn't finish that thought. So elegantly, beautifully evolved to pick one smell out of millions, it had far more trouble with simple logic.

The male was trying to get her attention again, speaking to her in a silent language she had never needed to learn. She just knew what he meant when he pushed out his tongue and licked his snout a little. She raised her tail. She put aside human thoughts and concerns. They were inessential. Meaningless. Prey was nearby—and she was a predator.

The wind stirred her hair and ruffled her cowl. She possessed two layers of fur, a dense, woolly undercoat and a much looser coat of guard hairs that stood out from her body and made her look bigger than she actually was. The guard hairs were stiff and they grabbed at the wind. She could feel them tingle as they rose away from her body, as her skin prickled with the sense of movement nearby. She was perfectly aware of everything around her, every small, trembling leaf, every insect crawling through the ground below.

She could feel the hunger in the ground, in the trees around her, and felt it matched by the tightness in her own belly. Summer was the starving time in the forest, when the caribou herds, the great food source for wolves, migrated still farther north to calve on open ground. The wolves had to find other sources of nourishment. Sometimes they could not and they starved to death.

She was a hunter, though. She could provide for herself—

once she learned how. She narrowed her eyes and felt for the prey. The ground trembled in time with her heartbeat and she felt where it was not solid, but hollow, where the prey had dug itself in for safety.

She could hardly stand it but *Wait, wait, wait,* the male was telling her, his fierce energy banked and hidden. Wait for it. Then the waiting was over. He opened his mouth in a broad, silent yawn. Then he snapped his jaws shut with an audible click.

The prey must have been aware of them. It must have smelled them, and dug itself even deeper into its hole. But that sound of such enormous teeth coming together must have terrified it. The sound must have driven it crazy.

A snowshoe hare shot up out of the ground and dashed between them, its gray summer coat flecked with mud. Its dark eyes rolled wildly in its head as its broad feet smashed at the ground.

The male was off like a shot after the prey. She came up close behind, staying to one side of the hare, instinctually knowing how to flank it. They moved like electricity along the ground, dodging around tree trunks, fluttering through shrubbery that rattled and shook but didn't slow them down. His mouth was wide open as he looked across at her, over the head of the doomed hare. He was showing all his teeth and the meaning was clear. He could have snapped up the prey easily, but he wanted her to take the kill.

Her body sang with excitement and hunger. She dug in harder, pushed herself that much faster and made contact. Without hesitation, without so much as a thought, she brought her jaws together around the hare's spine and lifted it clear off the ground. With the huge, powerful muscles in her neck she shook the animal until it was bloody and twitching. Her legs came up and she rolled to a stop in the leaf litter, her prize still locked inside her jaws. The hare's wild eye caught hers as it flopped in its death throes, but any idea of mercy or pity was foreign to her. She was a predator.

Her human side screamed in protest, but she just snarled it away.

He dashed up beside her and nosed her kill, excited by what she'd done, panting wildly. He did not bite into it right away, however. It was her prey and hers to do with as she saw fit. He waited for her to signal that she was willing to share. Then together they tore the hare apart and gobbled down its meat. She cracked its skull between her giant teeth and let the buttery softness of its brains slide down her throat. He crunched its long legs and dug the marrow out of its long bones with his tongue.

Yes, yes, yes! In triumph and exultation she tilted her head back and howled in delight.

When they were done with their meal they fell across each other, sated, bloated, barely able to move. She would have been happy to drift off into sleep and she did, in fact, doze a little. She was woken, however, when he batted at her stomach with his nose. She looked up and caught his eyes—then pricked up her ears.

There was a sound, a sound she didn't like gliding over the trees. A sound like someone was cutting the wind into pieces. She stared at him but he didn't have an answer for her, couldn't tell her what it was. Then she smelled it. It smelled of gasoline and metal. Human smells.

A desire similar to that she'd felt for the hare's blood awoke inside her. Similar, but not exactly the same. She hated that human smell. Hated it with a purity she'd never felt before. She began to rise to her legs—but he pushed at her again with his nose and she didn't move. The smelly human thing was high up in the air, flying like a bird. She could no more reach and kill it than she could snatch the moon from the sky. He wanted her to be aware of it, but also to know that some things were beyond her expansive powers.

In a moment the smell and the sound were gone, having passed over the face of the woods and disappeared. She lay back, easy and with a full belly, and thought no more of it. When he started nosing at her hindquarters, she did not turn to snap at him. It was only a friendly kind of sniffing, anyway. This time.

fourteen

They woke up stiff and naked—with Powell, also naked, draped across her legs. His—his penis was flopping across his thigh. It wasn't quite flaccid.

"Guh," she let out.

Her heart pounded in sheer unadulterated disgust. She thought she might throw up. When he'd put his hand on her shoulder, that was one thing, but this—she could not let herself get close to him. Not like that. "Jesus," she said, her whole body shivering, and not with the cold. She slid out from under him and dashed behind a tree. When she looked again his green eyes were open and staring at her but he lay still as a dead man on the forest floor. "This is not cool," she said. "This is definitely not cool."

He didn't cover himself up. He didn't even look down at himself. "Don't be so agitated," he told her. "You've never seen a man's thing before?"

"A man's thing? His thing? What are you, twelve years old?" She turned away and covered her face. When she looked again he hadn't moved. "Put that thing away, please. Now."

He waited a moment longer. Then he smiled with a certain degree of self-satisfaction. She didn't like it at all. Eventually he sat up and moved his legs so he wasn't so—so entirely naked.

"You knew we would be naked when we came back," he said, which sounded almost like an apology.

"I didn't think you would be stretched out all over me!"

He shrugged. "I can't control what my wolf does."

A new wave of disgust surged up from her stomach to the roof of her mouth. "Oh. Oh my God. We didn't. We definitely did not. Please tell me we didn't—"

"My memories are hazy at best. But no, I don't think so."

That was some kind of relief, anyway. She clutched her arms around herself, hiding her breasts, and said, "I can't do this for the rest of my life. Don't look at me!"

He put his hands up and covered his eyes. "Dzo will be here soon enough. I'll try not to look at you until you're dressed."

She sat down on a soft carpet of reindeer moss. Her arms broke out in gooseflesh, but at least this time she knew she wasn't going to die of hypothermia. She watched him for a while, watched him keep his hands pressed tight over his eyes, and started to feel a little guilty. She *had* been harsh, she decided. Everything he'd said had been true.

"I'm sorry," she said. Her stomach rumbled and she realized that maybe some of her nausea didn't come from the horror of waking up naked with Powell. She felt like she'd eaten something that didn't agree with her. With a sudden inpouring of wisdom she realized she did not want to find out what it might have been. "I know you didn't ask to get saddled with a newbie wolf who didn't even know how to hunt. I've been pretty abominable so far."

"It's understandable," Powell said. "You didn't ask for this either. I just hope you'll find it in your heart to forgive me."

She started to talk. Then she bit her lip hard enough to make it bleed.

She'd been about to take a step in that direction, had reflexively almost said yes, that she did forgive him, but then her old self, her purely human self, recoiled inside her head, squirmed with negation. *Not on your life,* she wanted to say. *Never.*

She decided to deflect the subject. Say anything, anything else. "I'm so far out of my element," she said. "Nothing up here makes sense to me. Compasses don't point north. This is midsummer, the days last eighteen hours, but it never really gets warm. And these trees. Why on earth do the trees point in all different directions? For my entire life I was under the impression that trees pointed straight up."

"These did too, originally." He rolled over onto his stomach, his hands still over his eyes. He wasn't technically showing her his butt. But she could see it if she wanted to. She told herself she 100 percent did not want to. "It's the permafrost that does it. That's soil where the groundwater is permanently frozen, and the groundwater never thaws, not even in summer—"

"I've seen a nature documentary before," she told him.

For a second he looked like he had no idea what she was talking about. He went on. "Some parts of the ground, the shadowy parts, stay frozen all year. Other parts thaw out and turn to mud, which sags." He held his two hands next to each other, then lowered one, which had the effect of making the other look higher. "The earth around here is fluid. Not stable at all, even if it looks solid right now. It just moves very slowly. If you could stay still long enough to watch it, say over the course of a year, you would see waves rolling through it like on the surface of the ocean. The miners and loggers who used to come through here called this the Drunken Forest."

Chey rested her chin on her kneecap. "You've been up here a long time, haven't you?"

"Nearly twelve years now. You learn plenty about a place by just being in it and paying attention. I've even come to love it."

"Why?" she asked.

"Well, it has its charms. For one thing, north of the Arctic Circle there are days every month when the moon never rises. Of course there are days when it doesn't set, either."

"No," she said. She caught her breath. This was one of the important questions. One she'd been asking herself for a long time. "I meant, why did you come up here in the first place? Dzo said the main reason was because there were no people up here for you to hurt. Fair enough. But if that's the main reason, it must not be the *only* reason."

"I've got others," he admitted, his voice suddenly rough. She looked around the tree and found him staring at her. "I don't know if I should trust you with that kind of information or not."

"Don't you think you owe me?" she asked. His eyes narrowed and she shifted uncomfortably. "This isn't just obnoxious curiosity. I have to understand you better if we're going to be stuck together for the rest of our lives."

"Don't be dramatic," he said, a little too quickly.

Hmm. For once she seemed to be getting through his armor. She decided to capitalize on the advantage. "Isn't that exactly what we're looking at? Dzo said it—you can't let me go. I might go south, back to civilization. Where I might hurt somebody. So you've got to keep me close, where you can watch me. This place," she said, indicating the whole of the North, "is one big prison cell, and we're bunkmates. You want me to forgive you for—everything. Why don't you start with a little honesty?"

She could see it was working, that she was persuading him.

She wanted him to say it, to admit why he had fled to this frozen place. If he would just confess to what he'd done it would go so far with her. He opened his mouth and started to speak, but just then they heard Dzo's truck honking through the woods, honking for them.

The spell was broken. "Maybe we'll talk about that later," he said, meaning they wouldn't. She knew that game.

They walked together naked through the trees, Powell in front so he wouldn't stare at her. She studied the angular shape of his back, the bones that stuck out beneath his shoulders, and wondered if she really could have connected with him anyway. She had to shake those thoughts out of her head. It had worked before to talk about other things. About the weirdness in his world. "Will you tell me something else, then?" she asked.

He sounded guarded when he grunted a yes back at her.

"Will you tell me how you got your wolf?"

He turned to face her and her arms went up to cover her breasts. He was looking right into her eyes, however. "Alright," he said. "I'll tell you that much."

fifteen

"**I** was born in Winnipeg a while back," Powell began, when they were seated in the back of Dzo's truck and headed for the house. "I had a pretty normal childhood. I played at tin soldiers like any boy, and worked some for my father, who was a grocer. Never went to much school, but I didn't know what I was missing, so I didn't complain. Then, when I was nineteen, I was called up to serve this country in the Great War," Powell said, facing away from her. "What you would call World War One, I suppose."

"Hold on," Chey said. She'd just thought of something. "This all happened when you were nineteen? The First World War started when you were nineteen?"

"I was born in eighteen ninety-five."

She shook her head. "You don't look a day over forty," she said. Except his eyes were old. They'd always looked old to her.

"We change almost every day. When that happens we don't just sprout hair and grow our teeth out. Every cell in our bodies is altered and renewed. Our cells never have time to age. It's true, Chey. I'm a hundred and eleven years old. And for most of that time I've been a wolf. I can guess your next question, but I don't have an answer. I don't know if we die of old age or not. I feel as healthy as I did the first time I changed, but beyond that I just don't know."

Chey's spine tingled at the thought of living that long running from one forsaken corner of the world to another. How long would her own life last, she wondered? Decades—maybe centuries of endless transformation lay before her. Of waking up naked in the frozen forest. Chey shivered and it wasn't because she was naked. She felt a pressing need to change the subject. "Did you wear one of those funny dish-shaped helmets?"

"Yes, I goddamned did," he said, the back of his neck turning red. It was the first time she'd ever heard him swear. "I wore a Mark One two-pound helmet. And I wore khaki leggings to keep my feet dry, but they never did. I don't know what you've been taught that war was about, or why we fought in it at all, but for me it was just about mud. Oh, there were some very pretty songs they had us sing about queen and country, but in the real day-to-day, when all was said and done, most of what I remember of the war was the smell of other men's feet and plenty of mud. Mud everywhere, and the Germans shelled the tar out of our mud, and we shelled theirs, and sometimes we took their mud away from them and sometimes we had to give it back. We dug down into the mud to try to get away from the explosions and then we crouched in our mud and waited to die. Every so often they told us to crawl over some barbed wire and shoot anything we saw. Everybody knew what that would mean, which was that most of us would not be coming back. This was the war when they first used machine guns, you see, and tanks, and aerial bombardment, and poison gas, and nobody knew yet how men in Mark One helmets and leggings were supposed to survive going up against all that, so a lot of us didn't. We did what we could to not think too much about it. There was always alcohol around, but cheap stuff, stuff people brewed in old coffee cans, and it would make your stomach sour for days. Then there were women. This was France, after all, and France was supposed to be full of pretty girls. Too bad they'd all packed off for less muddy places when the shooting started. Those who were left weren't the prettiest, but they were—well—more friendly, I suppose, than girls back home. Especially if it was the day after payroll came down the trench. You understand what I mean?"

Chey smiled. "Oh, yeah."

"One night like that my buddies and I borrowed a field car and just motored around for hours looking for anyone female who might enjoy some uniformed attention. Just when we were ready to turn back a mate of mine from Vancouver shouted out for me to stop. I looked ahead through the windshield and there she was, standing by the road as if she was just waiting for us. A woman, a God's honest French *jeune fille* like we always used to talk about finding but knew we never really would. Oh, she was beautiful. Long red hair and creamy skin and not a stitch of clothing on her."

"That must have been a surprise," Chey suggested.

"Oh, heavens, yes. Especially back then. You won't believe me, but in those days if you saw a girl's ankle you hurried back to your friends to tell them about it. When we saw that girl standing there in a state of nature, well. I suppose we thought she must be some kind of ghost or angel or something. None of us could figure it, how we got so lucky. Still, this was wartime. You saw crazy people around all the time. You know about shell shock?"

Chey frowned. "We call it PTSD now. Post-traumatic stress disorder."

Powell shrugged. "It was brand new back then, so we made

84

up our own name. Human beings weren't meant to see some of the things we saw on a daily basis. Bodies stuck in the wire that nobody was brave enough to fetch back. Whole chunks of French countryside disappearing in clouds of smoke, leaving craters behind. Good men shot by snipers half a mile away because they were foolish enough to light a cigarette at the wrong moment. People went crazy with the noise of the shells, and not just soldiers—plenty of civilians, too. When they got shell shock they would turn inside themselves. They would stop looking at your face and get real quiet. And then, sometimes, they would start crying, or screaming, or maybe they'd start fighting everyone they could get their hands on. Compared to that—this woman looked alright, she was just naked. We weren't about to hold it against her."

"So you were—how many of you were there?"

"Six of us, including myself," Powell said.

"Six virginal teenagers looking for prostitutes and you saw a beautiful naked woman standing by the side of the road. I assume you pulled over."

"Of course we did. I jumped out and ran up to her and took my cap off and asked her if she was alright and if she needed any assistance. She spoke English rather well, well enough to tell us a story we didn't believe at the time. Something she'd obviously thought up on the spot. She said thieves had accosted her and taken her clothes. If we would give her a ride home she said she would reward us."

Chey laughed. "Is this a horror story or a letter to *Penthouse* Forum?"

Powell stared at her with a lack of comprehension that made her realize he'd never heard of the magazine. He had been up in the north country a long time.

"When she spoke her voice sounded like church bells off in

85

the next valley, you know, a long way off. Almost like she wasn't talking to us, like she was barely aware we were there. Her name, she said, was Lucie, and she was very pleased to meet such well-mannered gentlemen. I think some of us had wicked ideas before she said that, but she shamed us into our best behavior. Back then a lady could do that, make you step back into line with just the tone of her voice. You knew that some people weren't to be trifled with. One of us offered her his greatcoat, which she took and put on, but then she didn't tie the belt, so you could still see you know what. I thought about tying it for her, but that seemed like a real liberty and I didn't want to impose. Instead, I opened the car door for her and she climbed into the seat beside me. I still remember the feel of her smooth, soft hip against my own. She directed us to her house then. It was about ten kilometers away in the shelter of a deep river valley. It was a castle. Not a chateau, not a villa, but a real medieval castle. It stood in pretty serious need of repair. A German shell had knocked in one of its towers. Still, it was a castle—and our mysterious guest turned out to be the daughter of the Baron de Clichy-sous-Vallée."

"Oh-ho, the plot thickens."

"We worried her father would come racing out with a pack of hounds and an old blunderbuss, maybe, and give us all what-for for offending his daughter's honor, but it turned out we didn't need to worry. The old man had gone off to fight as an officer in the cavalry. He had died, along with every single one of his men, leading a charge into a hail of machine gun fire.

"So there was no Baron. But the Baroness was at home, and she met us at the door in a dusty gown. She had brown hair and haunted eyes and she carried a golden candelabra with no candles in it. Like I said, we saw a lot of crazy people during the war. She looked maybe twenty or perhaps thirty years old and when I first saw her I thought she must be Lucie's sister. She was not.

"Lucie went to her rooms and threw on a gown from the last century. I mean the nineteenth century. The kind of thing Josephine might have worn to Napoleon's coronation, except that moths had been at it and there were gravy stains on the sleeves. I figured it was probably the best dress she had, and I wasn't about to say a word against it. For one thing, it left her shoulders bare and she had shoulders like . . . like . . ."

"Hmm?" Chey asked, but she could see that Powell was lost in a reverie. Remembering those shoulders. She cleared her throat noisily to get his attention.

"Right, well. When she came back down we were led inside into a banquet hall lined with tapestries. The roof was full of holes and rain had ruined most of the furniture, but there was meat on the table, roast mutton of a kind we never got in the trenches. There was wine, too, of a kind that does not exist anymore. My mates and I ate and drank our fill, and perhaps more.

"Lucie came and sat by me. For whatever reason I was the one she picked. The other fellows saw it and there were a lot of jealous looks around that table, which made Lucie shower me with even more attention, because she could tell how bad I felt. She always did love making me squirm. She hung on me all night, holding my elbow, serving me from the silver platters, making sure my wine goblet was always full. The other fellows tried to make time with the Baroness, but they might as well have been pitching woo with a howitzer for all the warmth or affection she gave them.

"When we were all finishing up, all drunk and stuffed full of food, Lucie leaned in very close until I could smell her perfume and she looked up into my eyes. She gave me a very complicated smile, lots of different things going on in that smile. Then she whispered in my ear that she had something to show me. She had washed her white face and in her old-fashioned gown she looked like some ghost from a story. Even as I rose from the table, even as the boys whistled and cheered me on, I felt as if I were under some enchantment. Perhaps I was."

Chey held her tongue.

"Lucie led me deep inside the castle, through dark and dank hallways, our only light coming from a single candle she carried in her hand. I saw hot wax roll across her knuckles, but she did not cry out, and I wondered who this spirit could be. She led me down a flight of stone stairs, into the cellars of the place. The vaulted ceilings were white with niter. The floor lay submerged under a couple centimeters of murky water. Her dress dragged through the muck, but before I could say anything she hurried on, faster and faster, and it was all I could do to keep up. We passed racks of wine bottles, some of which had burst because there was no wine steward anymore to tend to them. We passed piles of furniture stacked to the ceiling, pieces that would be priceless antiques today, but these were left to rot. We came at last, at long last, to a narrow room that contained only a single enormous cage. It stood three meters high and twice as wide and the bars were made of solid silver. In the candlelight they glimmered like mirrors.

"'The moon is rising,' Lucie told me. I didn't understand, of course. 'Will you be my guest for the night? The accommodations are more comfortable than they appear.' I stared at her, thinking she must be some kind of maniac. More than just crazy. I think you can guess what happened next."

"She changed," Chey said.

"She changed."

sixteen

ne of the truck's wheels fell down into a deep pothole and the two of them lifted off the bed and fell crashing back. Chey's hand jumped over to grab Powell's arm, for support. When she realized what she'd done she yanked it back quickly. He didn't seem to notice. He was wrapped up in telling his story.

"This beautiful French girl turned into a wolf before my eyes. I guess you've never seen the whole transformation—the first time you saw me change, you were changing too. It's a weird thing to see. The body turns ghostly and transparent. Almost like the human being is fading out of existence. You can see the skeleton melting like wax from a candle; you can see the entire body collapse in on itself. Then it seems to stagger back up to its feet and become solid again. Color and then solidity return—but in a new form. Suddenly you're staring a vicious animal in the face. Drunk as I was, as weird as that day was, I knew it wasn't just a trick of the light. This snarling, slavering thing was going to kill me and it was going to *hurt*.

"I stepped backward, away from this monster. Behind me the

silver cage stood open and inviting. Even as the she-wolf lunged for my throat—and believe me, she didn't waste a moment—I leapt back into the cage and slammed the door shut. The key was in the lock and I turned it with shaking fingers, locking myself in. For just a moment, though, that meant my hand was outside of the cage. She got her teeth into it. She clamped down. Then she tore it right off and swallowed it like a piece of meat.

"The pain was unbearable, of course. I screamed and fell back on the filthy straw at the bottom of the cage and screamed and kept screaming. You couldn't live in the trenches as long as I had without learning a little emergency medical aid, so I did what I could to stay alive. I wrapped my belt around my spurting wrist to try to stop the blood loss, and did my best not to panic. That wasn't exactly easy. The whole time the she-wolf was throwing herself at the cage, over and over, making the bars ring like bells. The pain just got bigger and bigger, but the horror I felt was almost worse. There was the horror of being alone with that wolf, which was pretty bad. But I saw soon enough that it couldn't get through the bars. They weren't that thick, but every time the wolf touched them she jumped back as if they were red hot and she'd been burned. So once I knew I was safe, my mind started wandering to other subjects. Like what had just happened to my hand. I imagined what it would be like to live the rest of my life, my normal human life, with only one hand. I'd seen plenty of amputees on the battlefield. Bits and pieces of soldiers were always being blown off. I'd never truly thought it could happen to me, but now I had a ragged stump staring me in the face, confronting me with the reality of it. What woman would ever want me again? How would I find work?

"While I lay there feeling sorry for myself my buddies were still upstairs. The Baroness de Clichy-sous-Vallée was tearing them to pieces. Maybe they tried to fight her off—we all had weapons with us, sidearms or trench knives at least—but they never stood a chance. Lucie had locked the big doors at either end of the hall and there was no escape. I saw what was left of them later and it wasn't much more than scraps of their uniforms and the occasional bone with shreds of meat still attached. Lucie, I came to realize, had gone out of her way to protect me from that fate. She had other plans for me. She liked me, you see, liked my face, and she wanted to keep me around for a good long time. At least until she got bored of me. She hadn't even wanted to turn me into a wolf, at least not right away—it was just bad luck that I'd reached for that key at the wrong moment. She couldn't control herself when her wolf was on her. None of us can."

"You sound like you forgive her," Chey said, a little startled.

"Not at first. But with time . . . when the moon set the Baroness and Lucie came downstairs and let me out of the cage. They saw at once what had happened to me and they knew I was part of their family. Instantly they treated me that way, even when I fought against them. Even when I called them horrible names and threatened to kill them. They knew better. They knew I would come around."

"The cage," Chey said. "Why did they have that cage?"

"You haven't guessed yet?" Powell asked. "Lucie was the black sheep of her family. So to speak. She'd been injured by a wolf some time before I met her. Some time centuries before I met her."

"What?"

"That story about the Baron riding into machine gun fire was only half true. He had been a cavalry officer—but he had died during a very different war, back in the seventeenth century.

"As for Lucie, she'd been alive since then, and she'd had her wolf since she was a child. She could barely remember a time when she'd been fully human. She got the curse when she was twelve years old, she told me."

"Most girls do," Chey told him.

Powell looked confused for a moment. Then he blushed and shook his head. "Ah, blast, you know that's not what I mean. I mean that's when she got her wolf."

Chey nodded. It had been too good to pass up, that was all.

"At the time that was about the age when she was expected to get married, so she'd been out being courted by the cream of French nobility. A bunch of young men in blue silk suits with wigs and painted faces. She despised them all. They took her hunting, and gave her a little spear with a garland of flowers around the point. They tied a fox to a tree and led her right to it so she could have the experience of what it was like to go hunting with the boys. She had thanked them profusely and with great charm and wit—anyway, that's how she put it—and then cut the fox's chain with her spear. The fox knew a good thing when it saw it and dashed off. She followed, riding so fast after it the boys couldn't keep up. She followed it over hills and well off her father's property, but she was having such fun she didn't worry about it. Then, when she finally cornered it, just when she was about to catch it and make it her pet—out of nowhere a giant wolf came charging out of a thicket and snapped the fox up in its jaws. Lucie spurred her horse and was off like a shot, but not before the wolf had taken most of the flesh off her back and arms.

"Her family found her tied to her saddle with her own reins. She was a tough little *jeune fille,* I will never say otherwise. They brought in doctors who could do nothing but put her to bed, assuming she would die by morning. Instead, she changed.

"I think she hurt somebody, that first time. Maybe killed some of the servants. She wouldn't say. She told me that she wanted to turn herself in but it would have shamed her family if people knew about what she was. At the time werewolves were being burned at the stake all over France and Germany, thousands of them every year, and some of them were even real. That would have been her fate if anyone even suspected what had happened. So instead she went to her mother, the first Baroness, who listened to everything she said and promptly went mad on the spot and drowned herself in the river. Somebody in the family stayed sane long enough to have that cage built, and laid down the law about how they would keep Lucie's secret. For twelve hours out of every day they locked her inside and waited for the moon to go down. She would smash against the bars, batter at them with her own muscles and bones, but she couldn't get free no matter how hard she tried. For generations one member of the female line of her family had tended to her, sat with her, prayed for her soul. Mother had passed the duty on to daughter, who had passed it on to her own daughter, and so on. The Baroness I met was the last of those attendants.

"When the war came, and the castle was abandoned by the rest of the family, it had become clear they couldn't take Lucie with them. Not unless they wanted to explain to the army authorities why they had a pretty naked girl locked up in an extremely expensive cage. The Baroness had volunteered to stay behind and take care of Lucie. Instead, the moment the two of them were alone, she turned to Lucie and said she wanted to make a deal.

"She'd been watching the wolf for years and she wanted it too. Like I said, she was crazy as a cat in a bathtub. She knew what she wanted, though. She wanted that strength and power. She said there was no need for cages anymore, that Lucie could go free now. In the anarchy of the war the two of them could hunt together as a pack. That Lucie could run free and hunt as she pleased. She was crazy enough to think that was what they were meant for. Lucie was crazy enough to think that was a great idea. So they made it happen. Lucie was the Baroness's great-great-great-aunt, you see, and when I met her the Baroness had only just changed for the second time. She needed to learn, just like I taught you, except Lucie thought she needed to learn how to hunt bigger game. So Lucie brought my buddies home for the Baroness to play with."

"But why did Lucie protect you?" Chey asked.

Powell's shoulders tightened. "Because the two of them wanted a mate."

seventeen

Dzo's truck rolled ever onward, back toward the little house. How far had the wolves run? Chey wondered. The light was already changing, the day getting away from them. Powell didn't seem to notice the time. He barely even glanced at her as he spoke. She recognized the look on his face from the many years she'd spent hanging out in bars—he was lonely. He hadn't spoken to anyone but Dzo in years. He wanted so badly to tell this story that it would have been an act of deliberate cruelty on her part if she asked him to stop, or even interrupted too much.

So she didn't.

"I thought I knew the rules. I thought I understood what I had become, but I was wrong. I don't suppose children in this day and age tell stories about werewolves to each other when their parents aren't looking. When I was a boy that was a favorite pastime: seeing who could scare the other boys with the most gruesome, the most vicious story, the best blood-curdling howl. So when Lucie and the Baroness imprisoned me I had reason to believe I knew what they wanted, that they were going to eat me. Why they should bother to change me into one of their

95

own kind first was not something I spent much time thinking on. I spent the first few days trying to remember everything my boyhood companions had told me about lycanthropes.

"There had been wolves like us in Europe for thousands of years, I recalled. The older stories suggested there was something called a wolf strap—a belt, or a girdle, and when a person put it on they could take the shape of a wolf. Whenever they wanted to they could take it off again and regain their human form. Later on, when I was free again, I wasted a lot of time research-ing the wolf strap, trying to find if such a thing existed. Maybe, I thought, the strap actually prevented the change. Maybe there was a way to make myself normal. No dice, I'm afraid. That part was just a myth.

"The werewolves of the Renaissance couldn't live in normal human society any more than you or I can. They changed, they ran free. They killed people. There were times when they almost overran the human population. In Germany and France in the sixteenth and seventeenth centuries there were thousands—tens of thousands—of werewolves burned at the stake or hanged or tortured to death. Church and political authorities shouted from the pulpits about an epidemic sweeping the land, about the wickedness of the people finally catching up with them. In some places whole villages were put to the torch because every last inhabitant was deemed to be a werewolf."

Chey whistled in disbelief.

"The strangest part is that werewolves were turning them-selves in. Confessing, in enormous numbers. I'm still not sure if there were that many wolves or if it was just mass hysteria. It didn't matter, often enough. Whenever the authorities caught a werewolf the punishment was always death. Traditionally they were buried with their heads cut off and their hearts impaled by a silver cross."

"Yikes."

"The burning and hanging wouldn't have killed them permanently. As soon as the moon rose their bodies would try to change, even inside their coffins. Those silver crosses would have finished them off. But not instantaneously."

Chey squinted very hard, trying not to think about what that meant.

"By eighteen hundred our kind of wolves were extinct, or so it was commonly believed. By my day they were nothing but old silly stories. But of course the wolves never went away—they just went into hiding. Lucie in her cage was not the only one. I've met others in my time, old beasts, legendary monsters. I met a duke's son in Spain who lived locked up inside a silver palace, a tiny house made entirely of silver in the courtyard of an enormous castle. He had servants who fed him with very long forks, through a barred window, and a valet who he had infected just to have someone inside with him to dress him and brush his hair. It seemed sometimes like every aristocratic family in Europe had at least one of us hidden away somewhere. It made a certain degree of sense, of course. Peasants who turned into wolves were hunted down without mercy. If you could afford a silver cage, though, you were allowed an amount of leniency. Under the feudal system these nobles were quite literally beyond the reach of law—no court in the land could condemn them. So they lived hidden away, sometimes for centuries. They were lunatics, all of them, of course. Their families saw them as obligations, as part of noblesse oblige, but really I think they were just afraid of their secrets being discovered. If they were careful enough they got away with it, and these old European families had learned to be very, very careful.

"Lucie and the Baroness weren't in the same league, of course. They were both crazy and had nobody sane around to keep them under control. Maybe that was another reason they wanted me with them. First, though, they had to tame me. They kept me locked in the cage for the first week, even as my body changed and changed again. When they worked together they were stronger than me, so what could I do? They fed me raw meat and filthy water until I went a little crazy myself. At one point a patrol came around looking for me and my pals. We'd been gone so long I assumed the front had moved on without us and that they'd marked us off as missing, assumed dead. When I heard soldiers moving around the half-ruined castle I thought maybe I was going to be rescued. I didn't even consider what that would mean. Lucie held her hand over my mouth when I started to scream. I tried to bite and even chew through her fingers, but she didn't even yelp. Eventually the soldiers left. When they were gone I knew there was no hope left for me. I was never going to escape."

"So you stopped trying, right?" She understood that feeling.

He shrugged. "Hatred is a funny thing. It's tough to keep it hot in your heart when you're faced with the truly mundane. I had realities I had to confront that got in the way of hating my captors. I wanted cooked food. I wanted to shave. I wanted to wash my clothing. All these things I could do, they said, but first I had to behave myself. Eventually I relented. I swore up and down I'd be good. They let me out of the cage, at first only when my wolf was on me. Later I was allowed to move around the castle, though they watched me. Eventually they began to trust me on my own. By then . . . by then I was a wolf, through and through. I had accepted what I had become, and I knew I could never go back. They didn't need to watch me anymore. I couldn't escape, because the most freedom I would ever have again was living with them, away from other human beings. That—that was when they started to discuss with me why I had been chosen. What was expected of me."

"You mentioned they were looking for a mate."

Powell actually turned red. His eyes stabbed into her as if he were angered by her interruption. Then they drifted, across her hair. Down to her breasts and then her hips for one flickering moment. *Jesus,* Chey thought. *He's—he's checking me out.*

"It must have been hard," she said. "I mean, difficult, to really hate them when they were, you know. Coming on to you."

He squirmed and his eyes drifted off of her body. "There was that, yes. Having two beautiful women as my captors was—well, I won't deny it. There was a certain excitement in the idea. Had they been men I might have fought a little harder."

"Did you have sex with them?" she asked, point blank.

"My God! It sounds so ugly when you say it like that," he said. He sat up very straight and looked out at the trees flashing by outside of the truck. "Yes," he admitted, turning his face into his shoulder.

"Both of them?"

"Yes!"

Chey just watched in fascination as he tried to recover himself. She took some real delight in his squirming. She wondered for the first time how much experience he might have had with sex. She thought he had probably been a virgin before he was cursed. Lucie and the Baroness might have been the only lovers he'd ever had.

Just as he'd mostly calmed down and looked relaxed again, she asked, "How were they? Any good?"

He looked away and blew air out of his mouth. He shifted on the truck bed as if his legs were falling asleep. Finally he looked straight up—then turned his frozen eyes on her. The discomfort was gone. He was going to talk about this, and she wasn't going to be able to torture him anymore. The sheer strength of his will scared her a little. "They were voracious. But I found it within

99

myself to satisfy them. Physically, at least. I could not truly love them, not the way they wanted—they were like vampires when it came to love, draining me every chance they got and always demanding more. There were endless fights and slow-burning jealousies and quite a bit of treachery. But we had sex, yes. We . . . fucked, if we're being blunt about such things. We fucked almost constantly. Sometimes as humans and sometime as wolves. Real wolves go on heat just like dogs, only for a few days of the year. The rest of the time they don't even think lustful thoughts. But like humans, werewolves are in a constant state of estrus. There is no bottom to their desires. Is that what you wanted to know?"

"Just trying to keep you honest," Chey said, a laugh in her voice she didn't really feel. She had challenged him and he had responded to her attack. This wasn't joking around. This wasn't a game they were playing. But she didn't want to bring that to the surface quite yet. Especially when she was losing.

Maybe he was tired of their sparring as well. He changed the subject quickly. "For the first few years we hunted with impunity. France was in the grips of chaos at the time. There really were no civilian authorities capable of stopping us, and the military had no interest in chasing down mythical creatures. But after the war ended that had to change. The Baroness was at least sane enough to realize we couldn't roam the countryside by moonlight anymore. We shared the cage when we were wolves and lived like humans when the moon was down, pretending to be a quietly decaying, formerly aristocratic French family. The local villagers supplied us with our needs and asked few ques-tions. If anyone noticed my accent was a bit off when I spoke, they just assumed I was a deserter from the war, which was true enough.

"We received only vague recollections of the terror and anger our wolves felt locked away like that. In dreams I would catch glimpses of our panic, though, and even in my quietest moments I felt claustrophobic and anxious. I was going insane, just as Lucie had over the decades. I didn't want to break down completely the way she had. I told them I wanted to leave. To come back to Canada, my homeland, and try to create some kind of life. There were real wolves there, I told them, there were places we could be free. The Baroness might have come with me, but Lucie took it worse than I expected."

"It was a messy breakup?"

"She tried to kill me," he told her. "I barely got away—and even then she tracked me. For years she followed me, sticking close to my shadow, waiting for me to slip up."

"Jesus," Chey said. "What happened?"

"Like I said," Powell told her, "hate's difficult to maintain. Even for crazy people. Love, though. Love doesn't die so easily. She's still out there somewhere. She's still chasing me, though for now I've escaped her. I haven't seen her in thirty years, but I know she and I are not done with each other yet."

eighteen

Powell drank some water from an old tin canteen and went on with his story. "I left the castle in nineteen twenty-one, I think. I had lost track of time—when you're not living in society, when every day is like every other, you stop paying attention to clocks and calendars. When I first came back to human civilization I was in a sort of fog and I wasn't entirely sure where I was, either. I quickly discovered it wasn't going to be easy fitting in. The moon rises when it's going to, and there's no way to hold back the change. I had to make sure I was someplace safe when it happened. That made it hard to make friends, and quite impossible to hold down a job. I slept rough for a lot of that time and spent my human hours pondering how I was going to get along, how I would ever make my own way in the world. I couldn't go back to my family, I knew. They wouldn't understand—and what if I ended up hurting one of them? I would have to create my own life, out of whole cloth. I don't know if you can imagine what that's like."

Chey shrugged. Maybe she had some small idea.

"Without a plan, without money, with this horrible curse

forcing me to take elaborate precautions for every day of my life, I fell from one bad circumstance into another. I followed the trains and asked everywhere if anyone knew a way to reverse my condition, but of course there was no good way for me to approach anyone who might actually know the answer. I went to scientists who wanted to study me—to experiment on me. I went to scholars of history who frankly disbelieved that I still existed. I went to priests who could only tell me that my immortal soul was forfeit, though their explanations as to why never made any sense to me.

"No one had anything tangible to offer me. I wandered around Europe for a while, but I'd been honest when I said I wanted to come back to Canada. Eventually I got enough courage together to try it.

"It wasn't easy crossing the ocean. I could hardly afford to buy a silver cage. Instead I stole a trunk, a big steamer trunk large enough that I could climb inside. I had a silver chain I had taken from Lucie's castle, and no matter how badly I needed money I managed never to pawn it. It was the only way I could keep my wolf from hurting anyone, you see. It wasn't very thick, but it didn't matter. When I would feel the change coming on I would climb into my trunk. Then I would wrap the chain around the outside in such a way that it held the trunk shut but could still be easily removed by a human hand. My wolf would try to get out, of course, but it was impossible—without hands the wolf couldn't pull the chain free. Stuck inside that confined space the wolf couldn't get enough leverage to kick the trunk to pieces, either. Every time I climbed into that trunk I worried the wolf would get out, all the same. I might hurt someone—for all I knew I might kill every human being on the ship, and as I was no seaman I would be left adrift on the ocean, unable to steer my way to any harbor. Far worse, there was the possibility I might get out, hurt only one person without killing them, and thereby spread my curse.

"My fears went unrealized. The other passengers and the crew knew there was something odd about me, but back then people weren't terrified of each other's mysteries so much, and no one asked any questions I couldn't answer. Two weeks after I'd departed I made landfall at Boston and from there I worked my way north, across the border. Back, at last, to 'our home and native land.'

"I know the southern part of the country is pretty well developed now, but there wasn't much of anything west of Ontario back then. This was sometime during the Depression, but before the second war. I found a cabin in the Barren Lands and tried that for a while. I was lonesome, but it was bearable—I thought I had found my place. Eventually, though, the cities of Ontario started to grow and spread out and new suburbs developed, whole new towns sprouting up where before there had never been anything but logging camps and the occasional hunter. When the land developers moved in I moved out, heading west. That became a pattern. I would live somewhere a while, maybe six months, maybe a whole year, but as soon as the loggers packed up and moved out I knew I would have to hurry on, sometimes with no warning. I roamed through the west until the west became British Columbia and the western coast, which was already growing itself, the cities there spreading back eastward. I changed direction, headed north, and then I roamed upcountry until I got here. Always running away, always foot-weary and wanting to finally settle down, to stop the running, always horrified of what might happen if I did. I know I'll have to leave even this desolate place eventually, but I think it'll be a while."

He stopped talking, then. His story was done. The sudden

silence was so strange that she sat up and looked right at him. "You've spent all this time alone? All those years in the backwoods with nobody?"

He shrugged. "There's Dzo. He and I met up in the seventies. He was living above a bar in Medicine Hat. It was kind of weird, actually. I had popped in for a quick beer—I allowed myself that small luxury sometimes, when I knew the moon wouldn't rise until much later. He was sitting on a bar stool eating peanuts out of a dish, but I knew something was up because he had another little dish full of water and he had to wash each peanut fastidiously before he popped it in his mouth. I knew, from long experience, that whenever I saw something weird my best bet was to turn around and walk away, but this seemed like harmless eccentricity, so I just pretended not to notice and held up a finger for service. It was too late, though. He saw me and pointed at me and said, 'Hey, you're a shape-shifter, right?' I looked around, expecting to be seized by the patrons of the bar. If they knew what I was, surely they would lock me up, or worse, I figured. I raised my hands in surrender and fled. My car was parked out back—I still had three hours to get back to my cabin before I changed. He came up and stood in front of my car and wouldn't let me leave. He had his mask on and a bag over his shoulder and he said he was coming with me. I tried to explain that I was just passing through. He just nodded and said he was mobile himself. I tried to explain it would be dangerous, that he should be afraid of me, but my threats just made him smile. No matter what I said, he wouldn't take no for an answer. Eventually I had to give in and let him tag along. We've been working together ever since."

"At least you had someone, then. Anyone. You must have missed your family pretty terribly," she said.

"Eh, families aren't what they're cracked up to be," he said, dismissively. There was a story there he wasn't interested in telling.

Chey had her own ideas, though. "Mine was pretty great, once," she said. She could feel the wolf inside of her, baring its teeth. She fought it back, kept her face clean of emotion. "Then things went to shit." Some ember of humanity in her heart flared up as soon as she'd said that. No matter what she'd been through, Powell's sheer life span meant he'd suffered a lot longer than she had. "I'm sorry. I know you've had it bad, too."

He shrugged. They said little more to each other until they were back at the cabin. When he jumped down from the truck bed he took a look at his watch. "The moon's down until about quarter to ten tonight. I don't know about you, but I wouldn't mind a bath and a bed." Her eyes must have flashed, because he grinned. "One at a time, of course. We have a big galvanized tub I bathe in, usually. Fill it up with water off the fire and it actually gets medium hot. I don't have much in the line of fancy soaps and notions, but what's mine is yours."

She nodded gratefully. It would feel good to get clean again.

"Listen," he said. "I know you probably don't want to think about this right now. But this life doesn't have to be so terrible as you think. It's been a long, long time since I had a place I could call my own for more than a season or two. I figure it'll be five years before we have to move on from here. If you're going to be sticking around"—her eyes definitely flashed at that, but he pressed on—"If you're going to be here a while, maybe we can start thinking about how to improve this place. Dig a well for sweet water, maybe even rig up a windmill to get some electricity. Don't say anything now. Just think about it. Your life doesn't have to be completely miserable."

Her face froze. Complete misery. When was the last time her life had been anything but? She tried to smile but felt like her skin was stretching painfully over her teeth. Instead she just turned away and walked toward the cabin. He headed for his smokehouse.

When he'd mentioned electricity it had made her think of her cell phone. She looked around to make sure Dzo wasn't watching, then pulled it out of her pocket to check to see if it still had any charge. She nearly dropped it when the screen lit up with the message:

SATELLITE
CONNECTION
ESTABLISHED

- you have (1)
message waiting -

nineteen

They announced, on returning to the little house in the woods, that the thing she wanted most in the world was a bath.

"I think we can make that happen," Powell told her. He shot her a look with one corner of his mouth turned up in what sort of resembled a smile. "Of course, if you want hot water, you're going to have to work for it." He led her around the side of the house and showed her a big galvanized tin washtub hanging from a hook. "It's big enough to sit down in." It was mottled white with age, but there were no holes in it. "I try to take a bath myself at least once a week. Though typically I just jump in a pond and scrub myself until my fingers go numb."

"All the comforts of home," Chey said, and reached up to grab the tub. "You going to help me with this?"

"No need," he told her.

She frowned, but then she lifted the tub off its hook with one hand. It felt far lighter than it had any right to be. She hefted it a couple of times and realized that it weighed quite a bit, actually, but that the muscles in her arm worked better than they ever had before. Somehow she'd gotten stronger since she'd changed.

"One of the few bright spots in your new existence," Powell told her.

Chey slung the tub over her shoulder and started heading toward the woods behind the house.

"Where are you going?" he asked her.

"Far enough away that I can have some privacy, if you don't mind. Don't worry. I won't go so far that I can't scream for help if I see a bear."

He shook his head, but he made no move to stop her. "You're still figuring this out. If a bear attacks you out there, scream so I know to come help the bear," he told her. She thought maybe he was going to leave her alone, but then he called for Dzo to come help her. The little man came jogging over and grabbed one handle of the tub, even though she didn't need the help. The message Powell was sending her was clear. Still, she was glad it was Dzo who was going to watch over her and not her fellow wolf. She had been worried Powell might insist on keeping an eye on her while she disrobed.

The two of them, Chey and Dzo, carried the tub out to just beyond the edge of the clearing and set it down on a spot relatively free of undergrowth. Then Dzo pushed the mask up onto the top of his head and grinned at her. "You're starting to like him, aren't you?" he asked. "Monty, I mean." He scraped out a fire ring and started to lay down a pile of thick logs with air space between them. "At least tell me you're not still mad at him."

Chey grabbed an armful of twigs and started piling them in a cone shape, just like she'd been taught in the Girl Guides. "He's not what I expected," she admitted. She caught herself almost immediately, but she forced herself not to look up, not to look at his eyes and see if he'd caught her.

He had, though. He stood up straight and squinted at her. "What do you mean by that?" he asked. "How could you have expectations about a guy you didn't know existed until two days ago?"

"I just meant when I first saw him," she said, trying to keep her voice slow and steady, "when you brought me here. I had no idea he was a wolf."

That seemed to do the trick. Dzo nodded happily and lit a crumpled page from a crossword puzzle book on fire. Blowing on it carefully, he tucked it inside her twig cone, then pushed in some dried leaves. The fire jumped up at once, then flickered back down as the kindling was exhausted. Fingerling flames touched at the logs and blackened them. Eventually they would catch. Dzo brought over an old fire-stained kettle and braced it on some rocks over the fire. "There's a stream about twenty meters that way where you can get water," he said, pointing into the woods. "Or you can just gather up snow off the ground, though it tends to be pretty muddy underneath."

"Beauty," she said, and gave him the warmest smile she had. After a minute she blinked at him. "That's—great. Maybe you can go now," she said. "So I can take my clothes off without you watching me."

He shrugged and flipped his mask down. "You need anything else, just holler." He started away, then stopped and looked back at her. She didn't mind, somehow, talking to him with his mask on. Maybe because she had no trouble imagining the expression on his face beneath it. It would be the same half-bemused, half-amused expression he always wore. She could see now that the mask, which before had just looked creepy, was actually carved to resemble that same expression.

"I will," she said, thinking he was just waiting for a reply. But he just stood there a while longer before he said anything more.

"He likes you, you know. I mean Monty."

"He does?" she asked. She hadn't even considered that.

"Sure. 'Course, he ain't seen a naked lady in more'n fifty years," he added, "so maybe he's just ruttin'." With that he traipsed away, back toward the cabin.

Chey watched him go. As soon as he was out of sight she poured out the kettle over the struggling fire, extinguishing it with a hiss. She would, indeed, have loved a bath just then, but there was no time. She unzipped her pocket and took out her cell phone. She pushed the "five" key three times and a GPS display came up. She looked at the trees, then back at the cabin. Then she dashed into the forest as fast as she could on human feet.

The two of them would leave her alone for at least an hour. They wouldn't dare come check on her in the tub for that long. Eventually they would wonder what was taking her so long and investigate. When they couldn't find her they would start searching. They couldn't just let her run away—Dzo had been quite clear on that, that they would track her down and drag her back if they had to. Once they came after her she would have very little time left. She had little faith in her own ability to evade them. Powell had been a wolf long enough to know how to track a woman through the woods, she was sure of that. With an hour's head start, though, maybe she could make it to the rendezvous and be back before that happened.

She'd forgotten how hard it was to move at any speed through the drunken forest on two feet, and she tripped three times before she was even out of visual range of the cabin. She slid down a slope of loose soil and weakly anchored reindeer moss and got a face full of snow at the bottom, but she got right back up and kept moving. Her course, as outlined on her cell phone's screen, took her along the high bank of an all-year

111

stream, a thundering rivulet that made it impossible for her to hear if anyone was pursuing her. Eventually she came around a thick stand of trees and found the source of the stream, a miniature lake as white and blue as the sky above, a brilliant mirror. On the far side of the water a red light burned angrily—a flare, giving off great clouds of pale smoke as it fizzed away. From the air that light would have been visible for kilometers, but the heavy tree cover made it impossible to see from the ground unless you were right at the shore of the lake.

She had to pick her way around the lake's edge, which took more time she didn't have. It would have taken her ten minutes to swim across, but it was far too cold for that—whether or not her changed body could handle the chill, she knew she wasn't prepared for it emotionally. Taking the long way around cost her another twenty minutes. She estimated she had eight minutes left before Dzo came to check on her and found her missing.

In the clearing on the far side of the lake a two-man helicopter sat like a giant dragonfly sunning itself on a clump of sparse grass. The pilot, an Indian in a padded vest, lay with his back against the big machine and his hands folded behind his head. He didn't even look up as she staggered into the clearing.

Bobby Fenech, on the other hand, jumped up as if he'd been bitten by a snake. He was wearing a leather bomber jacket over an orange polo shirt with the collar turned up. He had on a pair of wraparound aviator sunglasses, but he was just as soft- and harmless-looking as ever. His spiky hair stayed perfectly motionless even in the stiff breeze off the lake.

"Jesus, Chey, you don't just sneak up on a guy in my profession," he said. "Don't you know we're famous for our killer reflexes?"

"Hi, Bobby," she said, and leaned into his embrace. She let him lift her chin and kiss her. She had let him do a lot more than that before—and now was hardly the time to be squeamish. "Please tell me you got my message. About losing my pack."

He grinned evilly. "I can't believe you lost your weapon. Do you know how expensive these are?" he asked. He put a hand inside his jacket and pulled out a square black handgun. He ejected the magazine and handed it to her so she could check the ammunition.

The seven bullets lined up in the clip were black with tarnish, but she knew they were 995-grade silver underneath.

twenty

A duck slid in on the wind and flapped to a landing on the perfect mirror surface of the lake. Thick velvety ripples of black water hurried away from its body as it cruised serenely along. The breeze off the water made the quaking aspens rattle and shiver.

Chey's weapon swung through the air and sighted on the duck as if the handgun were mounted on ball bearings. It felt like her arm didn't move at all. She'd trained long and hard so it would feel like that.

"Remember," Fenech said, "you have to be close."

"I know. You told me already," she said, slipping the gun into her back pocket.

She knew the science involved. Normal lead bullets were soft enough that when they passed down the barrel of a gun they changed shape, slightly, conforming to the rifling on the inside of the barrel. They emerged from the muzzle spinning as a result, and that spin kept them traveling in a mostly straight line. Silver bullets were harder than lead and they didn't change their shape as easily. Because they didn't spin they were far more likely to deviate in mid-flight from the trajectory you wanted—which made them far less accurate, especially at any kind of range. She knew all this; she knew it better than he did, but he was going to tell her again anyway. Bobby was one of those people who liked to repeat things for emphasis, because he assumed other people's memories weren't as good as his. "At more than twenty meters you're unlikely to hit the side of a wood buffalo." He smiled at his own jest. "So you need to be close."

"Close," she said. "Got it."

His smile deepened a little. Turned warm. In his own way he really could be affectionate, even caring. "How are you?" he asked. "It can't have been easy getting this far. You look great, though. I kind of half expected to find you starving and frozen, but you look like you've been working out. You found out that life up north agrees with you?"

She nodded and bit her lip. How to tell him? Would he freak out? Would he shoot her on the spot?

"You know I always thought you were crazy for wanting to hike in like this."

"It was the only way," she said. "My cover story was that I was completely lost and near death. I had to look the part—enough to fool somebody who's lived in these woods for decades."

"Have you seen him yet?" Fenech asked. She hadn't said much in her message. He had no idea what had happened to her. "Did you make contact?"

"Yeah," she said. "Yeah, I made contact. He has a cabin about two kilometers from here in a little clearing. He lives there with another guy, a Dene Indian named Dzo."

She'd thought the pilot of the helicopter was asleep. When she mentioned Dzo's name, however, he let out a little grunt of humor.

115

"Something amuse you, Lester?" Fenech asked, a cockeyed grin on his face.

The pilot sat up a bit. His eyes were hidden under deep, pouchy lids, but they sparkled when they met Chey's gaze. "That's probably not his real name, is all," the pilot said.

Fenech turned halfway around. "It's not a common Dene name?"

The pilot shrugged. "In North Slavey language, that's the word for the musquash. The, you know, you call it the muskrat down south. Little furry thing. It's like if your name was Chipmunk."

"Is that so." Bobby stared at the pilot as if surprised he'd had the temerity to speak. Surprised, and slightly amused. "You know, Lester's a pretty funny name where I come from."

The pilot shrugged again and closed his eyes, done with the conversation.

"Bobby," she interjected, "let's worry about people's names later, okay? I made contact. I made really bad contact. There's been a complication with the plan."

Fenech's face hardened and he nodded. He was ready to hear it.

She sighed deeply. "He scratched my leg with one of his claws. While he was a wolf."

He looked down at her leg, concern growing across his face. "So you need medical attention? We'll fly you out of here right now," Fenech offered.

She shook her head. "No, Bobby, you don't understand. He scratched me, and that's all it takes. I'm one of them now."

She could see in his face he still didn't get it.

She swallowed painfully. There was a thickness in her throat she didn't fully understand.

"I'm a wolf, too, now," she said, and watched him take a step

116

back, just like she'd known he would. His face stayed perfectly still, but his eyes widened a little.

"Oh, boy," he said. He brought one hand up and scratched at his spiky hair, careful, even in this moment of shock, not to muss a single strand. "Oh, boy," he said again. "Alright. So . . ."

"So you just need to be aware of this," she said. "It doesn't have to change anything. I can still do what I came for."

"No. No, in light of this—this shocking revelation—I think we scrub the mission. I mean, we need to move forward but not—not like this. I know some guys I can bring in."

"You're going to call in the Mounties on this?" she shouted. She couldn't believe what she was hearing.

"Not exactly. Not any official police," he said carefully. "Just some guys I happen to know. I mean, that's what I wanted to do in the first place."

"No," Chey insisted.

"No?" he asked, and it was an actual question. "Because it looks like maybe you've screwed this up. In the worst way possible."

"No," she repeated. "This is my operation. I fucking deserve it."

He might have started in on her again if Lester the pilot hadn't cleared his throat just then.

"If you two are at a good stopping place," he said, "you might notice we've got guests."

Fenech and Chey swiveled in unison to look down the side of the lake. Something was moving toward them, bouncing and lurching through the brush, weaving around the tree trunks. It was Dzo's rusted truck crawling over broken terrain down there, its windshield catching sporadic winks of sunlight as it rumbled through the shadows.

Powell leaned out of the driver's side window and shouted

117

her name. The soft syllable flapped around in the treetops and echoed off the surface of the lake.

"Chey," he yelled again. "I just want to talk to you, that's all," he called.

Chey muttered a curse and turned to look at her handler, but Fenech's eyes were invisible behind his sunglasses. He was smiling, but she had no idea what that meant.

"When you said you made contact," he told her, "I assumed that meant you'd set up a position and had him visually. I didn't think you'd been properly introduced. Does he know about me? Did you tell him you already had a boyfriend?"

Chey tried to keep her face blank of expression. She would not let him take this away from her. Not now. Not after what she had done, not after what she had become, just to get this far. "I had no weapon at the time. I needed to get close. I did what I had to."

Dzo slewed his vehicle around to a stop where a line of trees blocked further progress around the lake. Powell didn't wait for a full stop, but jumped out of the truck while it was still slowing down. His legs caught the earth and grabbed it, propelling him toward her a lot faster than she'd been able to cover the same distance. He had seen her, perhaps, or maybe he'd just spotted the helicopter. He came loping around the side of the lake and then stopped twenty meters away. He looked more confused than anything else. "Chey," he said, closing the gap. Ten meters. Eight. "Chey, you can't leave me now. You know that. Who the hell are these people?"

"Bobby," she said, "I'd like you to meet—"

"I don't want to meet him. You know what I want," Fenech said.

She nodded and drew her weapon. Powell was six meters away. She sighted on his forehead.

"Chey?" he asked.

part two

on the yellowhead highway

twenty-one

Most people's lives change very slowly, more slowly than the seasons. Some people are born into the life they're going to lead and nothing much ever comes along to force them to change. For Cheyenne Clark, change came about in the space of thirty very bad seconds.

It happened when she was younger. Much younger. It happened one day when she and her dad were driving in their car.

It was at the end of a vacation. They were coming down out of Jasper National Park, where her dad had shown her the glaciers. Just the two of them—she was on holiday from school and he was between jobs, but he'd scraped enough together for the trip of a lifetime. Her mother hadn't been able to get time off from work, but frankly, she'd looked relieved when they packed up the car, waved good-bye, and pulled out of the drive—glad enough to have the house to herself for a while, to have some time off from looking after the both of them. For Chey and her dad it had been a time to bond, something they'd never had much of before. The park was half a continent away from home

121

and they'd driven the whole way there, which meant a lot of time to talk to each other and reconnect.

That was the summer she'd started to really think about what it was going to be like to be an adult, and her dad had answered all of her stupid questions. He'd told her stories about his own youth, in America, and his time in the army there, which sounded like going to a summer camp you couldn't leave. In exchange she'd told him all about her life, about school and her friends, and she'd even told him about her first kiss, with a sweaty Quebecois boy who had called her *mademoiselle* and then bragged, afterward, that he'd gotten his hand up under her shirt even though he really hadn't.

As for the park itself, it had turned out to be a lot of fun. The two of them had ridden in a snowmobile as big as a bus and out of the window she'd seen a herd of deer. They'd had a week in the park, and though she'd been dreading the trip all spring, now that it was over she wished she could have stayed there for a month.

It was on the drive back that things changed.

It was July 25, 1994, and Chey was twelve years old. They'd been driving for days already and the car was full of discarded fast food wrappers and empty plastic water bottles and it had started to smell a little. Her dad let her put in an Ace of Base CD, and he even said it wasn't half bad. It was that or the radio, and there was nothing on that far west but country music and talk radio about ice fishing and hockey.

He was wearing his red Melton jacket that smelled like cigarettes even though he'd quit the year before. He hadn't shaved in three days and his face was dark with stubble. Afterward she would not be able to remember much of what they talked about in the car that day. There had been so many long, deep conversations already, and the promise of plenty more to come—they

122

were nearly a thousand kilometers from home, and had days of driving ahead of them—and most of that day, she thought, they had lapsed into a kind of companionable silence, the two of them sharing a half-breathed laugh now and again, her father occasionally pointing through the windshield at a flight of geese or a particularly stunning stretch of landscape.

She was sure, however, that she was the first one who saw the wolf. "Oh, Dad, look at that," she said, pressing up against her window until her breath fogged on the glass. He stamped on the brakes, maybe thinking she'd seen some obstruction in the road. They hadn't quite stopped when the wolf leapt onto the highway and smashed into the front end of the car.

There was a really loud bang as metal crumpled under the impact. Chey slid to one side in her seat and screamed as the car rocked on its tires.

"Honey, shh," her dad said. "Shh," his big hairy hand catching her across her chin as he reached to steady her. Maybe he'd reached over to try to grab her shoulder, but his eyes were fixed on the animal in front of them.

The sun had set, but still a trace of orange lingered on the horizon. The moon was up, a narrow crescent. In the distance the mountains were slowly turning into silhouettes, already heavy with night. The wolf sat in the road in front of the car with its head turned to one side, not moving at all.

Chey breathed heavily. She was very scared.

"It's alright," her dad said. "It was just a little accident. It didn't see us coming."

The wolf slowly stood up and took a loping step to the side, away from the car. Then it shook its head violently as if trying to shake water out of its ears. It turned its face to look at them, and its frosty green eyes were full of undeniable malice.

"Just don't scream, okay?" Chey's dad said. "Just don't make any noise, and I'm sure it will leave us alone. It's hurt. It's going to be scared, but—"

The wolf tilted its head back and let out a roaring yowl, sounding more like a mountain lion than a dog. Tears jumped out of Chey's eyes and she pulled her knees up to her chin.

"I'm going—" he stopped as she started to whine for him to not go anywhere, to stay with her. It was a primal sound that came out of her, not any coherent speech. She couldn't have held it in if she'd tried. "It's okay," he said. "I'm not going anywhere. I'm just going to put the car in drive and—"

The wolf bounded up onto the car's hood and smashed at the windshield with its wide face. They both screamed then. A crack clicked and rattled across the glass as the wolf reared back, wrinkling its nose. It brought up its massive paws and slapped them against the glass and the windshield shivered, cracks radiating outward, cobwebs of broken glass emanating from where it struck. It brought its face close again and howled in at them, and its breath froze on the windshield, fogged it up. The wolf threw itself at the barrier one last time and the glass just evaporated out of its frame in a winking cascade of light and noise.

The wolf's giant teeth came inside, inside the car with them. The teeth were white and yellow and the animal's lips were black, drawn back to bare the teeth. Those white, white teeth turned red as they sank into her dad's neck; she heard her dad trying to talk; he made a gurgling sound as he tried to tell her something. The wolf yanked backward and her dad's body strained against his seat belt. Safety glass was everywhere, in the leg wells, on the dashboard, in her hair. The wolf yanked again and her dad's throat came out in pieces. His eyes were still watching her.

They looked calm, those eyes. Totally in control. He was still trying to convince her that everything was okay. His eyes were lying to her.

The wolf's green eyes showed nothing but the truth.

She was screaming. She screamed and screamed, but the wolf didn't even seem to hear her.

Her dad kept trying to speak. His lips moved, and he lifted his hand toward her, but he couldn't seem to get it high enough. It fell back against the seat between them with a soft thud. Blood came up out of his neck and ran down his shirt. The wolf lunged forward again and got its teeth into his shoulder and his chest. It pulled, and pulled, and her dad slid out of his seat belt, his arms and legs bobbing, and the wolf dragged him down into the road.

Then—she was alone in the car. Her dad was just—just gone, along with the wolf.

The silence would have been perfect if it had not been for the CD playing on the sound system. She reached over and switched it off.

Cool air came in through the hole in the windshield, a breeze that touched the wetness on her face. Chey sat up a little and looked forward.

Outside, in the fan of the headlights, the wolf was tearing at her dad's body. Tearing pieces off of him and swallowing them convulsively. Eating him. The wolf looked up, its face covered in blood except for those wintry eyes. Those hateful eyes. They looked right into Chey and judged her and found her wanting. They despised her.

In a minute, those eyes said, *I'll be done here. Then I'm coming for you.*

twenty-two

Her dad—her dad was dead. Dead. He was—he was dead.

It was like the moment when the airplane lands, and the pressure in your ears is intense and you can't hear anything. And then your ears pop and it all comes rushing back. Time started moving again, and everything was real.

Chey screamed and screamed. She thrust her hands into her eyes so she wouldn't see, pressed her face against her shoulder.

Screamed some more.

It didn't change anything. It didn't help. Breath whistled in and out of her lungs, but she was just sitting there. She was just sitting there doing nothing.

She was still about to die. The wolf was still going to tear her apart and—and—

She was still screaming as she unfastened her seat belt, but at least she was moving. Achieving something. She was going to open her door, very slowly, and get out. And then she was going to run as fast as she could.

She would run until she found someone else, somebody who could help her. Somebody who could make it all okay.

Somehow. She didn't have to worry about the details, about how anything could ever be okay again, because when she found this person, this hypothetical Good Samaritan, they would have the answers. All she had to do was get out and run.

Except that wasn't going to happen, was it? She could run as fast as her body was capable of and it wouldn't be enough. She knew it wouldn't. The wolf wouldn't just let her get away. The wolf would outrun her. It would catch her, and finish her off.

That was what the wolf wanted. And the wolf had all the power. It had those teeth, and it had claws, and it had millions upon millions of years of evolution on its side. It would be very, very good at chasing down little girls in the dark and tearing them to pieces. That was one reason why people had invented fire, and guns, and cities—as a way of protecting themselves from—from monsters that ran in the darkness.

She had none of those things at her command. If she played this game the way the wolf played it, she was going to die.

But there had to be something she could do. Something other than running for it. She thought again of the mythical person out there in the night who was going to make every-thing okay. That person was too far away to help her. She needed to help herself.

Which meant that first, she had to start thinking. She had to stop screaming so she could hear her own thoughts. Somehow she found it within herself to stop screaming.

When she'd managed that, she could hear other things again. She could hear bones cracking in between those giant teeth. That nearly made her start screaming again. She needed some-thing—she needed to find something that would help her not scream. That would help her think. She looked around at the broken glass and the torn vinyl upholstery in the car.

She glanced over at all the blood on the driver's seat. Her dad's blood. His seat belt hung slack and stretched out across the blood. So much blood.

She had an idea. It was not a brilliant epiphany, not a moment of genius. But it was a good, solid thought at a time when her brain was barely functioning, so she clutched to it like a mountaineer clutching to the last, poorly seated piton, because the other option is to drop away into nothing.

The next step was to make herself move. To put her plan into action. Her whole body shivered, though she was not particularly cold. She slid across the seat, slid her legs down into the leg well on the driver's side.

She was twelve years old—she'd never driven a car before, had no idea how. She'd played video games where you had to drive a car. She looked down and saw two pedals. She thought there were supposed to be three. Weren't there supposed to be three? She stepped on one of them with all her weight and the car bobbed back and forth a little.

In the headlights the wolf tore something stringy out of her dad's torso. She wasn't sure, but it looked like one of his arms was missing. Would the wolf wait until it had finished eating before it came for her? Maybe it thought it had all the time in the world. Maybe it wanted to enjoy its meal.

Chey almost threw up. But that wouldn't have been helpful just then. It was not part of her plan.

She pressed down tentatively on the other pedal, the one she hadn't tried yet, and the car surged around her but it didn't go anywhere. She held down her foot and the engine made an angry whirring sound. It was enough to get the wolf's attention. It pulled its face out of her father's side and took a step around the side of the car.

She had managed to make it think it needed to come for her

now. She'd managed to make herself its priority. That wasn't helpful at all.

"Get away," Chey screamed. "Get away!" If neither pedal worked she had no idea what to do next. She was certain she was pressing the accelerator but—but why wouldn't the car go? She stepped on the pedal again and again the car roared. The headlights flickered but—

What had her dad said? Right before the wolf got him? He had said he was going to put the car into drive. What did that mean?

The wolf took another step. It was coming up around to the driver's side door. Was it grinning at her?

She grabbed a stick on the side of the steering wheel—she'd seen her dad move it before—and yanked it down as hard as she could. The windshield wipers swept up, but then the one on her side got stuck in the broken glass and just sort of flopped there. The other one beat back and forth madly. She pushed the stick back up.

The wolf reared up and put both paws on her windowsill. It licked at the window next to her face. Jesus, she thought, it was playing with her. It wanted to scare her.

"I'm already scared, you, you asshole!" she screamed at it. Then she grabbed another stick and pushed it down. The car jumped underneath her and started rolling backward. Shit! She looked back and saw the side of the road there, saw a ditch. A big letter *R* had appeared on the control panel. It had to mean *reverse*.

The wolf trotted away from her. It got maybe five meters away. She stepped on the brake pedal and the car stopped. Everybody stopped.

From the side of the road the wolf watched her with lethal curiosity. It looked like it was considering its next move. Very soon, she was certain, it would decide to stop playing games and get down to business.

She studied the stick and the dashboard and she figured out how to push it up two stops until it said *D*, for *drive*. There was a *1* and a *2* as well, but she had no idea what they meant.

Standing on the brake pedal, her legs not quite long enough to reach comfortably, she flipped the stick up to *D*. The car bobbed again and she looked over and saw the wolf. It was leaning back on its hind legs, ready to jump at the car again. To drag her out just like it had dragged her dad.

Just as the wolf bounded toward her she shifted all her weight from the brake to the accelerator. The car lurched forward and she swung the steering wheel around to get back on the road. The wolf slashed at the side of the car and she heard metal ring and tear. The car's rear fender came off with a clang and a rattling clatter as it bounced on the asphalt. She didn't dare let go of the accelerator—she just kept pushing it harder, as the car rushed along underneath her, dragging her forward so hard she had to clutch at the steering wheel with every muscle in her arms. She looked back in the mirror and saw the animal falling away behind her in the red wash of her taillights.

That was the last she saw of it.

Except . . . some nights, when she couldn't sleep—which was pretty much every night after that—some nights she would sit in the dark and replay her escape. She would go over it in her head, each event, every little thing that had happened. Her hands would involuntarily reach for the gearshift; her feet would press down against the sheets, hunting for the pedals. And she would remember looking in the rearview one last time and—

—she swore to herself every time it was a false memory, a guilt complex, her imagination running away with her but—

—just for a second, just for a split second she would see her dad lying in the middle of the road, covered in blood and gore, and before she looked away, before tears made it impossible to see anything, she would watch him sit up and reach for her with his remaining hand. Reach out, begging her to come back and get him.

twenty-three

She drove until she found people. Good, kind people who took her in and let her tell the story as best she could, and who tried to understand what had happened to her and help her in any way they could. But not the people she'd imagined, the people who could make everything okay. Over time she began to realize those people did not, and could not, exist.

After the police were through with her, they put her on the phone with her mom, who told her not to worry. That everything was going to be okay. On the phone it sounded like her mom was a long, long way away.

Chey got to fly home in first class. She slept through the flight and the stewardesses had been advised ahead of time not to wake her until they had to, and then someone came and led her through security to her mom, who just stood there watching her for a while, studying her. Maybe looking for signs of injury. Maybe just watching to see if her husband would come off the plane as well, even though everyone knew he wouldn't. There wasn't even a coffin to ship back, because the body still hadn't been recovered. Eventually her mom hugged her, and rubbed her back, but she didn't say anything. She just led Chey to the car, and drove in very uncomfortable silence back to their house.

Chey went home, except home wasn't there anymore. Not home like she remembered it.

She was in the papers for a while, and even on TV a couple of times. Her mom wouldn't let her give any interviews, though, so quickly enough the media attention dried up. On the other hand the police wouldn't take no for an answer, and for weeks afterward they would come to the door at night, right after Chey had finished dinner and cleared the plates, and she would have to sit down with a man in a uniform and answer questions. Sometimes they brought pictures, photographs of different kinds of wolves. None of them looked like the one who attacked the car, and she wondered what it would have meant if one of them had. Was it like a police lineup? Was she supposed to pick the wolf out of the usual suspects? Once the police brought pictures of the crime scene, of the stretch of road where it had happened. She just nodded and said yes, that was what it looked like. Neither the car nor her dad's body was in the picture.

Her mom hated it when Chey had to look at the pictures. Chey claimed it was okay, that it didn't bother her, but that wasn't really true. She just said it for her mom's benefit. She couldn't sleep after she saw the pictures. Not for whole days on end.

Chey tried to ask her own questions, but the police didn't like to answer them, even when they could. They did tell her that her dad hadn't felt much pain at all, that he had been in shock when he died and probably wasn't even aware of what was happening. They also confirmed what she'd thought, that it wasn't any kind of ordinary wolf that had attacked them. That it was a lycanthrope. That was the word they used. The Assailant was believed to be a Lycanthrope. Just like the car was a Late Model Vehicle, and her dad was the Decedent Victim.

133

Lycanthropes fit a certain profile of Assailant. There were Protocols for dealing with Lycanthropes. There were statistics on Lycanthropes—no more than three Fatal Attacks in the last twenty years, a believed Global Population of no more than a thousand Individuals, most of them in Europe now. There were whole three-ring binders of information on what to do when investigating a Lycanthrope Sighting.

The police carried out a Thorough Investigation. They formed a Searching Party and they swept the country around the Incident Area. They turned up No Result—the Lycanthrope was never found.

The police had done what they could. Chey never blamed them—why would they even want to find the wolf? Who would ever want to face such a thing if they didn't have to? The main detective on the case was good enough to recommend a therapist for Chey, and so her mom took her to a little office downtown with dusty potted plants in a window with shades that were always drawn. The therapist was a very skinny, very pale man with blond hair who recommended they meet three times a week, at least until they saw how much help she needed. Her mom just nodded and wrote a check.

They had a funeral for her dad. The police had finally collected his body, but they held onto his remains for the duration of their investigation. Chey's mom had not protested. Chey's mom bought an empty coffin and arranged for a service. All of her relatives came up and touched the wood of the coffin and some of them cried. Chey got to stand with her mom at the door of the chapel, wearing a black dress that buttoned at her neck. She got to shake all their hands and thank them for coming.

Back at the house they had a reception and the same people showed up, but there was a lot less crying. People in suits and dresses filled up the tiny rooms, pressed up against the walls balancing paper plates full of food or plastic cups full of soda. They spoke in whispers or at least in low voices, but the combined sound was loud enough to hurt Chey's ears. She really wanted to just run back to her room and go to bed, but it was covered in coats and bags, so she couldn't.

All of her aunts and adult cousins had to make her go through the same ritual that was boring after the first time. They would pat her head or hug her to their waists and tell her how brave she was and how the hurt would go away with time. She would nod morosely and look like she was about to cry and eventually they would let her go. After a couple hours of that she couldn't even hear them anymore, but it didn't matter. She could respond without paying any attention at all. Then the doorbell rang and she ran to get it, because it got her away from all the sad people who were trying to talk to her. "Such a good girl," someone said behind her. "A time like this and she's still so well-behaved. I would be in hysterics."

She opened the door and looked out into the daylight. A tall man in a military uniform stood there, holding a peaked hat in his hands. He was maybe fifty years old and he had a fuzz of iron-colored hair on his head. Chey had never seen a man with hair that short. It startled her, but she tried not to show it on her face.

"Cheyenne," he said, and bowed forward a little to hold out his hand. "I doubt you remember me, but I'm your uncle Bannerman. Your father's American brother."

She nodded politely and shook his hand. He smiled at her, a cold little smile without anything at all hiding behind it. She asked him to come in and he disappeared, making the rounds, greeting everyone. A couple of Chey's aunts tried to grab him up into bear hugs, but he deflected them easily with a neat little trick. He held his hat in front of his body. If they hugged him they would have crushed the hat, and nobody wanted that. Chey was impressed. She wished she had thought to wear a hat.

She lost track of Uncle Bannerman then, but near the end of the reception he found her. She supposed he wanted to tell her how sorry he was for her loss, and she assumed the correct position, eyes downcast. Instead he squatted down next to her and wouldn't look away until she met his gaze.

"I wanted to say something to you, specifically," he said. When she didn't reply he just went on. "I was very impressed with how you escaped."

She squinted. Nobody at the reception had mentioned any of that. The day was supposed to be about her dad. "I had to do something or I would have died," she said, trying to dismiss him.

"Not everyone would have had the presence of mind to make that connection. Very few people would have had the resolution to carry it out." He smiled at her and started to stand up. It was all he'd wanted to say.

A question came out of her then like a belch. She had no control over it. She actively fought it. This man was her dad's brother, after all. His grief would be very real, too, and she needed to be sensitive to that. But she had to ask.

"Is this how people die?" she demanded. "They just disappear. And then nothing. There's nothing there."

He looked at her with very hard eyes, as if trying to decide what to say to her. "That's exactly how it happens," he told her.

"A person just goes away." Her voice was getting louder. She couldn't seem to control it. "A person is there, one day, and the next he doesn't exist. Even if he's your dad. Because nobody is safe. Ever."

More than a few black-clad aunts turned to look. But Uncle

136

Bannerman just held her gaze and wouldn't let go. He said nothing, just looked at her. Finally he took a handkerchief out of his pocket, not a tissue but a real cloth handkerchief, and gave it to her. She hadn't realized she was crying.

twenty-four

For a couple of weeks Chey's mom walked around the house like a ghost. She would walk into a room and look around as if she didn't recognize it. She didn't talk much and when she did it was just to say she was alright, she was fine, she was just tired. She worked pretty hard at boxing up all of Chey's father's stuff. Most of it went to the local church, even though the Clark family had never been particularly religious. Other things were just thrown away. Everything he'd ever owned had to be seen to. The car that the wolf had attacked was still out there, still out west sitting in a police station parking lot. Chey's mom asked them to donate it to a good charity, but there were insurance problems with that, so every day for a week she had to make phone calls and send letters and emails until eventually somebody agreed to take responsibility for the car. Her dad's will was pretty simple; everything went to her mom, but it turned out that even a really simple will took a lot of work to execute. A lawyer came to the house a couple of times. He brought Chey a box of chocolates, which was weird, but she thanked him politely and even ate a few while he watched and smiled.

Eventually Chey's mom went back to work. She was a para-legal at a firm of business lawyers. She said she desperately didn't want to go back, that she wanted to stay home with Chey and help her, but Chey said she would be okay on her own. It was another lie, and her mom even said she knew it was a lie, but when Chey didn't say anything more, her mom said it was alright, that she would go to work, that they would find a way to make things okay together. The first day back she called Chey at least a dozen times just to see how she was doing. That night she came home and fell asleep on the couch and Chey could smell alcohol on her. But that didn't turn out to be a long-term thing. After a couple days back on her job Chey's mom wasn't wandering around the house anymore. She looked more like her old self.

It took Chey a while longer to figure things out.

The neighbor's dog was a little schnauzer with whiskers hanging down from its face. It didn't look anything like a wolf, but still, every time it barked, she would jump. Her heart would race and she would hug herself, pull herself into a ball. When they walked around town, when her mom would take her to do the shopping and she saw a dog, she would cross the street.

She didn't sleep much. Maybe a few hours every night. Her grades started dropping at school because she kept falling asleep during algebra. She tried all kinds of tricks to stay awake. She jammed pencil points into her thighs, bit her tongue, anything, but it never seemed to work.

The therapist gave her tranquilizers so she could sleep and Prozac so she wouldn't just sleep all day. The combination made Chey feel like live eels were swimming around and around inside her skull, so after a while she only pretended to take the pills and hid them in the back of her desk drawer.

The therapist was supposed to be somebody she could talk to, but she had nothing to say. She would go and sit in his office and not say anything, thinking she could just wait him out. For a couple of sessions that was exactly what happened—he just waited until her time was up, then sent her home. After a while, though, he started asking her questions. Weird questions that made her feel angry or upset and she didn't know why.

He asked her about dogs a lot. He told her that he owned a dog, a dalmatian. He asked if she'd like him to bring his dog to the office so she could pet it. She said no thank you. He got a very knowing look on his face and lifted his eyebrows like he expected her to say something more. She didn't. He never mentioned his dalmatian again.

During one session he started asking her questions she definitely didn't like. This time he wouldn't take silence for an answer, though. He wanted to know what she remembered about her father. He wanted to know what her father had looked like, and she thought that would be easy, but then she couldn't quite remember. Then he asked her if she ever thought about how her father had died and she had to admit that she did.

"Do you ever get excited when you think about that?" he asked. Her heart jumped in her chest when he said that. She stared at him as hard as she could, but he just sat back in his chair and waited for her answer. "This is really important, Chey," he said to her. "I think this might be a breakthrough. I want to show you a picture," he said. "I want you to tell me if this picture is arousing." He pulled a piece of paper out of his pocket, a folded sheet torn from the pages of a magazine. Carefully he unfolded it and passed it to her. It was a picture of a wolf with snow on its muzzle.

She told her mom about what had happened, and then Chey didn't have to go to therapy anymore.

She tried to be a normal kid, then. Tried her hardest to just fit in and do okay. Tried to act like a spinny chick and flirt with boys and get invited to parties. It never felt quite right, but it did lead to one unexpected bonus. At the parties there was always alcohol. She discovered that two or three beers would ensure she slept the whole night through.

twenty-five

When she was sixteen years old Chey went down to Colorado for the summer. Uncle Bannerman met her at the airport in Denver in his uniform. As far as she knew, he always wore it. He was in the American army somehow, but she didn't really understand when he tried to explain his exact job. He took her up into the mountains, where he'd already set up a camp with two small tents and a fire ring.

"We're going to live up here for two months," he said. "No telephones, no Internet, no friends from school." He took off his uniform jacket and tie and put them in a plastic bag in the back of his car. Chey was confused and kind of frightened—she'd had no idea this was coming. "Your mother tells me she found pot in your school bag," he said. "That won't happen again. Correct?"

"I guess," she said. She hadn't liked pot anyway. It made her feel weird and fuzzy and that made her paranoid—she kept looking at all the shadows in the room and they kept changing like they were moving. Circling her. "Yeah, whatever."

"When you speak to me you will call me *sir*," he told her. He wasn't joking around. "She tells me you're running with a bad crowd. Older girls who already have bad habits."

She squirmed and kicked at the dirt before answering. "Maybe. But they know how to fight," she said, figuring that if anybody would understand it would be him. "I thought they could teach me how, too. I mean, sir."

"Fighting *is* a bad habit," he told her, which didn't make a lot of sense since he was in the army. His eyes softened a little, though. "Cheyenne," he said to her, "there is a difference between getting in fights and learning how to defend yourself."

She could only look at him. He got it—he understood what she'd wanted to learn. What she'd been trying to figure out by spending so much time with the tough girls. She was amazed. She hadn't really thought it through that carefully herself.

"Enough of that. Let's focus on what's ahead of us, not what's behind. This summer you're going to live rough. You're going to stay up here with me and we're not going to leave until I say we can. It's up to you how you spend your time here. You can help me out. You can gather all of our firewood and do the washing up every night. Alternatively, you can do no work at all. You can sit around camp and stare into space. Your choice."

If it had been anyone else she would have told them to fuck off. She would have run away at night and hitchhiked into town. But this was Uncle Bannerman. He had never lied to her, even when he probably should have. And he had never treated her like a baby. It meant more to her than she could say. So she scrubbed his dishes and she washed out his clothes in the stream and she called him sir.

She made a lot of mistakes the first couple of days. She gathered green wood that took forever to start burning and gave off huge clouds of black smoke. She wore a hole right through one of her uncle's shirts by scraping at a bad stain with a rock. He never had a harsh word for her, but he didn't hug her and tell her it was alright, either—he just showed her what she'd done wrong, and how to do it better the next time. At night she would lie on the hard ground with just a blanket underneath her, and her whole body would hurt. She missed her friends, missed television and pizza and dressing in decent clothes. She cried sometimes and wished she had her mom there. Sometimes she thought about running away after all, about hiking down to the highway under cover of darkness and hitchhiking her way back to Canada. The idea made her even more scared. Scared because she thought there was something she was supposed to do here, to learn, and that if she ran away from it she would never get another chance to find out what it was. Sometimes she would cry herself to sleep, like a baby.

But the next day she would wake up, perhaps stiff and groaning, but stronger. Every day she worked at the camp made her stronger.

One morning on her daily firewood expedition she found a deadfall, the rotting hulk of a fir tree that had crashed through half an acre of forest, rolling downhill and smashing up saplings as it slid. It was all red and wet with sap and teeming with insects. With her hatchet she broke it down into nearly half a cord of firewood. Her arms lifted again and again to let the hatchet fall, to let the wood split where it wanted. Her arms just never seemed to grow tired. When she dragged the accumulated firewood back to camp in a travois, Uncle Bannerman looked up at her with real surprise. He was sitting drinking coffee out of a tin cup. She tried not to meet his gaze as she stacked the cut wood carefully under a blue tarp.

"Why'd you do all that?" he asked her. "That's more than we need for tonight. That's enough wood for a week, at least."

"Yes, sir," she said. "But I figured it might rain tomorrow, and this way I won't have to go looking for twigs in the mud."

"Hmph," he said, his eyebrows rising. "Good thinking."

It was—it made her feel—she didn't know how it made her feel. But it was good; she felt good that she'd gotten that much praise out of him. It was good.

After all that hard work she was sweaty and covered in sap, so they drove down to a little park where the water was warm enough to go swimming. There was a little changing cabin and he went first. He looked ridiculous in swim trunks, but she managed not to laugh. She went next and put on her black one-piece suit. She came out of the changing cabin and saw him and waved. He came walking over, but then his face hardened and he stopped in place.

She looked down at herself, thinking maybe her suit was too revealing or something. Then she realized what he was looking at. Her new tattoo. She'd lied about her age and had it done at a place way downtown. Her mom had never seen it—nobody but her friends ever had. It was done in brown ink and it was pretty simple, just the silhouette of a wolf's paw print on the top of her left breast.

"It's nothing, sir," she said, looking at her feet.

"It's an obscenity," he told her. His arms stuck out from his sides and his hands were balled in fists. If he hadn't been so angry he would have looked ridiculous. "Why on earth would you do such a thing?"

She tried to put it in words but she couldn't. Years later she would think of the right answer. *Because the wolf was stronger than me,* she would have told him. *Because I wanted its strength.* At the time all she could do was break down in tears. Most people would have given up then, and maybe even reached for her, tried to comfort her. Uncle Bannerman just stood there and waited for her to finish.

The next day he took her to the airport and sent her home.

twenty-six

At nineteen she found herself in Edmonton, Alberta, nearly a thousand kilometers from where her mother lived. She told herself she wanted to get as far away from the crazy old bat as possible. There had been some pretty epic fights between them just before she left—screaming fights. Worse, even. She had punched her mother in the nose, not all that hard. There hadn't been any blood. But it was going to be a long time before she could go back there.

Edmonton was okay. It was huge, but it always felt half empty. There were big parks to roam around in and plenty of cheap places to live. She tried at first to live with a couple of girls her age in a nice place near Old Strathcona, which was safe and clean. After six months, though, she found she couldn't live with other people. They wanted to sleep at night, while she got by with only a few hours during the day. After the forty or fifty thousandth time they knocked on her door at three A.M. and told her to turn her stereo off, she moved out.

She got a room of her own, then, above a car body repair shop. She had to listen to metal screaming and tearing all day long, but that wasn't too bad. It only sounded a little like the way the car sounded when the wolf clawed it. Anyway, the rent was next to nothing.

She got a job as a bartender, which fit her sleep schedule better than being a secretary or working in a retail shop. She had worried at first that being around so much alcohol would be a problem, even though she didn't drink much at all anymore. She'd stopped drinking herself to sleep back in high school, after she started waking up places she didn't recognize, but toward the end of that part of her life she'd really started worrying she was an alcoholic. It turned out the alcohol wasn't as big a temptation as she'd thought it was going to be, and the work was pretty easy and it paid well. She didn't mind pouring shots for the Ukrainians in cowboy hats and the real cowboys in baseball caps who surged in and out of the place every night, as reliable and reassuring as the tide. She didn't mind their filthy jokes, or the rude comments. She'd never really worried about things people said. It was what they did you had to watch out for.

The bar had a reputation as being a real tough joint, but for the three female bartenders there was no safer place in the world. They kept bouncers at the table next to the door all night, big guys who drank for free but never very much. If anything went wrong the bartenders would slip out back and share a smoke while the on-duty bouncer took care of it. When she started Chey hadn't believed that one guy—no matter how big he might be—could keep a lid on so many rowdies. She quickly learned there was an art to it. Good bouncers didn't wait for a fight to break out. They watched the crowd and they could see right away who was going to be trouble: the ones who laughed too loud or who didn't laugh at all, the real nasty shit-kickers who started fights for entertainment, the skinny little ones who looked like they wanted to prove something. Just as trouble was

148

about to begin the bouncer would jump in, grab the idiot's arm, and haul him outside before he even knew what was happening. It was truly rare that a punch ever got thrown—things usually ended well before that point.

That was how you kept yourself from being victimized, Chey realized. It was how you kept from being prey. You found out where the would-be predators were and you dragged them out of their dens when they didn't expect it. She made a mental note.

Not all of the men who came to the bar were after violence, of course. Occasionally somebody would grab her ass or make a stupid pass at her. Occasionally, if she was bored, or horny, or she wasn't ready to go to sleep at closing time, she would go home with one of them. The bouncers wouldn't let her leave with anybody who might hurt her, so she knew she would be safe. She had a couple of rules to make sure none of the men ever got a second date. Nobody ever came back to her place, and she always drove her own car—no matter what they said. Some of them told her they wanted to be her boyfriend. Some said they wanted to marry her. She never stuck around long enough for them to sober up and decide if they'd meant it or not.

A lot of the guys asked her about her tattoo, but she just shook her head and smiled in reply. Very rarely somebody would recognize her. Werewolf enthusiasts, she thought of them. Men attracted to the idea that she'd been to the far side of the predator–prey relationship and come back in one piece. These guys were in it for more than just curiosity—they had to be, to know who she was. She didn't look the same as she had when she was twelve, when she was in the papers. She had no idea how they figured out who she was, but she didn't bother finding out, either. She had rules for dealing with that kind of guy, as well. They got a drink on the house, and then they got politely told to shut up. If they didn't shut up they got told to go home. If they didn't go home, she called in the bouncer.

Work didn't end until four or five in the morning, when the cleaners would come in and the bar back would put all the chairs up on the tables. The regulars who stayed that late got to drink for free in exchange for washing glasses. The bartenders left as soon as the doors were locked.

Most nights Chey drove straight home, but sometimes she knew she wasn't going to be able to sleep, so she did something else. There's not a lot to do in western Canada at five in the morning if you're not a farmer, though. Sometimes she drove around town, looking at the lights with the radio on low and soft. Sometimes she drove out to the edge of town, or beyond. One night she caught herself driving half-asleep as the sun came up, and she pulled over onto the side of a highway. She had no idea how far she was from home. Up ahead she saw a sign saying she was on Highway 16. There was another sign below that showing a man's head in silhouette, painted a bright yellow. It couldn't be more literal.

She was on the Yellowhead Highway. The road that ran from British Columbia all the way to Manitoba. She knew it best for the stretch between Edmonton and Jasper National Park. The stretch where her father had died.

She breathed a curse and pulled a road map out of the side pocket of her car door. She studied the landscape, looking for clues as to where she was, but she couldn't figure it out. It looked like there might be a little town ahead of her, so she drove slowly toward the slumbering cottages and convenience stores where the Coke signs were the only lights still on. When she saw the name of the local bar—the Chesterton Arms—she stamped on the brakes and closed her eyes and waited until she could think straight again. Chesterton. That was the town she'd driven into when she was twelve years old, the town where she'd told the local police about what had happened. It was the safe place she'd gone to when she was running away from the wolf.

She thought about getting out of the car and going into the bakery down the street. That was the first place she'd come to when she arrived, back then. People work at bakeries all night, making bread for the next day, so there had been a light on inside and she had seen people moving around in there. She had walked in, thinking she would ask to use their phone. She hadn't been able to talk, but they were smart enough in the bakery to sit her down and feed her fresh doughnuts while they called the police. They had been nice people in there.

She could go in, now, years later, and ask who was working. They might remember her—or they might not; maybe the people there weren't the same. With a shudder she realized she didn't know what she would say, if she saw the same bakers, the same night manager. She couldn't remember their names, anyway.

She turned around and drove back to Edmonton with the radio turned up. She didn't want to think about how she'd gotten out there, 150 kilometers from home. She didn't want to think that her subconscious could control her like that. She drove home, she pulled the heavy drapes closed across her windows, and she swallowed three Ambiens with a can of flat ginger ale.

twenty-seven

ife changed again on July 25, 2003. Chey was twenty-one
years old. Though she'd done nothing in remembrance, nor
did she even want to think about it, she was conscious of the fact
that it was the ninth anniversary of her father's death.

One reason people go to the same bar every night is because
every night is exactly the same. That night started like any other.
She was pulling Labatt Blues for the workingmen and Alley Kat
microbrews for the more discriminating customers. She was
laughing and generally having a good time, making jokes with
the regulars, eating some fried fish one of them had brought her
from the chip shop next door. She had just taken an order for
a table full of mixed drinks when Bobby Fenech pushed
through the door and the smoke in the air rolled under the
lights. Well, it did that when anyone walked in, when the warm
air in the bar surged out into the cool night. For whatever
reason, she happened to be looking up at that exact moment
and she saw him. The swirling smoke seemed to wrap around
him like a cape.

He looked like the kind of person who would work on that

effect. The kind of man who liked to make a dramatic entrance, whether or not he could back it up.

He wasn't a big guy, really, but he sort of puffed himself out, the way a cat's fur will stand on end to make it look bigger. He had on a heavy-duty leather jacket and boots with steel-reinforced laces, as if he'd just hiked down out of the hills. If he was all business on his feet, though, he was ready to party upstairs. His hair glowed with mousse and ended in sharp triangular points that stuck straight up. He was maybe thirty-five years old, though there was a weird boyish air around him. Maybe it was the shit-eating grin on his face. He came up to the bar and leaned up against it, his hands grasping the brass rail around the edge.

Chey smiled at him—he looked like he might be a big spender—and finished the order she'd been working on. Then she turned and gave him the nod.

He raised his voice over the general din of conversation and the Aerosmith song on the jukebox. "What do you have that's Mexican and bottled?" he asked. "I can't stand domestic beer. I prefer my piss-water imported."

Her eyebrows drew together in consternation but his grin didn't falter. The bouncer by the door, three hundred pounds of Eastern European muscle named Arkady, gave her a glance. But it was a questioning glance, not a warning glance. She shook her head and Arkady relaxed a fractional amount. She was pretty sure this newcomer was just trying to be funny.

"Corona good enough?" she asked, reaching for the bottle. He nodded and she tapped it down on the bar, flipped off the cap and shoved a lime wedge down the neck in one quick motion. "Three dollars," she said, holding up three fingers in case he couldn't hear her over the crowd noise.

He took out a hundred and draped it across the top of his

bottle. "You see me running low, just give'r and don't ask questions," he smiled. "Whatever's left when I leave you keep for yourself."

Chey had been tending bar long enough at that point to know how to react. "That's very generous, thank you," she said. "I'll be sure to take care of you tonight." She grabbed the bill off the top of his bottle. "At least until you leave."

He said something low and probably insulting, but she decided not to hear it. It was a busy night and she had orders to fill, so she moved on. He kept an eye on her and she knew he wanted to talk further. She was trying to decide whether she wanted to listen when he finished his first beer and she went to replace it with another.

He grabbed the nearly empty bottle away from her and tilted it to his mouth. As if he was offended she would take away the bottle when there was still one last swig of backwash in it. When she bent to get the next beer she could feel his eyes on her chest. On her breasts. Nothing new or surprising there, except she got the sense he was more interested in her tattoo than her skin.

That moved him into the category of people she'd rather not talk to. She was about to grab his hundred back out of the till and return it, to tell him his first beer was on the house as long as it was also his last. Before she could, though, he set down his bottle and spoke.

"They never found it," he said. His grin was still in place.

Chey thought about asking him what the hell he was talking about. No point, though. He could only be talking about one thing. She popped open his second beer. She didn't say a word.

"They did a pretty thorough search, surprisingly. Most local copshops would have written that one off as an act of God. The good people of Chesterton, though, they really tried. They called in the big guns. The Mounties sent helicopters out into the bush and brought in real live bloodhounds when the aerial search turned up nothing. They found a caribou carcass a ways north of there that looked like maybe it was his handiwork. Only two kinds of animals could rip up a buck like that. Either a grizzly or a . . . werewolf."

"Yeah," she said. "Okay. That's enough." Arkady the bouncer sat up in his chair. "We have a policy here for people who want to talk about things they don't understand. I get a free smoke break, and you get a free beer. There's only one catch. You finish the beer and you leave before I come back."

"Alright," he said. "If that's what you want. Listen, though, I brought you something. Something I think you might like to have." He started reaching into his pocket. Arkady grabbed his wrist and pulled it back out, twisted it around behind his back. A slip of paper or maybe an index card fell across the bar and Chey picked it up.

She flipped it over and saw it was a photograph. It looked like it had been taken from out of the window of an airplane. It showed a patch of waving grass from above. In the middle of the picture was a wolf rearing up on its hind legs, its massive paws batting at the camera. Its eyes were an icy green that made her whole body tense up.

"Wait," she said, and looked up.

Arkady had the weirdo in a neck lock. He wasn't going anywhere. He wasn't struggling, either, which was strange, but then he'd only had one beer. Maybe he was smart enough to understand what the bouncer could do with just a little pressure. "Wait," she said again. "This picture looks recent."

"It was taken two weeks ago by a bush pilot flying up near the Arctic Circle. A guy who sees real wolves all the time. He knew the difference and so he took that shot and brought it to me, because it's my job to look at pictures like that. It took me all this time to connect that thing with your daddy. And then to you."

Chey flicked the photo back and forth between her hands. Trying to make a decision.

The weirdo raised his eyebrows, making his face look open and honest. She didn't trust that face, not one bit. But she trusted the picture. Those eyes. She couldn't remember her father's face, but she remembered those eyes.

Chey nodded at Arkady and the bouncer let go.

"My name's Robert Fenech," the weirdo said, sitting back down on his bar stool. His grin was back. "I'm an intelligence operative with the government. And I'd like my free drink now."

twenty-eight

Three days later she woke up and rolled out of a motel room bed in Ottawa. Bobby lay asleep under half of a sheet, one arm slumped off the side of the bed, his knuckles buried in shag carpeting.

Chey showered as quietly as she could and then got dressed. Bobby didn't stir. She went to the drapes across the window of their room and pulled them open a little. Across the street she saw a convenience store, a chemist's, the parking lot for the local Canadian Tire. Everything had the same muted, grayish colors that blended together. Bilingual signs crowded the sidewalks. She was back in Ontario, alright.

It had been so many years. Her mother still lived in Kitchener. A couple hundred kilometers away, but in the same province at least. She hadn't spoken to her mother in six months and she wondered if she ought to call her—but it was still too early.

Chey and Bobby had flown in the night before and taken the little room because they were too tired to find anything better. Then Bobby had wanted to fool around, and she'd been too tired to put him off.

No, that wasn't quite true. As much as she wanted to pretend that she wasn't attracted to Bobby, she couldn't convince herself. He was a little daft looking and a little obnoxious, sure. But he got her. When she'd told him about sleep-driving to Chesterton he'd just nodded and held her hand. When she told him about how ashamed she'd been when Uncle Bannerman saw her tattoo he had showed her his own tattoo, a sloppy black Molson logo on his bicep that a high school friend had done with a hot sewing needle. And when she told him she was still afraid of dogs he hadn't laughed.

Then there was the fact that he knew more about lycanthropes than she did. He could teach her things. That was his ultimate turn-on.

"Couldn't sleep?" he asked, his head still buried in a pillow. He brought up his dangling hand and ran it through the spikes of his hair. They were crusty with old mousse and he scratched at the scalp underneath.

"I'm too excited," she confessed.

He turned his head enough to smile at her. "You're doing a good thing," he said. He pushed his butt up in the air, getting his knees up underneath him, then sprang out of bed and whooped as he jumped into the shower. "Today's going to be a good day."

A car came for them promptly at nine, a white sedan with a government seal on the driver's side door. They drove along the St. Lawrence River to spy headquarters, the Canadian Security Intelligence Service building. The building was a three-sided monolith with big mirrored windows surrounded by a miniature park. It looked pretty impressive from the highway.

Maybe Bobby had seen it one too many times. "You know, America's got the Pentagon. That's got *five* sides. Even the CIA building in Virginia has four."

Inside they passed through a metal detector and were fitted

for security cards. Chey had worn her best outfit, a black velvet skirt and a purple blazer. When they clipped the VISITOR pass on her she felt like Gillian Anderson in *The X-Files*. It was all she could do not to giggle.

A woman with permed hair and thick glasses led them down a long corridor and then they went inside a conference room where a lot of men and women in suits waited to shake Chey's hand. They seemed really happy to meet her. She forgot all of their names as soon as she heard them. Once everybody was seated another man came in and put a tape recorder on the wood-grain table. He explained that everything she said was going to be recorded for later use and she agreed that was okay with her.

The newcomer, who had not been introduced to her, started asking her questions then. Most of them were pretty basic. He wanted to know the date and the time of the attack. He apologized before he asked her a series of simple questions about how, exactly, her father had died. She didn't mind answering.

"It went right for his throat, for—" she couldn't remember the word. "For the artery here," she said, and drew a finger across her neck.

"That's the jugular vein," one of the other men offered. Chey smiled her thanks.

The next bunch of questions surprised her: questions about her life since the attack. A woman dressed like a doctor asked her if she'd ever grown any hair in unnatural places. She did laugh, then. They asked her if she had ever experienced an occurrence of unusual strength or fast reflexes.

"Well, I exercise a lot," she told them, looking around to see their reaction. A couple of them frowned. "I don't sleep very well, you see. So I need something to do with all that extra time."

The man with the recorder suggested that they move on. It turned out he only had one more question. "At any time since the attack have you been contacted by the lycanthrope? In any way? I want you to take time and think about this. There's the possibility of what we call subtle communication."

"Subtle?" she asked.

The man with the recorder shrugged. "For instance, telepathy. Or maybe a telehypnotic suggestion. Have you ever done something, especially when you were tired or in a trancelike state, that you can't explain?"

She looked over at Bobby, excited. "Yes," she said, her hands grabbing at the table edge. "Yes." And she told them everything about her sleep-driving.

Some of the men glanced at each other and her heart sank, because she thought she knew what they were thinking. *That doesn't sound like telepathy. That sounds like crazy.*

They had a lot more questions after that, but she couldn't help but think she'd blown her big chance. Whenever she glanced at Bobby, though, he nodded confidently. Encouragingly. It helped her get through the endless session.

When she was done the men all stood up. She didn't understand what they were doing. Then she stood up and they all started shaking her hand. "The CSIS is extremely grateful for your help," one of them said. Another repeated the same message in French. She started shaking their hands.

"Wait," she chirped. She couldn't believe that was all they wanted. "Wait, I'd like to ask you something. If I may."

They had already started filing out of the conference room. Now they stopped and looked at her patiently.

"If you catch him." She swallowed painfully. "If you catch it. The lycanthrope, I mean. Is there any way you could let me talk to it? I don't mean privately. You can have anyone there you

160

think should be there, or just listen in if you want. I want to ask it a question, you see. I want to know if it hated my father or if it was just hungry."

The men and women looked at each other, not at her. The same look as before. Now they definitely thought she was crazy.

"Look, I know it's weird. But it would help me so much," she pleaded.

Finally the man with the recorder cleared his throat and put a hand on her upper arm. "Ms. Clark, I'm so sorry if we gave you the wrong idea. This was just a backgrounder session. For informational purposes only."

She shook her head. She didn't understand.

"Mr. Fenech will explain, I'm sure," he said, and then they all left.

An hour later the car took her and Bobby back to the motel. Chey sat down in a chair and smoothed out the wrinkles in her skirt. Bobby tore all the sheets off the bed and threw them at the TV set.

"Goddamned grits!" he shouted. "I shit on all the Green Party bilingual wine-sipping owl-hugging dolphinfuckers who run this country! I knew this would happen."

Chey exhaled deeply before she spoke. "What happened? You said the government wanted my help."

"Yeah, and I was right." He threw the plastic ice bucket at the tempered glass windows. It bounced off without leaving a mark. "They wanted you to help them not make a decision. What you said in there should have gotten me the paperwork I needed to go up to the Arctic and give this animal a sterling silver enema. Instead they took what you gave them as a sign that they needed to do more fact finding. Maybe form a new committee on Lycanthrope Relations. *Lycanthropes!* I hate that fucking word. It's Greek or something, right? It's one of those *science* words. It's the name of a *medical condition*. This isn't some kind of cancer that only baby seals can get. It's a godforsaken monster. Why can't anybody ever say the word *werewolf* with a straight face?"

"So they're not going to do anything?" Chey asked.

"They never do," he told her. Then he tried to pull the curtains off the curtain rod. They wouldn't come loose.

twenty-nine

"How about a Cuban cigar, Captain?" Bobby asked, waving one at Uncle Bannerman. Chey's heart sank. She jumped up onto a wooden fence and sat down on the top rail. She didn't have high hopes for this introduction to start with—she had known all along that the two men weren't going to click—but it seemed almost like Bobby wanted this to fail. "You can't get these down here in the States, right? There's nothing like them." He rubbed the cigar under his own nose and breathed out joyfully.

"Thank you, no. I don't smoke." Her uncle was dressed in his ranch clothes. Flannel shirt, jeans, perfectly clean work boots. He didn't wear his uniform anymore—he was retired now, retired with honor and a nice pension after he cleaned up some bad prison riot or something with no casualties. He had transitioned to private life pretty smoothly and had bought a ranch where he raised Appaloosas. He had a bag of carrots with him and he was methodically feeding them, one after another, to his favorite animal, Vulcan, who kept flicking his tail back and forth.

It was 2006, the year the Canadian government went to the

Conservatives, and it seemed like maybe, finally, they had a chance. If they were discreet about it. They needed Uncle Bannerman's help, though, so the two of them had flown down to Colorado to ask him in person. It was January and there were patches of snow on the ground and Chey wished they could just go inside and get warm.

Bobby bit off the end of his cigar and spit it into the grass. Bannerman followed the projectile with his eyes and stared at where it hit the ground, probably memorizing the location where it fell so he could pick it up later. Bobby put the cigar in his mouth unlit and started sucking on it.

"Do you need a match?" Bannerman asked.

"Fuck no. You think I want lung cancer? I just like the taste."

Bannerman looked away. "You can get mouth cancer just as easily." He shook his head, clearly ready to give up. "Cheyenne told me that you wanted to ask me for a favor. I suppose I should let you ask, at least."

"Yeah. I need your help with killing a werewolf."

Bannerman didn't react to that at all. He fed the last carrot to his horse and then wadded up the bag and put it in his pocket.

"It's a matter of public safety," Bobby tried to explain. "Canadian citizens are at risk and you can help me put an end to that. Surely you can appreciate that. This asshole ate your own brother."

This time Bannerman winced visibly. Then he collected himself and reached up and patted Vulcan on his forelock. The horse snorted and kicked at the icy ground.

Bobby tried a new tack. "This is kind of my life's work. Can you understand that? You're at the end of a pretty distinguished career. I'm at the start of mine."

"I served my country to the best of my abilities, that's all." Bannerman ran his hands down the horse's mane a few times and then clucked at him with his tongue. The horse knew exactly what that meant and he ran off toward the far side of his enclosure, his hooves kicking up bright sprays of snow. "Tell me now, please, what exactly it is you want me to do for you."

"One phone call. That's all," Bobby said. "You were a pretty important guy over at the Colorado National Guard. I want you to call somebody high up over at the Guard base at Buckley. Somebody who can authorize registering a civilian for a crash course in basic training without asking a lot of questions."

"You want me to enroll one of your intelligence operatives in our boot camp. Well, that's very interesting, and it suggests to me that you're not telling me the whole story. The last time I checked the Canadian Forces have a perfectly good training camp at Saint-Jean in Quebec. But for some reason you can't put your agent into that camp."

"Yeah, about that." Bobby raised his hands in confession. "It's a freelance job I'm running. Very much on the hush-hush side. I have somebody who's perfect for what I want to do but they've never shot a gun before. See, we don't just let anybody get firearms training up north. We're funny that way."

Uncle Bannerman nodded. "I happen to know someone who can make that happen. Dare I ask who your operative happens to be? Or is that classified?"

Bobby scratched his head for a while. "Now, that's kind of the funny part. You see, I've been trying to run this show for years now. I've been begging my people for one good guy, one smart guy who could carry this out. I've been tied up in red tape for so long, though, that I had to go low budget on this one. I had to ask for volunteers. People whose lives have been damaged by this particular animal. People who would be willing to put themselves at some mild risk to get within silver bullet range of a werewolf."

165

His eyes slid sideways. Bannerman followed his glance. Soon they were both looking right at Chey.

Then Bannerman started laughing. It was a sound Chey had never heard before, and she nearly fell off the fence.

When he had finished laughing he rubbed at his eyes and then looked right at Bobby. "You, Mr. Fenech, are insane. Get off my property now."

"Wait—wait—just listen for a second," Bobby pleaded.

"And you, Cheyenne, have apparently never listened to anything I've tried to teach you. I'll tell you what I'll do for you. I'll buy you a plane ticket so you can go home and see your mother. Or you can stay here if you like. I can always use some help around here—I'm getting old and the horses need plenty of attention."

"Fucking hold on, just give me a chance," Bobby said.

"No." Bannerman folded his arms across his chest. "I believe I asked you to leave. I'm not too withered to make you go," he said.

"Chey, try to talk to this guy, will you?" Bobby asked. He ran his hands across the sides of his head, careful not to mess up his spikes. "It looks like I'm not getting through to him."

Chey jumped down from the fence and started walking away from the two of them. "Give up, Bobby," she said. "He's not the kind of guy you can talk around to your side. It's one of the reasons I respect him so much." Her face burned with shame and she just wanted to leave.

"Chey," Bobby wheedled, but she kept walking.

"There's a firing range just up the road. For fifty bucks they'll give me a basic firearms safety course," she said. "I checked. I kind of figured I knew his answer already."

"Cheyenne," her uncle said. There was ice in his voice. She stopped where she was, but she didn't turn around. She thought

166

he was going to forbid her from going up to the Arctic. She should have known better. He didn't have a right to forbid her anything and he was not the kind of man to meddle where he didn't have a right. "Is this really your idea?" he asked. "This jumped-up spy didn't talk you into this?"

"I don't sleep, Uncle. I haven't slept a full night since I was twelve years old," she said. She figured that all the times she passed out drunk didn't count. "Every time I see a Chihuahua I lose my shit. The wolf ate my father, but that wasn't all—he fucked up my life, too. I need to make this right."

"If you go up there you're just going to get yourself killed. You can't fight a lycanthrope. They're stronger than we are."

"I know something stronger," Bobby suggested. "A silver bullet. I have a guy in Medicine Hat, a silversmith, who's making them for me right now. Of course, if she can't fire a gun then a silver anti-tank round isn't going to do her much good."

"You're a vile little squirt of a man, Mr. Fenech," Bannerman said. Then he took his cell phone out of his pocket and started dialing.

thirty

$\mathscr{A}$lmost—almost done. The ten-kilometer run ended in the obstacle course. Hand over hand, swinging on an overgrown jungle gym. Crawling under wire. Chey came through the tires puffing, but she had enough strength left to grab the top of the wall. She got one leg over and jumped down the other side just like she'd been trained. Sergeant Horrocks, her drill instructor, started screaming at her as soon as she was through the mud. "If you can't get those legs up higher you're going to do the whole fucking thing over again," he said. He was a tough little man with curly white hair and during her six weeks of training she had never heard him say one word in a conversational tone. With the sergeant it was either screaming or contemptuous silence.

She ran up to a table and tied a blindfold around her face. She had fifty-five seconds left. With sweaty hands she picked up the pieces of her weapon off the table. Receiver, barrel, clip. She slapped the handgun together, stripped it down, put it together again. Then she pulled off the blindfold and stood at attention until Sergeant Horrocks screamed at her to stop.

Her heart was racing. Her body burned with pain. She was done.

"Pretty shabby, but it's a passing score," the sergeant announced. "Alright, you're done."

And that was it. She walked over to where Bobby and Uncle Bannerman were sitting in camp chairs and dropped to the grass in front of them. She didn't have the strength to say anything and they didn't offer any congratulations. They were deep in conversation and barely seemed to notice she was there. The same conversation they'd been having, over and over, since the two of them had met.

"This is your brilliant plan. To send one woman against a monster."

"One determined survivor, intent on healing her broken psyche. A highly trained survivor now, thanks to you."

"She's not even twenty-five years old and now you're both going to throw away her life. Do you know that she's afraid of dogs?" Bannerman asked. "How is she supposed to get close enough to a lycanthrope to shoot it when she's terrified of dogs?"

"It's not in its wolf form all the time. Sometimes it's just as human as you or me. At least it looks that way."

Bannerman harrumphed. "It will still be stronger and faster than her. It will still be a killer. She's not even a soldier, with or without basic training."

"If I could send soldiers I would. I'd love to send in an infantry regiment," Bobby said. "I'd love to send in an air strike. But this is one clever animal. He'd see that coming and just move on before we arrived."

"You'd also have to get official sanction to do that," Bannerman added. "And that's something you'll never have."

"Yeah, there is that. Look. I've made this as easy as I can. We wait until high summer when she won't freeze to death up there. She goes in looking like a lost eco-tourist, in case anyone asks. We think the werewolf might have human accomplices watching out for him. She'll have the perfect cover story. All she has to do is get close enough for one shot and then she's done."

"Except that she'll have to exfiltrate from some bad country. Is she going to shoot the accomplices as well?"

Bobby waved a hand in front of his face as if he were batting at flies. "I'll have a helicopter ready to evacuate her at short notice. This is a survivable mission. You think I want to lose her like that? She's my girlfriend."

"She's a sacrifice. I don't know what you're getting out of this, but I know you're willing to let her be killed."

Chey's heart skipped a beat when she heard that. But she wasn't going to stop now. She sat up and looked at them.

"Why are you so gung-ho about this lycanthrope?" Bannerman asked.

"Like I said, it's a public safety issue. I don't want any more Canadians to get eaten." But he couldn't even keep a straight face when he said it. Bobby had never really told her what his interest in this was. She realized she'd never really asked.

"Tell me the truth, son." Bannerman's face had turned to stone. His eyes were like sharpened pieces of flint.

Chey knew that look. Even Bobby couldn't stand up to it and keep bullshitting.

"Alright," he said. "You want to know? It's about oil."

"I beg your pardon?" her uncle asked.

Bobby shrugged. "Not terribly original. I know that. But important all the same. I've got satellite intelligence saying there's an untapped oil reserve right on the Arctic Circle. Maybe six hundred million barrels, they say. And it's not tied up in oil sands or shale that cost more to get it out than it's worth. This is the real thing, liquid crude. There's only one problem. There's a werewolf on top of it. If we start sending up guys to drill for this jackpot then some of them are going to get eaten. The big boys in Ottawa prefer their oil blood-free. So they'll never okay drilling. Then there's the terrorism angle, because in my business these days there's always got to be a terrorism angle, right? You know all about that. If we can start producing all of our own oil, if we can be less dependent on the Middle East, Canada becomes more secure."

"Please," Bannerman snorted.

Bobby's mouth was a firm line. "We're dealing with intangibles here, sure. But in a reality-based way, once this asshole's dead, every single person in my country gets a little bit safer."

"And no one in the world except my niece can make that happen," Bannerman said. He was about to scoff his last scoff, to send Bobby away. He was about to give up on everything she'd worked so hard for. All the things she needed if she was ever going to have a real life. She sat up and looked at him, even as he was opening his mouth to tell Bobby to leave and never come back. She pleaded with him with her eyes. Not the way she might plead with some other man, not with begging eyes, but instead with the eyes of an adult. The eyes of someone capable of making her own decisions.

Bannerman drew in a long and difficult breath. Then he met her gaze. "Cheyenne," he said. "Is this what you really want? You really want to throw your life away just for a chance to kill this lycanthrope?"

She didn't let herself blink. "Yes," she said.

part three

western prairie

thitty-one

The breeze off the tiny lake shook the pine needles, made the limbs of the trees bounce and sway. Sunlight danced on the water.

Chey adjusted her stance. Then she lifted her weapon and pointed it right at Powell's forehead. He looked surprised but not very frightened. Her hand started to shake but she fought the tremor down. One shot was all it would take. He would be dead. She would finally be stronger than the wolf.

She wished she'd had time to talk with him more. She had so many questions she wanted him to answer.

"Chey," he said, slowly. He was going to try to talk her down.

Her father hadn't been given a chance to talk. "You never gave my father a chance!" she screamed. She was losing control; she could feel it. She needed to act quickly or she was going to fuck this up.

"Your father?" Powell asked.

"His name was Royal Clark. He was a good man. You wouldn't know that, of course. You didn't seem particularly

175

interested in his character at the time. You seemed more interested in how his guts tasted. You attacked our car twelve years ago and you ate him."

"Oh, boy," he said.

"Tell me you remember him," she said. "Tell me you know who I'm talking about. I know you were never introduced, but surely you remember his red jacket. That's pretty much all I remember now. Tell me!"

If he confessed, if he said he remembered, and that he was sorry, then it would all be over. Then she could just kill him and she could sleep again.

"I'm sorry, Chey," he said.

Her body sagged a little. She thought she might swoon. He was confessing, he was apologizing for what he'd done, just like she'd wanted—

Except he wasn't finished.

"I'm sorry, but I don't remember him at all."

Quite suddenly she became aware of the solidity, the square rigid reality of the gun in her hand. Now, she thought. Now now now! She tried to squeeze the trigger. It didn't move. Nothing happened.

She closed her eyes in shame and horror. The weapon's safety was still on.

For a lurching, drunken moment no one moved. Everyone tried to figure out what had just happened. Powell's face darkened and his arms lifted from his sides. He lowered his head and put a foot forward.

Then everyone moved at once.

Chey's thumb moved down to disengage the safety. Her aim slipped away from Powell's face.

Lester, the Inuvialuit pilot, dashed around the side of his helicopter, trying to get to safety.

Bobby shoved a hand into his leather jacket, clearly reaching for a gun of his own.

In the distance Dzo spun out on the logging road and drove his rusted truck back into the impenetrable woods.

But before any of that had really happened, before Chey could even breathe, Powell moved.

She knew that even in their human forms wolves were faster than any normal person. She had that strength and that quickness in her own legs and arms. She'd never really tried it out, though. She'd never tested her new limits.

Powell had possessed that speed for nearly a hundred years. He must have known what his body could do, what it could achieve if put to the test. He didn't hesitate. He just moved, flowed across the clearing. One of his hands batted at Chey's arm hard enough to dislocate her wrist. Her handgun went flying. Powell didn't stop to watch it fall. Momentum carried him onward, his feet digging in the soil, his legs pumping. He brought his shoulder around and collided with Bobby hard enough to make them both yowl in pain. Bobby's yowl was sharper. He smashed to the ground and rolled into a ball. Powell kept moving, his feet a blur, until he came up against the side of the helicopter with a clang. He looked through the Plexiglas bubble of its cockpit. Chey could see Lester back there, crouched low, his face and eyes wide.

"Don't try anything," Powell grunted at the pilot.

"Yeah, okay," Lester said, nodding agreeably.

Chey looked around. Her arm stung with pain but she could ignore that for a couple of seconds. She had better be able to ignore it long enough to find the gun again. There—its black angular shape stuck out prominently on a crust of snow. It was only a few meters away. She bent her knees and tried to jump for it.

She didn't even get to take a step. Powell pushed off the helicopter and nearly flew back across the clearing to tackle her legs. The ground tilted upward and her cheek smashed into it. Her teeth rattled in her skull.

Powell pushed her face deeper into the soil with one hand. With the other he grabbed her hurt wrist and gave it a good twist.

Yellow stars exploded behind her eyes. It hurt so much that vomit rushed up her throat and she had to swallow uncomfortably or choke.

"You want to kill me," he said to her, his voice thick with emotion. "Well, maybe I deserve it. But first you had to lie to me. I took you into my house and this is the thanks I get. I should kill *you*. I will, the next time I see you."

He twisted her hand again, all the way around this time. Her shoulders shook and bucked beneath his grasp, her jaws clacked in her head. The pain was sending her into shock. Cold flashed through her body, cold as fierce as when she'd been submerged in the freshet. Cold like the time she'd woken naked in the tundra after her first change.

He let her go. She couldn't move except to shiver, to convulse in pain and cold.

When she'd recovered herself enough to sit up he was gone.

thirty-two

Pain ate at her. It was like a small animal lodged in her abdomen, chewing on her stomach. Nausea made her eyes bulge, made her sweat even in the cold air.

Slowly Chey raised her arm to look at her wrist. The skin of her forearm was red and purple, while the hand itself looked limp, like a doll's hand. It dangled at the end of her arm. She tried to close her fingers and they twitched but refused to do as she asked. She tried to lift the hand but it wouldn't move at all.

The pain grumbled inside of her and told her to lie down. It told her to go to sleep. If she hadn't been half wolf, she probably wouldn't have had a choice. Whatever she thought of the curse Powell had given her, it did have some compensations.

It wasn't permanent, she told herself. As soon as she changed again her body would heal the injury. As soon as she changed again . . .

She had some thinking to do. She had to make a plan. The pain was going to have to wait.

She stumbled up onto her feet and walked toward where Bobby lay curled up on the ground. He was conscious, but his face was twisted in a grimace of hurt. "Lester," she shouted. "Lester, come over here."

"Is he gone?" the pilot asked, coming around the side of his helicopter. "Do you think he might come back?"

She shook her head. "He's too smart for that. Come on, help me with Bobby."

Together they pulled Fenech up into a sitting position. The operative clutched at his chest, but Chey found he was weak as a kitten when she took his hands away. She pulled at the neck of his polo shirt and looked inside. A wide blue bruise had already formed around his sternum. Powell had tackled him pretty hard. "Can you talk?" Chey asked. "Can you say something?"

"Frigging squatch," he moaned. "That frigging squatch!"

"I guess you're going to live," she said, and squatted down next to him.

She stared out at the water, unsure of what to say next. The sun was still high over the trees, but she figured it had to be getting on to nine o'clock. She could have checked the clock on her cell phone, but that would have involved reaching into her pocket with her broken hand.

"Listen," she said finally, "I'm sorry, but—"

"Hold on." Bobby patted the needles around him with his hands, then turned up his sunglasses. They must have fallen off when Powell hit him. The right lens was badly scratched, but he polished them on his shirt anyway and then pulled them over his eyes. "Okay," he said. "Chey, you know how I feel about you. You know that I trust you. So when I ask you my next question, I want you to please not take it the wrong way."

"Alright," she said, making it half question.

"Are you fucking stupid?" he demanded. "Did you know the safety was on? Because I seem to remember that was part of

180

your training. The training I had to go through *so much* shit to convince your ratass uncle to give you."

"I fucked up, I know," she said. "But it wasn't conscious. Look, next time—"

He held a finger to his lips. "The fact that you think there's going to be a next time is actually pretty funny. I might even laugh, if I didn't think it would rupture my spleen. Let me say this one more time—"

"Wait, wait, you—"

"You're fired, Chey! You're off the team. I'm going to get some friends of mine up here and we will actually kill that frigging squatch. That's what's going to happen. I have been working on this project way too long to let you end it like this. Lester, get the camp stuff out. I don't think the squatch is coming back tonight, not if he knows we're packing silver. Chey, you can help me go sit down inside the whirlybird. I think I'd prefer a padded seat to these fucking rocks."

Every time she moved pain rumbled through Chey like the tremors that come before a volcano lets loose. She nearly fell over. She helped Bobby stand up, though, and limp toward the helicopter. Lester did as he'd been asked, hauling a stack of nylon bags out of the helicopter's cargo compartment.

"Bobby," she said, when he was sitting down inside the helicopter.

"Save it."

"Bobby, there's something we need to think about."

His head rolled to one side until he was looking at her.

"I'm going to change," she said.

His brow furrowed.

"In about an hour, I think, the moon is going to come up again. Every time the moon comes up I change. Into a wolf."

He nodded, but he didn't seem terribly concerned.

181

"When that happens," she said, "I'm going to do everything in my power to kill you and Lester." He started to protest and she raised her good hand to stop him. "It's not an optional thing. When I change I kill anything human that I see. I think I should get out of here. Run off into the woods. I'll get as far away as I can before it happens, and maybe that'll be enough. Maybe if I get far enough I won't smell you guys when I'm a wolf. Maybe."

He nodded and sat up a little, grimacing in pain as he did so. "I've got a better idea," he told her. "Lester!" he shouted. "Open up the blue bag." To her he confided, "I had kind of this crazy notion that we might catch your new friend unawares. That we might be able to take him alive."

Lester pulled open the blue bag and a length of metal chain slithered out. Bright silver chain, with a thick manacle on one end.

"Do you think it'll fit?" Bobby asked.

thitty-thtee

The two men made camp and built a cheery little fire. The white smoke that lifted off the blaze mixed with the mist off the water and the yellowish twilight. That butterscotch quality of the evening had lingered for hours and it still wasn't dark—it was near midsummer in the Arctic and that meant some very short nights—but the air had turned frosty and damp and the dancing fire chased away some of the gloom.

It was half past nine, already. The moon was going to rise at 9:45.

She caught Lester checking his watch more than once. Bobby, though, kept his eyes on her the whole time. Even as he got up to throw another sap-heavy log on the fire he watched.

"You hungry?" he asked, and she almost jumped. She'd gotten used to the silence. "We've got some powdered eggs and coffee. Instant, you know, but it's still Timmy Ho's best, and it'll probably smell like civilization. I can't remember, do you take sugar?"

The breath leaked out of her with a whimpering sound.

"I guess not," he said, and sat down by the fire. To watch.

Her body grew light, almost insubstantial. Her clothes hung

on her like formless sacks, then dripped to the floor of the clearing. She watched her broken wrist. The hand there lifted of its own accord—it looked like a balloon filling up with air. She could feel the bones inside twanging and grating on each other. It didn't hurt much—nothing hurt, or felt like anything much. She felt like she were made of some softer substance than flesh and bones. She felt like she might have floated away if not for the incredibly heavy chain around her ankle that held her down. That didn't fall off, even when she stood naked and ghostly and tearing at it, pulling at it—

Silver light. The world filled up with silver light. It was 9:47 P.M. Moonrise.

Her body shook with joy, her fur fluffing out and her bones popping happily. She dug at the ground with her claws and then lifted her muzzle to the wind to howl in pure pleasure.

Her nostrils twitched. Her throat tasted smoke—fire—wood burning nearby. Her eyes tried to focus and though her vision was not her best sense, she could still see the yellow splash of flame in the middle of the clearing. She could still see—them.

Men. Men. Men, hated men. *Men,* she panted. *Men.* She could taste their blood already. Though not as much as she would have liked. Visions of tearing them up and feasting on their entrails struck sparks in her heart and her head. Desires she had not felt before blossomed inside of her, filled her up, made her body race.

Men—two of them. They stood around their little fire as if it could protect them, their bodies crouched as if they might run. They were afraid of her.

They should be. A growl rumbled in her throat, low, but like the thundering pulse of a waterfall muted only by distance.

They shouted at one another and at her. Grunting, grumbling noises that meant nothing to her. They sounded sickly. They made the kind of sounds a stomach full of rotten meat might make. Her lips pulled back from her teeth as she took a step toward them. Another step, closer, her paws flat on the ground, her body low for the pounce, another step—

Searing pain burst through her leg, like a hot knife pressed against the bone. She yelped in horror and fell back, curled around herself, looked for the source of the terrible cutting agony. Her tongue lapped at her leg and she tasted fire there. She sniffed at the injury and smelled something new, new to her at least. Something she'd never encountered before and yet—and yet in her bones she understood immediately what it was. Silver. Silver the color of the moon, the color of the orb that ruled her.

A band of it wrapped around her hind leg. The band was tied around a tree with a rope of silver. She could never break that cord. If she tried to bite through it her teeth would snap, her gums would bleed. It was stronger than she was. She understood at once that she was trapped, and she knew it was the men who had trapped her.

She had not thought it possible that she could hate the men any more than she did already, that she could long for their throats between her teeth with any more rage and longing than she'd already known. But it was possible indeed. Every cell in her body burned with the need. And yet even as she wanted and begged and growled and fought and needed, she was stuck in place; she could not pounce, or run, or fight. A whimper leaked out of her that sounded pathetic, she knew, but she couldn't help it. *Let go, go, go, go,* she panted, the rhythm of her anger and her dread rattling in the hollow parts of her skull. *Free, free, free me, free!*

One of the men, the paler of the two, walked toward her, his knees bent. Ready to jump away if she snapped at him. If she could move, if she could just get loose for one moment, she would tear apart his face and his chest and lap at the blood of his hot heart. Closer he came, his hands outstretched as if to soothe her. Fool! And yet even with bloodlust smearing its gory paws across her eyes she knew she could not hurt him, not unless he came a little closer, closer, closer, little closer, closer—

He stopped just outside her range. She swatted at him anyway out of sheer need, but he was out of reach. He made some more of those hateful sounds at her, but where before the clanging human syllables had been harsh and grating, these were soft and low like the fur of a woodchuck's belly.

She couldn't reach him. She couldn't bite through the chain. Her growls were pointless, impotent.

Then she thought of something. Even as he spoke to her in those soft and rumbling tones, even as he studied her with his eyes, she licked the metal one more time, the silver like searing ice on her tongue. Then she got her muzzle and her enormous teeth around her own ankle and with one quick snap she bit through the bone. There was pain as her leg tore, as her skin and her muscles snapped apart, there was pain as her paw came off like so much dead meat. But the band of silver on her leg fell away and suddenly, instantly, she was free.

thirty-four

They woke face down in a snowdrift, her hands gripping the earth like claws. Her body ached and pulsed—a maddening tingle in her left leg made her cry out.

She rolled over and stared up at the sky. The sun was high above but its light couldn't seem to warm her. Her breath turned to mist inside of her mouth.

She sat up—her body complaining, her neck popping noisily—and grabbed at her leg, kneading the muscles there, trying to get her circulation going. She felt a real shock when her hands met the skin of her calf and found it blistered and raw. She looked down and saw what looked like a burn scar there. That was where the silver chain had bound her. She knew silver could kill her, kill the wolf. Maybe even just being in contact with the metal was enough to hurt her.

Wait, she thought. Something was wrong. Bobby had chained her up so she wouldn't hurt him or Lester. The chain had held her even when she transformed—she could remember that much. But now it was gone. Had Bobby released her while she slept?

Except then why was she not in the clearing by the little lake? She looked around, nearly forgetting she was naked, and called Bobby's name. There was no sign of the helicopter. She must have traveled some distance while she was in her wolf form.

She brushed snow off her arms and her chest with shaking hands and rose creakily to her feet. She wasn't going to freeze to death, she knew that much now, but her body still rebelled at the cold air around her, the cold earth beneath her feet. It wanted clothing and shelter.

She took a step and got another shock. A bad one, a really bad one. The snowdrift around her was splattered with red blood. What looked like gallons of it.

Her hands pressed against her mouth. Her chest tightened—what—where—had that blood come from?

Oh, God, she thought. Oh, no.

Somehow she'd gotten free of the chain. She'd gotten free right in the midst of the two men. Her wolf was faster than any human, stronger. Bobby had silver bullets but—but maybe she had attacked before he could draw his weapon.

Murder, she thought. *Murder, murder, murderer, murderer,* her brain gibbered. But no, she thought, no, she had to calm down. She didn't actually know what had happened. She had vague memories of snarling and snapping and running through the woods. She could taste blood in her mouth still—the obvious conclusion, the most plausible scenario was that she had killed the two men and maybe . . . maybe she had eaten them—

She fell to her knees and retched into the snow. A little red blood flecked the white, but after a moment her body was just fluttering with dry heaves.

If she had killed Bobby and Lester then that made her exactly the same thing as her demon, as the trauma that had devoured her life. The thing she had sought to destroy for so many years, the thing that had destroyed her. It made her no better than Powell.

Chey had on many occasions in her life been haunted by memories and questions. If there was one thing she knew how to do it was cope with horror. Not fix it, not resolve it, just cope. She knew what she needed to do. She needed to focus on her immediate situation. She needed to get to a place of safety.

She started walking. It helped—moving over the rough ground required a certain amount of concentration. Picking her way through the dense undergrowth took mental energy away from the parts of her brain that just wanted her to sit down and scream. Still. She had no compass, no map. She wasn't sure where she actually was, nor did she know where she wanted to go. She couldn't go back to Powell's cabin, could she? The wolf knew who she was now. He would be on his guard and he would probably attack her—kill her—on sight.

She could head back to the little lake—assuming she could find it again—but what would she discover there? Broken bones with the marrow sucked out? Bobby's wraparound sunglasses, the lenses shattered on the rocks?

Shelter was the main thing. She needed to get inside someplace warm. She needed clothes, if only to help her feel human again. Such things would be in short supply in the drunken forest, she knew, but there had to be something.

There was, and she found it purely by accident. The only real idea she had was to try to get to higher ground, where she might be able to see better. Climbing a sinuous ridge, she stumbled right into a cleared path, one of the meandering logging roads Dzo used. The way was overgrown and full of tiny saplings—clearly it hadn't been used for years—but it had been cleared by human hands once, and that was something. She headed southward, toward the sun, and followed the path no matter how it turned or bent back on itself. She climbed a tree from time to time to try to look around. With her new strength it was a lot easier than when she'd climbed to escape from Powell's wolf. Nothing presented itself to her from the treetops, though, except a chaotic expanse of more trees.

The road seemed to run on for kilometer after kilometer. After what felt like hours Chey began to think she'd made a mistake, that she was doomed to wander the logging road until she transformed again. At her lowest moment she stopped and looked up, one last time. And there, between two trees, she finally saw what she was looking for. A squat bunkhouse elevated on a scaffold of rusted metal girders. A tower—a fire lookout. It wasn't much, but it had four walls and a roof. She ran through the trees and climbed up the rickety stairs two at a time.

thirty-five

They discovered the limits of her new domain pretty quickly. The fire tower comprised a single square room twenty feet on a side. It had a pitched wooden roof through which she could see sunlight peeking in. The walls were painted a peeling green, and were cut away at waist height so they could be opened upward like shutters. The walls, floor, and ceiling were covered in block-letter graffiti carved into the wood with a pocketknife. Very little of it was legible or made any sense— mostly it was just names and dates, presumably memorials left by the people who had stood lonely watch high above the trees, making sure they didn't all burn down. Chey propped open one of the shutters even though it let in a gust of frigid air and made her feel even chillier. She took a long look at what her prede- cessors in the tower would have seen. The drunken forest all around rolled and pitched like an ocean frozen in mid-heave. In the distance she could see sparkling light bouncing off some water, but she couldn't be sure if it was the lake where Bobby had set up his camp. Powell's cabin was nowhere in sight. Beyond that she had no points of reference—beyond those two locations the forest was a unicellular seething mass, an entity without boundaries or form. She let the shutter fall back with a bang that made her wince.

A big footlocker along one wall proved to be locked up tight. Chey tugged at the latches a little as if they would come loose in her hands, but the metal locks were solid, perhaps rusted in place. Chey inhaled deeply—she wasn't going to let even such a tiny mystery go unsolved if she could help it. Then she used all of her wolf-given strength and tore the locker open, sending pieces of the lock flying around the small room.

Inside the locker were kerosene lamps (but no kerosene), boxes of firestarters, tin plates and cups, and other camping supplies. Underneath the supplies she found an old sweater with a bad tear down one sleeve and struggled into it. It was far too big for her and came down to mid-thigh. She pawed wildly through the other contents of the locker, looking for more clothes, but didn't turn anything up. There were some old books, but they smelled musty and when Chey picked one up the cover was damp and spotted with mold. The pages stuck together in one thick, gloppy block.

On the far side of the room stood a table and a pair of folding chairs. There was a big electrical outlet under the table—perhaps there had been a radio once—and a single light bulb hung from the ceiling, but the power had been cut off. With the shutters down the room was dark and oppressive. With the shutters up the wind tore right through and cut her to the bone. She compromised by bracing one shutter halfway open, then sat down in one of the folding chairs. It creaked badly under even her relatively slight weight—rust had been working at its joints for years.

If she sat very still it didn't make any noise. She experimented with drawing her feet up underneath her, sitting almost in lotus position on the chair. She pulled the sweater down over her knees, stretching it out.

She had no idea what to do next. If Bobby and Lester were dead, if Powell was going to kill her the next time he saw her—she couldn't stick around. She knew she was going to have to leave if she wanted to survive. Still, she couldn't very well walk back to civilization. And even if she did she would just be putting people at risk. What would she do, walk into a hospital and ask to be treated for lycanthropy? There was no cure. Powell had been quite clear on that—he'd been looking for one for a hundred years, he'd said.

She bit off all her fingernails, thinking her way through her situation. Then she jumped up and tore open the footlocker and took out one of the books. It was called *Black Sun,* by somebody called Edward Abbey. She'd never heard of him, but she didn't care. She tore off the cover, then started peeling the pages apart one by one. Carefully she arranged them on the floor, left to right, then across when she ran out of room. The paper felt slimy in her fingers but it crumbled if she rumpled it too much. She was careful not to rumple it. She figured she could dry out the pages and then read them one by one over by the propped-open shutter where the light was better.

Before she had fifty pages laid out to dry silver light came and carried her away.

thirty-six

She came to, naked and stiff, on the floor of the fire tower. It was nearly pitch dark inside but she recognized the texture of the floorboards under her cheek and her stomach.

It was somewhat reassuring to find herself in the same place she'd been before. She was a little surprised, though, to find herself still there—surely her wolf would have wanted to get down to the forest floor, to get out among the trees and run and hunt. Then she noticed the trapdoor that led to the stairwell. It opened easily; in fact it was on a spring, so you barely had to tug with one finger on a ring to make it pop open. Of course, what's easy for a human finger might not even be possible for a wolf's paw.

Rising to her feet, she pushed open one of the shutters to let in some morning light. Then she turned around and jumped in surprise.

The wolf had been busy while she was out.

It must have gone wild when it realized it couldn't escape through the trapdoor. The walls of the small room were gouged, scarred with claw marks, scratches whole meters long, some

194

deep enough to put her finger inside. The graffiti left behind by the tower's human occupants were obliterated by the scratches. The table and the chairs had been broken into pieces, while the footlocker had been smashed up against one wall, its contents strewn across the room, battered and trampled. Nothing remained of the Edward Abbey book except tiny scraps of paper that littered the floor like big moldy snowflakes.

She understood, of course. They had been human things. Maybe they even smelled, to the wolf, like their previous owners still. Trapped and alone, the wolf had resorted to the one thing it really understood, which was destruction.

The smell of the wolf was thick in the tiny room. A little like wet dog, a little sharper than that. Chey pushed all the shutters open and let in a frozen wind to try to disperse the funk. Then she sat down on the floor—the chairs were useless, broken—and put her head in her hands.

She didn't even hear the helicopter at first because she was too sunken into her own depression. It wasn't a particularly loud sound, either, not one that demanded attention. Just a rhythmic chattering carried on the wind. As it grew closer she did look up, but she had no idea what she was listening to. Then the light coming in through the shutters changed and she jumped up.

Out over the treetops, maybe five hundred meters away, Bobby's helicopter zoomed past in a long arc. It was curving inward to get a better look at the fire tower. Chey waved her arms and shouted, then thought to open and close the shutters rapidly as a signal. The helicopter tilted backward and stopped to hover in midair, then slowly moved closer. She redoubled her efforts until the pilot waggled his vehicle back and forth to tell her she'd been seen. He hunted around for a minute, then started to descend toward a clearing she could make out in the distance.

Chey didn't waste any time. She rushed down the stairs and across the forest floor, her bare feet aching from the cold in the ground, from sharp rocks and pinecones and broken branches. She stumbled and tripped, but she ran as fast as she could toward the clearing.

When she arrived Bobby and Lester were both waiting for her. They didn't look like they'd been hurt at all.

"Oh, thank God," she said. "I thought I'd killed you!"

Bobby wasn't smiling. "You very nearly did," he told her. "I thought I was pretty clever bringing that chain along."

"What happened?" she asked. "What did I do?"

"You don't remember at all?" he asked. He glanced down at her legs. Involuntarily she took a step backward. "I really should have thought it through better. You did what wolves in traps are famous for doing. You gnawed off your own leg. Except, there wasn't a lot of gnawing involved. Then you came for us like you wanted to swallow us whole."

"How—how did you get away?" she asked. What she really wanted to ask was why he hadn't just shot her. He had a pistol full of silver bullets, after all. No one could have blamed him for defending himself.

"The second you changed you started straining against the manacle. I had a bad feeling, so I told Lester to get the chopper warmed up. When I saw what you were going to do we jumped in and took off. You still came for us and you even jumped at us but, well, with only one hind leg you didn't get much air."

Chey put an arm across her mouth. She could hardly believe it. "I'm so sorry," she said, and moved to reach for him, to grab his hands, to hug him.

It was his turn to step backward. Maybe he was afraid she would scratch him and pass on the curse. Maybe he was just afraid of her.

She stood there for a moment with her hands out. She needed something from him, something she couldn't ask for. Maybe not ever again. But he was still alive—he and Lester were both still alive. That had to be enough. She backed off until he looked a little more comfortable and stood there, hugging herself in the cold.

"Do you have any food?" she asked.

thitty-seven

"**T**here's something you need to see," Bobby told her. Fenech, she thought. She should start thinking of him by that name, since it was clear that whatever had once been between them was over. It was hard, though. She watched him as he turned and walked away from her and she thought about how she knew exactly what it would feel like to run up behind him and run her fingers over the top of his spiky hair.

"Lester, get this thing ready, okay?" he snapped. It looked like he might have had a bad morning.

The pilot ducked his head and ran to his helicopter. He was ready to go by the time the other two got there. "Might be there's room for three in here, as long as we're all friends," he assured her. He held open the Plexiglas door on the side of the bubble cockpit and moved around some of the baggage for her. Chey clambered into the space behind the two seats and sat with her knees up around her chin. She had to hold down the front of her sweater to keep from flashing the two men.

Then Bobby and Lester got inside and pulled the door shut. The air in the cockpit changed, subtly, and Chey found her breathing came a little faster. She didn't know what to make of that. Once Lester had them off the ground and she could look out at the blue sky and the trees below them she was pretty much fine, she decided.

Lester and Bobby had headphone sets so they could talk to each other over the roar of the engine. She had to make do with her hands over her ears just to keep from being deafened. Still, when she saw where they were headed she tried to shout over the noise and warn them away.

Ignoring her pleas, Lester descended toward the clearing by Powell's cabin. The rotorwash stirred up a ton of pine needles and curled brown leaves as they set down gently on the almost-level ground. As the engine wound down she grabbed Bobby's shoulder and said, "This is a lousy idea. He's probably lurking nearby, waiting for you to mess with his stuff."

"Good. If he is I can shoot him," Bobby told her. He shrugged violently.

They piled out of the helicopter and moved across the front of the house, Chey craning her head back and forth to try to pick up any stray noise.

"Relax," Bobby finally told her. "I've already been through this place once and he didn't pop out of the woodwork to get me." He pointed and she saw that the front door of the cabin stood open. She could only see shadows inside, but she understood what he was trying to tell her. Powell had moved on—as he always had before. Had he run off to the north? There wasn't much farther he could go.

"You think he's gone for good?" she asked.

"No," he told her, "I don't think he'll leave until he's dealt with you and me. That's what I would do. But what the hell do I know? I skipped Werewolf Psychology 101 when I was at McGill."

"Maybe—" Chey hated the sound of her own voice as she said, "maybe we should leave. Go back south, I mean."

He turned to look at her then, and she realized that he hadn't really made eye contact since they'd been reunited. He looked right into her eyes then and smiled a tiny, cold smile. "Chey, this guy's a killer."

"I know," she said, "but—"

"Come on," he told her. "Maybe you need a little reminder why we're up here." He led her around the side of the house to where the two small outbuildings stood. She remembered how one used to have smoke leaking out of its eaves. She had assumed he was curing meat in there. "There's a big tank of diesel fuel in that shed," Bobby told her, pointing to the other one. "Some tools, some firewood. No big surprise. When we looked in here, though," he said, pointing to the smokehouse, "well, that's where all the nasty is."

She expected him to walk over to the shed and throw open the door, but he didn't. So she stepped up and pulled it open herself. She wasn't immediately clear on what he'd found so exciting about its contents. It had occurred to her that instead of a smokehouse it might be a sweat lodge. What she found couldn't be far off that guess. A small fire pit sat in the center of the tiny space and there were various implements lying near it— a smudge stick, an eagle feather, a copper bowl—that looked like the magical tools an ancient Paleo-Indian shaman might use. Hanging from a rack on the ceiling were long strips of tanned leather like belts with no buckles, dozens of them. Interspersed among them hung similar strips of fur. Wolf fur in various different colors.

Powell had been making wolf straps. She remembered him telling her about the lycanthropes of Germany, who supposedly could change from wolf to human by putting on magical belts.

He'd said he'd looked into the old legend and found nothing there. She hadn't realized that he had tried to make his own wolf strap, but it made perfect sense now that she saw the proof.

"Yeah," she said. "He told me he's been looking for a cure for decades now." She left out the fact that he had failed at everything he'd tried. "What's the big deal, though? So he works with leather."

Bobby stood by the side of the shed, not really looking inside. "That's not cowhide he's got there," he told her. "That stuff is human skin. It wouldn't surprise me if some of it came off your dad."

thirty-eight

Bobby gave her back her old clothes—he'd gathered them up from the campsite at the tiny lake. She'd almost forgotten how cold she was until she pulled her parka back on and felt warmth, real human warmth caress her. It made a big difference, though even getting warm didn't seem to shake the hollow feeling she had, the strange high-pitched emptiness in her stomach and her limbs.

She tried not to think about it. She helped Lester build a fire out front of the cabin. She couldn't help but look up among the trees. She tried to focus on the wood in front of her, concentrate on building a little pyramid of medium-sized branches, but then Lester cleared his throat and she realized she was scanning the dark rank of trees again. Looking for Powell.

He wanted to kill her. He had killed other people before. She had plenty of reason to be frightened of him. Right?

Skin—human skin—hanging in his sweat lodge. What had Powell been up to? She didn't like to imagine it. She'd come north to kill him. She had wanted to confront him, thinking she knew what kind of monster he was. She'd started to think things were more complicated than that. That there was something to him . . . something human. The straps told a different story, though.

She watched the trees. Waiting. It was only a matter of time before he came back. To finish things with her. Maybe to finish her off.

The little kindnesses he'd shown her—taking her into his home, teaching her the ropes of lycanthropy. Had those been the gestures of a human being reaching out to the only other person in the world who might understand him? Or had it been an initiation? Had he just been recruiting her into his own world of blood and horror? Breaking things to her slowly, so she wouldn't get scared off. What dark secrets had he hidden from her? And then she had betrayed him—a creature capable of such violence.

Maybe she'd made a very bad mistake when she didn't shoot him. Maybe it was destiny catching up with her. Making up for the day twelve years earlier when she should have died.

Things moved out in the woods. Occasionally a pine needle would flutter down through the branches and be swallowed by the gloom between the trunks. A bird would take off, bursting up into the air with a snapping sound of desperate wings, then catch itself on the breeze and swoop off in silence. One of the trees would creak and pop. Those trees froze in winter and thawed only slowly, one growth ring at a time, and when the ice broke inside them it would sound like they were ready to fall. These sounds made her jump, made her heart race a little faster. A squirrel rattled up a tall birch, skidding circles around the bark. She nearly cried out.

Lester put some water on to boil, made some instant oatmeal. She ate, and felt a little better—and then Bobby came over and squatted next to her. He studied her face as if trying to figure out how she would react to what he said next.

She didn't like it.

"We need to start thinking about this thing in a rational way. We need a medium-range plan, at least. The moon will be up at eight fifty-six tonight," he told her. He showed her a piece of yellow legal-sized paper covered in two rows of numbers. He tapped it and she saw written there the number 2056.

"Already?" she asked, trying to keep her voice low. "It feels like I just . . . woke up."

"Since you changed back to your human form," he said. He had a way of saying things like that. He made them sound real. Like facts, facts that had to be dealt with. "The moon set at twelve fourteen today." He tapped his paper again. The other row said 1214.

"That's not enough," she said. "I mean, that doesn't seem right. How much human time did I get today?"

"About eight and a half hours," he told her. "It's gone seven o'clock now. I need you to help me prepare for tonight."

Chey's spine shivered. She remembered Powell telling her that this far north the moon cycles were weird. He'd said their human time would grow shorter as the month went past, but she hadn't expected the transition to be so noticeable. "How much time will I have tomorrow?" she asked. Human time, she meant, but unlike Bobby she couldn't say those words out loud and take them seriously.

"Six hours," he told her. "We need to be ready."

She nodded. Six hours. Her wolf would have three quarters of the day to itself. She grew jealous suddenly. It was her life the animal was devouring. "And the day after that?"

"Four. Come with me, please."

She finally let him take her arm, lift her to her feet.

Four hours, out of twenty-four. Powell had said there were days coming up when the moon wouldn't set. When it would never drop below the horizon. It would dip and rise and dip again but never quite go away.

Chey suddenly felt weak. She felt like she was about to die. Bobby took her through the woods, along the logging trail. Sometimes he had to hold her up, his shoulder in her armpit.

"I need to call my uncle," she said. She wasn't thinking clearly. "I need to get my uncle to come help me. He can fix this." Her voice sounded shrill and insignificant in her own ears. Like the buzz of a black fly. She hated it, hated her weakness. She had been strong before—she'd been as strong as a wolf. What had happened?

They walked for a kilometer like that, maybe two. Ahead of her she saw the little turnoff for the fire tower. She hadn't realized how close it was to Powell's cabin.

"You're going to put me back up there?" she asked. She struggled to regain herself, to put some iron back in her bones. "Bobby?"

He didn't look at her. He was looking up at the silhouette of the fire tower. The sun was setting in its measured way and there were already long shadows striping the road. "I know you don't like this, Chey," he told her. He sounded sincere and she loved him a little for that. For the fact that despite all the horror and the violence that swirled around them, he could still care a little about her feelings. She remembered how much she owed him. Without him she couldn't have gotten as far as she had. She couldn't have made any sense of her life at all.

"You need to walk a ways in my shoes," he told her. "Lester and I have a right to be safe. Don't we? And I've got the guys coming in from Selkirk tomorrow morning. This is going to suck for you. But it's the only way."

Chey breathed in the smell of musty pine needles. She would be safe up there. Everybody would be safe if she was up there.

It had held her wolf just fine the night before—it would work again.

"I understand," she said, and started climbing the stairs.

"Good girl," he called up at her. She spun around to half-laugh, half-snarl at him, to shoot him a good-natured glare, but he was already walking back toward the cabin.

thitty-nine

Silver light came and passed behind her eyes and then Chey was down on the floor, naked and grunting, her fingers raw, the nails broken as she scratched and scrabbled and gnawed with her teeth at the wooden floorboards. Her cheek burned as she pushed her face harder and harder against the floor, and her hair got in her eyes. She whined and whimpered as her fingers dug and dug but got nowhere against the old dry wood.

Then she sat up fast enough to give herself a head rush. What—what had she been doing? It was dark in the fire tower, but she didn't want to get up to open the shutters, not when she didn't know what she would find. She'd had a shock the last time she'd woken up in that position and found the place torn to pieces by her wolf.

Her hands were stiff and sore. Carefully she unbent her fingers, smoothed out her palms. Then she reached down and touched the floor. There had been scratches there before, but now there were distinct gouges. Four narrow trenches, some of them deep enough to fit her fingertip inside.

In the dark she pulled on her clothes, then stood up and

hesitantly opened one of the shutters. Outside afternoon sunlight stretched in long rays through a haze of pollen. The golden spores filled the air between the trees like mist. She could hear people down there, maybe more people than just Bobby and Lester. She heard the repeated dull sound of a hammer at work. In a second, she thought, she would go down and join the other human beings. Yes. That would be nice. First, though, she had to make sure her wolf hadn't destroyed her one place of refuge.

Slowly Chey turned around. It wasn't as bad as she'd expected. The gouges were there, yes, but only in a few places. Her wolf hadn't dug its way through the floor. She'd been worried it might have found a way out—though she remembered almost nothing of the last eighteen hours, she knew the wolf had desperately, almost pitifully, wanted to escape the tower. The floorboards were too thick for that, it seemed.

Chey smoothed out her wild hair and rubbed dried drool off the corner of her mouth. Maybe she could have a bath in Powell's big galvanized tin tub. Maybe she could convince Bobby and Lester to heat up enough water so that the bath would actually be warm. She reached down and pulled the ring of the trapdoor, ready, she thought, to rejoin polite company.

The trapdoor lifted half a centimeter, then stopped fast. Even with her better-than-human strength she couldn't lift it any further. The explanation was obvious, even if she didn't want to believe it. Bobby had locked her inside the tower.

She couldn't stay up there another minute or she knew she would lose her shit. She had to get out.

Chey beat and pounded on the trapdoor, then ran to the open shutter and yelled down for someone to come let her out—anyone. She heard someone clambering up the metal stairs below and then the sound of a padlock being released. When the door opened she saw an unfamiliar face rise up toward her in greeting.

"You'll be the screecher, then," the face said. It belonged to a middle-aged man with a square jaw and a nearly shaved head. He was wide through the shoulders and his hands were enormous. She watched them grip the edge of the trapdoor as he pulled himself up. "Frank Pickersgill, pleased to meetcha."

He held out one of those big hands and she put her own into the meaty grip. He did not squeeze her hand in greeting as much as he just enclosed it, the way Chey might have held the hand of a baby.

"You're a friend of Bobby's," she said. "I mean Mr. Fenech. Is he around?"

"Out at the lake, coordinating. Supervising, you know," Pickersgill said, shaking his head a little back and forth as if he thought Bobby's talents were better employed elsewhere. "He'll be glad to hear you're back on your feet."

"He locked me in," Chey said, then looked away from Pickersgill's eyes very quickly. Maybe too quickly, she thought.

"Ah, well, that was just a safety precaution," the big man told her. He climbed all the way up inside the tower and Chey saw he was well over two meters tall. The floorboards, which had held up against the worst her wolf could do to them, creaked a little when he sat down with his legs dangling through the trap.

Chey nodded. She supposed she understood that. Though so far her wolf hadn't been able to open the trapdoor, she could sympathize with Bobby if he worried that sometime it might just figure out the trick. "I have to go down now," she said, because the fire tower's walls were just too close.

She scrambled down the stairs and heard Pickersgill descending behind her. His bulk made the metal skeleton of the tower shake and groan. At the bottom she wondered what she should do. She felt like just running—running as far as her legs would take her. She just didn't know which direction. She turned around, swiveling to look every which way, drinking in the open air. Then she noticed the pipes.

While her wolf had been clawing up the tower floor someone, probably Pickersgill, had been busy hammering lengths of PVC pipe into the ground. There were around a dozen of them, spread in a circle around the base of the tower, each a few meters apart from the next. They were driven in at a sharp angle to the ground and they pointed outward, making her think of the cannon on a pirate ship. A strange smell issued from the pipe nearest to her. She stepped closer and leaned down to sniff as if she were smelling a rose. The scent was a lot more pungent and musky than that, however. In fact, she thought she recognized it. She touched the edge of the pipe, started to reach inside. What was that smell? It was the smell of—of—

"Not for you, sister," a man said, grabbing her arm and pulling it away from the pipe. "Not unless you're ready to die."

forty

The stranger's hand on her arm felt like a pair of pliers were being closed on her wrist. She had no choice but to pull her hand back. Chey was astounded—she'd had no idea the man was near her, hadn't heard him coming up behind her.

She shook the pain out of her hand. Then held it out again, to shake. She glanced down at the PVC pipe at her feet. Its smell still tantalized her. "What is that, wolf musk?" she asked. She had it now. It smelled exactly like Powell's hair. Like a lycanthrope.

The sneaky guy stared at her for a long time before taking her hand. Then he bent down slowly from the waist and kissed it. "Bruce," he said, "Bruce Pickersgill. I think you've already been introduced to my brother."

He was smaller than the near-giant Frank Pickersgill, considerably smaller, and his shoulders were thin and narrow, but there was a smoky kind of intelligence in his eyes she hadn't seen in his brother's. He had a pencil-thin mustache and he wore a parka with a beaver fur collar that smelled like old smoke. He had a pair of pistols low on his hips, like a gunfighter, though the guns themselves were matte black and square in shape, just like the one Bobby had given her. She didn't doubt they were full of silver bullets.

"Pleased to meet you," she said.

"We came in this morning," he told her, "while you were up there howling away. We didn't have a chance to be properly introduced then." He held her with his eyes while he reached into his pocket. She half expected him to pull a knife on her. Instead his fingers flicked out with a business card between them.

WESTERN PRAIRIE CANID MANAGEMENT LLC, she read. 67 YEARS COMBINED EXPERTISE!

"Canids are what—dogs?" she asked.

"Doglike mammals," he told her. "Predatory beasts. Mostly we get called in by shepherds who don't like coyotes worrying their flocks. Lots of outfits do that. My brothers and I, though, we specialize in larger pest animals. Coydogs, bears, and the occasional wolf pack."

She nodded. She understood how these men "managed" such animals, she guessed. They killed them in the fastest, cheapest way possible. "I take it Bobby explained to you what I have become, Mr. Pickersgill."

"Bruce, please." He nodded. "That's why I didn't want you touching the mechanism."

She bent down to look at the PVC pipe. The smell of Powell on it had to be artificial, she decided. There was no way he would have gotten close enough to these guys to let them take a sample of his personal body odor. "What is this thing?" she asked, gesturing at the pipe but being careful not to touch it.

"That," Bruce Pickersgill said, his eyes very sharp, "is what we in the trade call a *getter*. It's a modified kind of coyote getter, big enough for your average exotic canid."

Chey figured she knew what kind of exotic canids he was talking about. "How does it work?"

A smile inched across his face like a worm crawling through the decayed insides of an apple. "At the bottom of that pipe is a rifle cartridge, a .38 to be exact. That's wired to a spring-up top. When your target animal pokes its nose into the lip of the pipe, it triggers the cartridge, which goes boom, and fires a pellet up into their face. If you're lucky it goes right down the target's throat. If not it'll get embedded in their jaw or face."

"Nice." Chey grimaced. "What kind of pellet?" She was almost afraid to ask.

Bruce scratched at his mustache. "Well, for your timber wolves, for your coyotes, for your coydogs, feral dogs, what have you, we usually use sodium fluoroacetate, what's called 1080 in the trade. With that you get some convulsions, you get uncontrolled running, and then vomiting and death follow pretty quick."

Chey winced. "Jesus. But even that wouldn't kill this kind of wolf," she said.

Bruce's face smoothed out in happiness. "We love a good challenge at Western Prairie. My brother spends long, lonely nights in his workshop dreaming up new mechanicals and testing new baits and lures. For this job he really shone. We tested a getter with a silver bullet in it, but on the five experimental animals we used only one of them was sufficiently wounded to guarantee a clean kill. So Bruce thought up something new. The pellets we're using today are full of colloidal silver, that's silver particles in a water solution. For people like me and—well, for Homo sapiens, anyway, the stuff's all but harmless. It might turn our skin blue if we got too big a snort. But for your exotic canid it's deadly poison."

Chey's hand twitched. She had come very close to setting off one of the getters. The silver pellet inside would kill her in human or in wolf form. And the smell, the smell of the lure—"You've got some kind of bait on these," she said. "A musk."

"Genuine wolf matrix," he said happily. "That's a patented formula right there. We call it Canine Curiosity and it works great on most canid sets. We make it with a rue oil base with lovage oil on top. That's a traditional canid passion simulator."

"Uh-huh," she said, getting about half of that.

"Then we grind up some authentic precaudal gland and add that in. That might be what you smell the most, because it's pretty fresh."

"That's disgusting," she said, unable to keep her reaction inside.

He shrugged. "It's what works, normally."

"You've put a lot of thought into this," Chey said.

"We've been preparing for this job for the last six months," he told her. "A population-control assignment like this, you don't just fly in with what you have on hand; you need to make everything custom."

She frowned. Because that meant—"I thought Mr. Fenech just called you in yesterday." She was confused. "Six months ago, he and I were still figuring out our original plan."

Pickersgill shrugged. "Maybe he just wanted to be prepared, like a good Boy Scout. I gotta say, though, the way he was talking, made it sound like we were the main plan, and you were a side bet." He shrugged. "No offense meant, but you're just a slip of a girl. You really think he expected you to take down this canid alone?"

"Yes, I did," she said.

Something connected in Chey's mind. Something she very much didn't like. Bobby had told her she would finally have her chance at revenge. That she would be allowed to go in alone and kill Powell. He'd never so much as hinted before that he had another angle working at the same time. And Pickersgill had a point—if he had all this technology at his disposal, why would he even need Chey in the first place?

Unless—unless he had never really expected her to succeed. Never really thought she could kill Powell. Maybe he'd thought of her just as a way to find the werewolf in the first place. To bring him out into the open.

Maybe he'd thought of her as bait. From the beginning.

No, she told herself. She was being paranoid, that was all. Bobby really cared for her. He would never put her in danger just to flush Powell out of hiding.

"This is how Bobby's going to protect me from him," she said. It sounded even to her own ears as if she was trying to convince herself. Pickersgill didn't respond. She thought, suddenly, of Powell, moving silently through the darkness. She thought of him looking for her, searching for her so he could kill her. She visualized him sticking his nose into one of the getters, his head tilted to one side, his tongue out to taste the lure, one paw up on the pipe. And then bang. Her life's long nightmare would be over.

She could hardly believe it.

Would he really be so curious? It had almost worked on her, even in her human form. But he was a lot older than she was. He was a lot more canny. "What if he doesn't go for it?"

"Well, then, Tony over there shoots him in the back of the head," Bruce explained.

A man sat in a tamarisk tree not ten meters away. A man with a very big shotgun. He was tied to the tree trunk with bungee cords. He had camouflaged himself with twigs and leaves so well that she saw him only because he waved down at her with one sweeping arm motion. Chey nearly jumped. "Is he your brother, too?" she asked, trying to mask her alarm.

"Half-brother," Bruce said. "Same ma, different dad. Meet Tony Balfour, my shootist."

Chey looked back up at the sniper. "Hi," she said.

Balfour gave her about three-tenths of a smile.

"He doesn't talk much," Bruce explained.

fotty-one

ruce Pickersgill took Chey down to the tiny lake on the back of an ATV. It was one of two vehicles the exterminators had brought with them. When she arrived she found Bobby and Lester unloading a small seaplane with the Western Prairie Canid Management logo on its side. The logo showed a stylized wolf head howling at a crescent moon.

"That's a strange logo for what you do," she said, as Bruce helped her off the ATV.

"Oh? Why's that?" he asked.

She squinted at him. "You guys hate wolves," she tried to explain.

"Heck, no," he told her, leading her over to the landing site. "I wouldn't say that at all. I'd say we have a healthy respect for them. The wolf is a beautiful animal; all of the canids are." He looked up as if he were trying to remember something. "I think Tony's pop's even got a pet coydog, back at home. We just provide an important service for livestock ranchers."

Chey decided she had better things to do than psychoanalyze the three brothers. She dashed ahead to where Bobby was drinking Pepsi out of a three-liter bottle. He had a number of white paper bags on top of a crate before him and as she got closer he took a golden brown pastry out of one of them.

"Oh boy," she said, as he beckoned her forward. Maybe he did care for her after all. "Is that what I think it is?"

"This," he announced, "is an authentic jam-buster from Tim Hortons. I can't be expected to guess what you think a given thing is," Bobby told her. He held it out and she grabbed it away from him. The icing sugar got all over her fingers and down the front of her sweater, but she didn't care. The thick, super-sweet jelly inside spurted the top of her mouth and she sighed in deep bliss. It was exactly as she remembered.

Everything came rushing back with that taste—hot showers, air-conditioning, good roads, and nationalized health care. As she chewed on the doughnut she was back, back in Edmonton, back in her mother's house growing up, even.

"I got addicted to these back in the real world," she said. "When you don't sleep much you need to eat more, and the only place open late at night is Tim's. I would sit in the parking lot staring up at the sign, wondering where the apostrophe went. Then I would taste one of these and forget why I cared. You don't understand, Bobby—this is the taste of home. Please tell me you have eleven more of these in those bags."

"They're not all for you," he told her, but then he pushed a bag across the top of the crate at her. She tore it open and found a mixed variety of doughnuts and Timbits inside. She didn't waste time devouring them. For one thing, she hadn't eaten in twenty-four hours.

"You've met the boys," Bobby said while she ate. "I'm glad. I want you to feel like you're part of this operation, Chey. I really do."

She nodded in agreement.

"When I kill Powell, I want you to be there. I want to give you that satisfaction. Did they show you the traps?"

"They're called getters," she said.

Bobby nodded and picked up a crowbar. He started tearing open a crate while she watched. "Honestly I don't think he'll be stupid enough to fall for those. And the lure they're using is all wrong—it's meant for timber wolves, not werewolves. But maybe we'll get lucky. But then we have another kind of bait for him. We have you."

She nearly choked on a cruller. "What?" she managed to say. It was what she'd been thinking, before. It was the worst thing she'd ever thought, and here he was saying it out loud. The doughnut in her mouth was suddenly dry and tough.

"He wants you, Chey. He wants to rip your throat out. Last night—you won't remember this, I guess. Last night you were up in that tower howling like a fucking dog for twelve hours straight. We could hear you over this far; we could hear you at the cabin. Lester slept right through it, but poor old me, I couldn't catch a single z. I wandered over to the tower, thinking I'd try talking to you—though God knows why I thought that would help; my presence would probably have just made you yowl more. And that's when I saw it."

"It? What did you see? Don't tell me you saw Powell," Chey breathed. She glanced around at the trees behind her.

"I saw his tracks in a snowdrift. Like wolf tracks, but bigger. Wider. I looked around and found them on the other side of the tower, too. I found them all over the place. The whole night while you were howling he was circling you, desperate to get at you. Your howling summoned him."

"Oh."

"Come on, don't look so pale," he said, clapping her on the shoulder. "You were perfectly safe. I even locked you in, just in case he tried to open the trapdoor. And don't you see what this means? I was worried he was just going to run off and escape us. He's done that before. But not this time. No, he won't leave until he's gotten to you. Or until we kill him. Now, with the boys here, I figure we've finally got him. It's all but done."

Chey swallowed the mass of thick dough at the back of her throat. When she spoke sugar puffed out of her mouth. "If you think they're good enough. The Pickersgills, I mean."

"It's Balfour I've got my money on," he told her. "I've been hunting with him. The guy's a menace to vermin." His face softened. "You're still with me, Chey, right?" he asked. "I mean, you want to help me get the asshole who ate your dad. Or maybe you've changed. Maybe becoming a werewolf has changed your perspective."

Chey nodded. "It has. It's helped me understand just how dangerous Powell is."

"So you'll help me," he said, looking at her over the lenses of his sunglasses.

"Yeah. But Bobby—I have one question."

"Of course," he said, opening the top of his crate. Inside were boxes of ammunition—bullets, shotgun shells, rifle cartridges. All of it silver. He'd told her his gunsmith took days just to make a handful of silver bullets. How long ago had he put in the order for all this ordnance, she wondered?

"What happens to me, when Powell is dead?"

He laid his crowbar gently down. "I guess that depends on how you feel then. On what you want, what kind of life you think you want to try to have."

It wasn't exactly what she'd wanted to hear.

forty-two

The six hours between moonset and moonrise went by in a flash. Especially because she knew the next day would be even shorter. And then—well, maybe by then it would all be over.

Bobby came with her back to the fire tower. He had a padlock in his hand so he could lock her inside. She tried not to think about what her wolf was going to do when it found itself locked up, again.

Lucie, the French lycanthrope who had given her curse to Powell, had gone mad from being confined when the moon was up. Of course, she'd been doing it for centuries. Chey wasn't sure she could live any kind of life that long without going crazy.

Then again, she'd had so little practice at life. What did she know?

Bobby knew exactly when the moon would come up. He offered to sit with her until nearly the last minute. She wanted to tell him not to bother, that he didn't have to coddle her like that. Instead she tried to hug him, to hold him close, to force him to be nearer to her. Physically near her.

"I understand you need some human contact," he told her, gently pushing her away. "But it's not so safe anymore. I don't know if you can pass on your infection to me when you're in human form. But I won't take that chance, Chey."

"No," she agreed. It occurred to her that she could grab him and pull him close, make him embrace her. She was strong enough. But no.

"It's not fair to me," he said, even though she'd already agreed. Did he see in her eyes how much she needed him? If she was honest with herself, she didn't even like him all that much, had never found him particularly lovable. But she needed somebody, anybody, to understand. To tell her she wasn't a monster.

She hated herself a little for feeling that way. She could imagine her wolf's reaction to those feelings—her lips pulled back over a snarl, her ears back in disgust. But she was still human, too.

She hung her head in shame. After a minute she looked up again. "I want to thank you, Bobby. While I still have the chance."

"You make it sound like you're going to die," he said, scolding her.

She shook her head. "Maybe it's like dying, if just for a couple of days. But pretty soon I won't be able to talk. And I really do want to thank you. You got me up here, you got me closer than anyone ever could have. You knew exactly what I needed, what was holding me back. And you tried to fix me. Heal me, I mean."

"I had my own reasons for wanting him dead," he grumbled, but not loud enough that she couldn't pretend he'd kept quiet.

"Whatever happens," she said, "we tried, right? A lot of people have wrecked lives but they never try to put things right. This was a silly thing to do, I know that. But at least we tried. Because you believed in me."

222

He did reach over, then, and rubbed her back a little. She wanted to reach up and take his hand—surely, surely that would be okay? But no, she knew it wouldn't. If she reached for him he would pull away again.

"You . . . did believe in me. Right?"

He exhaled noisily. "I believed you believed in yourself."

That just confused her. She needed to know, now. She needed to know that he'd been behind her all along, that he really had thought of her as the best person to take down the werewolf. "You hired the Pickersgills a long time ago. You had your gunsmith make all kinds of bullets. I saw them," she said.

"I don't know what you're getting at—" he began, but she reached over to put a finger across his lips. He jerked backward as if she were trying to stab him.

"Just tell me the truth," she said. "Did you actually think I was going to get Powell? Or did you just send me up here to draw him out?"

He looked at her for a while, his eyes studying her as if he were trying to decide what answer would get him the best return on his investment of lies and truths. His hesitation infuriated her, made her want to drag her nails across his face, because it told her exactly what she wanted to know, far better than any measured response he might come up with.

"Chey, I—" he said.

"Never mind," she growled. "Don't—don't say it."

"Don't make this all about you," he told her. "That's not the way to handle this."

She turned away from him in disgust. "How much longer do I have?" she asked. "This is so hard when I don't have a clock or anything. I wake up and it's midafternoon. Or it's first thing in the morning. I wake up and—I guess it's not really like waking at all."

223

He glanced at his watch. "We have a couple of minutes. There's something I wanted to talk to you about," he said.

She sighed. As much as she needed human companionship right now, she really wanted him to shut up. "Yes?"

"Tomorrow," he said. "You'll only have four hours of human time."

She nodded, understanding. "I want to make the most of it. Have a bath, have at least two real meals. I want to read a book, if you brought any with you. Anything to make me feel more human before I go under for five days straight."

Bobby grimaced. "Actually—I was thinking maybe you could just stay up here. The whole time."

"But—why?" she asked.

"It's just safer for all of us that way. I mean, four hours isn't a lot of time. We could lose track or something."

She shook her head. No. No, that wasn't fair, it wasn't acceptable!

"I'll see what I can do about getting you that book. I think the Pickersgills brought up some magazines; maybe they'll loan you one. Though the last time you had some reading material you just kind of tore it up."

He meant the Edward Abbey book. The one she'd found in the fire tower and tried to dry out so she could read it. The wolf had torn the printed words to shreds, as surely as if they'd been human bodies.

That was what it did when she tried to lock it up. It destroyed the things she needed to stay sane, because that was the only way it could hurt her.

"No," she said. "No. I won't stay up here. I refuse."

"Okay, time's up," he said, before she could protest any more. He climbed down through the trap and before she could even say good-bye he was fitting the padlock.

Chey knelt over the trap and knocked on the closed door. Rapped on it with hard knuckles. "Bobby," she said, "you son of a bitch, you can't just leave it like that and expect me to—"

But then silver light flooded her brain.

Later she came to crying, screaming. She came to not quite human. The walls around her—the walls—they were closing in—the walls—how long—how long had she been imprisoned—how long had the wolf howled—the walls—she shrieked; she pushed into a corner of the little room, tears wet on her face—the walls—the walls—

Come on, Chey, she thought. *Calm down. Just—calm down.*

She focused on her breathing. Focused on the darkness, seeing it as the absence of light, not as some dark fluid that was pressing in on her, drowning her.

Breathe in, breathe out.

Eventually, feeling just a little weak in the knees, she pulled her clothes on. Then she opened one of the shutters to let some light inside.

Four hours. She had four hours left. Or less—how long had it taken her to calm down? How long had she been screaming? How much of her time had she—

She was leaning on the edge of the wall, craning her head out into the fresh air. "Let me out," she demanded. It came out of her like a moan. "Let me out; I don't have much time left. I don't want to be up here. Let me—" Her hands were braced on the wood and they felt very strange. She looked down at them, at the wood she could see right through them. It was like her hands were made of translucent glass. Or—no—as if they were made of fog, of mist.

The silver light came again and found her screaming.

forty-three

The wolf howled.

The wolf felt as if she had always howled.

The wolf had gone a little bit crazy.

Not crazy like a human being goes crazy. Like an animal. There were two parts of her, of her self, of her mind. The thinking part of her brain, the part that could solve problems and that kept her out of trouble, grew less active with each passing hour. The instinctual part of her, the older half of her brain, rose up, its hackles high, and demanded more and more of her mental energy. Anger and fear and desperation had built up in the crenellations of her brain like wax building up in her ears, horror and hate and pain added to every day she was locked in the human place, magnified by the moonlight that leaked in through tiny cracks in the ceiling and the shutters. Multiplied—her hatred and her rage and her torment were multiplied, jacked up by a power of ten, because she knew a human female had been inside her square little cell the last time she'd slept. She could smell it on the floor, on the walls. She licked the wood and tasted the human, the oily sourness of the female's skin, the unbearable thickness of her artificial scent. She hated, hated, hated the human, wanted to snap her neck, wanted to grind her bones between her teeth. Where was she? Was she nearby? Was she—was she?

Was she still here? Hiding somewhere? The wolf felt the female human like she was under the wolf's very skin.

She paced the corners of her cell, ran from wall to wall. There wasn't enough room, wasn't enough, wasn't, wasn't, wasn't. She panted with the fear, the fear, the fear. Her legs cramped and her head bowed—her body filled all the available space. Her rage filled every square centimeter. It made the walls stretch and buckle as if she could escape just by needing it badly enough.

Finally she sank down to lie on her belly, her tongue out, her breathing slowing. And still she howled.

The human, the other human, the male, was he near? The one who had chained her leg, the one she'd nearly devoured. He had done this to her—he had imprisoned her in this terrible place. She could smell him! Was he nearby? She would tear him apart! She would, she would, she would. She would.

No, the human was nowhere near. She knew as much. Still, his stink, his cologne, was smeared on the walls, and the floor. Still he stung her nose, her eyes.

Still she howled.

She howled. She was a creature that howled. It was all she had left in this prison. The howls came out of her like the pure distilled essence of her anguish, long, rumbling horrors that ripped out from her throat, from her belly, over her teeth, rumbling in her chest, shaking in her, and out into the air.

She howled—and nothing changed. The howling achieved nothing.

For four days straight she howled, even as her body hungered and grew weak. Even as her brain dried out in her skull and she forgot why she was howling.

Still she howled.

And then one night she heard the other wolf, out there in the dark—howling back.

Her massive jaws snapped shut. Her ears perked up. The rest of her body lay perfectly still. She made no sound at all as she listened. She knew she had no reason to want him near; she knew he would try to kill her if he could. But he was another wolf, another creature like her. Another, another, someone like her, another. She listened—she craned her ears forward and she listened, desperate to hear him.

A roaring howl rattled through the forest, bouncing off the tree trunks. A searching wail. Then it was gone.

Her body had little sound left in it, so little energy left, so little to call on. She yelped. Whimpered. She leapt up and pushed and scratched at the walls until one of the shutters slipped open and she shoved her muzzle out into the dark air, her tongue tasting the wind.

Again—the answering howl. Her undercoat stood up away from her skin as if it were straining toward that sound. That long, stretched-out, lonely sound. He was looking for her, searching for her. She whimpered.

Below her she heard metal clinking, a fire crackling. She heard humans moving around excitedly. Had they heard the answer? They must have. She could hear them hurriedly extinguishing their fire. She could hear them moving out into the trees, their hands full of metal, their voices low, their grunting words meaning nothing to her.

The answer came again. She dug deep, dug into the last flickering embers of her strength, and let out a warbling yowl. Enough sound to guide him, enough for him to find her through the woods. Enough to lead him to her. She slipped backward, her body spent, and collapsed on the wooden floor, one foreleg over her muzzle.

Later on she heard gunshots, and her tail flicked across the floor, but she was too weak to prick up her ears.

For another day and a night she lay on the floor of the fire tower, rolling over when she could, too weak, too hungry, to do more than pant and wait, and pant, and try to sleep.

She lacked the strength to make a single noise, but in the hidden chambers of her heart, she howled, and howled, and howled.

fotty-fout

Eventually Chey woke in silver light.

Her mouth was smeared across the floor. Her hands were underneath her, crushed under her own weight. It felt like there was no blood in them—they tingled painfully. Unbearably.

Her eyes felt like raisins. Dried up, cracked and broken. She rolled over and the effort made her squint. She was so hungry, it felt like insects had colonized her abdomen, that they had hollowed her out and left a gaping void where her stomach had been. So hungry.

"Hungry," she moaned. She had a voice at least. A voice meant she was human again. It was getting hard to tell, sometimes. "Hungry," she said again, and her throat cracked. No one could have heard her—she didn't expect them to. But she was hungry.

She had no idea what time it was, or how many days had passed. Her thoughts were loose and small and she couldn't get the mental energy together to make the simplest of logical jumps.

"Hungry." She hadn't even thought it that time. It just came out of her like a fetid belch.

Without water, without food—shouldn't she have died already? But no. The curse wouldn't let her die.

She closed her eyes. Maybe she changed, maybe she didn't. All she saw was darkness.

When she opened her eyes again she felt a little better. There was a sound—a soothing sound. Tapping. Something was tapping on the roof. Lots of people, tapping very gently. There was a whole crowd of them up there, and they were—

A droplet of water seeped through the shingles over her head and dropped to scatter the dust near her face. Oh, she thought. It was raining. She closed her eyes again.

Up, moving, she smashed against the wall of the tower, slammed against it again, trying to knock the tower over, trying to break out. Her hands grabbed at the wood and pulled and shook and—and—she couldn't—couldn't catch her breath—she sank down to the floor again and—and closed her eyes.

Water was dripping down one wall. A thin, thready stream of it that wove around the splinters and pooled in the wolf-scratches. She watched it intently, raised her hands to touch it, lowered them again. As if by touching the stream of water she would make it stop. As if it was there just to tease her.

Her mouth burned. Her eyes felt like hard-boiled eggs, swollen inside her head. It hurt to move them from side to side. It felt like her eye sockets were full of sand, and every time she moved her eyes she could feel them getting scratched up back there.

The tiny ribbon of water never stopped. She leaned forward. Touched her tongue to the moistness. The water felt like ice on her cracked and swollen skin. It splashed across the inside of her mouth, wet her teeth. She laughed, it felt so good. She pressed her mouth against the wooden wall and sucked, sucked like an animal.

Like a gerbil in a cage sucking at its water bottle.

She didn't fucking care.

"I don't fucking care, alright?" she asked nobody. Because nobody was there. She sucked more water off the wall.

When she was done she dropped back to the floor. And closed her eyes. She had a smile on her face.

Knock, knock. She opened her eyes but didn't move. Knock, knock. Someone was knocking—no, she'd thought the rain was people tapping on the roof, but—knock, knock.

"I'm here," she screeched, and rolled over. She realized she was naked. She realized she didn't have the strength to call out like that. She shouted again. "Please! I'm here! And I'm human!"

The trapdoor creaked open on its spring. A hand, a very human hand, reached up through the dark hole and pushed a plastic bag up onto her floor. Then the hand drew back and the door shut again.

She reached for the door, tried to get to it. She could barely crawl across the floor. It was already closed. The arm—she'd seen the arm; it hadn't just been a hallucination. She was sure of it. The arm had been tanned and brown. It had been Lester's arm.

"Lester," she called. "Come on, Lester, it's safe. You can come in. Lester! Look, I know I'm dangerous. I know I'm scary. But I'm also a human being. It's not okay, Lester. It's not okay to leave people alone like this! It's not fucking appropriate! Lester! Come back. Just, come back. Please. Come back."

She pressed her face up against the wood of the trapdoor. Pressed against it with her nose, her cheek. She was sobbing. Was he there? She could visualize his face, inches away from hers. Looking up, through the wood, just like she was looking down through the wood at him.

She heard the padlock click into place. She felt the fire tower shake a little as he rumbled down the stairs. Then nothing. If

232

she'd had more strength she could have gotten up on her feet, thrown the shutters open. Screamed after him. If she'd had more strength, but she didn't. She had no more strength at all.

She wept until she was dry again, and then she closed her eyes.

Later she opened the plastic bag. There were some sandwiches inside, all the same. Ham with a wilted leaf of lettuce on white bread. She ate two of them right away, crammed them into her mouth, chewed just enough that she wouldn't choke, swallowed them in great painful lumps. Then she started to get sick to her stomach. It was too much, too fast. If she threw up it would only make her feel worse. She put the rest aside. Promised herself she would wait and eat them later.

Her body grumbled and bitched at her. But she could feel her stomach starting up again. Starting the process of digestion.

The bag also held two magazines. An outdated copy of *Outdoor Life,* and a relatively new *Flare,* which surprised her. What did the Pickersgills want with a fashion magazine? Then she noticed that half the pages were stuck together.

She put it aside and picked up the bag to see what else they'd given her. The bag was so heavy it slipped through her fingers. She picked it open and took out the last of the contents. A pistol. A black, square pistol. She ejected the magazine and found there was one silver bullet inside.

forty-five

They lifted the pistol in her hand and studied it as if there were some hidden message engraved on it. Some explanation of why it had been placed in the bag with the sandwiches and magazines.

When she actually thought about it, though, there really was only one conclusion to be made. A pistol with a single bullet in it is useful for a small variety of things, and only one of them made sense given where she was. And how alone she was.

The pistol was Bobby's final gift. The last residue of whatever he might have once felt for her. He was being merciful. The thought made her grin crazily. She had never meant anything to him, not really. She couldn't have. She was just convenient, a way to bring Powell out into the open.

His apparent affection for her—the words he'd spoken when they were quiet, when, after sex, she would reach for him—those words weren't sincere. They were calculated, intended to achieve a certain effect, and in that regard they'd been very successful. He had a problem—Powell—and she had presented a solution. That was the closest thing to affection he'd felt for her, that she was useful.

He hadn't expected her to get scratched. To join the club. Now that she had, she had become a new problem. And the pistol was what he'd come up with. The silver bullet was the solution. He was going to let her solve herself.

She lifted the pistol to shoulder height. She wondered if it mattered if she shot herself in the heart or the head. Blowing her brains out might hurt fractionally less—before she even knew what was happening she would just be gone, a puff of smoke blown away on a stiff breeze. If she shot herself in the heart it might take a couple of seconds for her to die. Excruciating, burning seconds.

Yet wasn't the heart more traditional? That was how the stories usually went. Or was she thinking of vampires? Yes, of course. It made no difference where she shot herself. It was just "Silver bullet plus lycanthrope equals no more lycanthrope." Just that simple.

Then again—what if she was wrong about that? She had never actually seen a wolf killed by a silver bullet. What if she shot herself in the head and it didn't work? What if she had to lie there in her blood and scattered brains until she changed again?

She lifted the weapon as nonchalantly as she could and tapped the muzzle against the side of her head. Then she started laughing and put the gun carefully back down on the floor.

She kept laughing until she realized she couldn't stop. Then she clutched her hands over her mouth and rolled up into a ball and tried to squeeze herself shut before her mind leaked out all over the floor.

She picked up the gun again. Contemplated just doing it. Finishing the whole sorry mess of her life the only way left to her. But her stomach was growling. She was still hungry—ravenous, after five days with nothing to eat. Maybe a last meal would help. Give her the strength to do what she had to do. The food might help her think more clearly, and . . . and she reached down and found nothing but a piece of wet ham lying on the floorboards. The stale bread and wilted lettuce leaf were gone.

"You can have that part," Dzo said. "I'm a vegetarian, remember?"

It was so natural, so perfectly ordinary for him to be sitting in the corner nibbling at a piece of bread, that she didn't scream. She just turned to look at him with half a smile on her face. He was sprawled across the floor with his mask tilted up, his furs spread out around him, making him look as flabby as a bear about to go into hibernation.

"Powell's gone off, and told me I couldn't follow, which left me kind of at loose ends. Thought I'd pop in and see how the lady shape-shifter was doing," he said, as if she'd asked what he was doing there. He looked at the gun that was dangling loosely in her hand. "Not so hot, it looks like."

"I've been a little . . . upset," she said. She was crying, she realized. She couldn't make herself stop. As dehydrated as she might be, her body seemed to still have a few tears left in it. "Don't try to stop me," she told him, almost begging him to do just that, and lifted the gun. Felt its weight.

"Why would I do that?" he asked, all innocence.

"You're not human," she said, as if she'd just realized it. She had no idea what he was, but he definitely wasn't human. Some kind of ancient Indian spirit or something. "You can't possibly understand what I'm going through."

"Because I'm not human, right."

She nodded slowly. "They hate me now. They want me to die.

236

I can never go home, never feel safe around another human being, ever again."

"And that's enough to make you want to die?" Dzo shrugged. "Weird. Monty didn't feel that way."

"But look at him! Alone up here! All alone, with just—just you for company. Which, no offense, is not what I consider enough."

"None taken," he said, and she could see he genuinely meant it.

"I can't be alone. Not forever. I'll go crazy. Just as crazy as I did being locked up in here. I'll start thinking that maybe I was wrong, that people can understand me after all. I'll head south, just to see another human being. I'll kill somebody."

"Yeah, it's tough being a lone wolf. You need a pack."

"What?" she asked, as she lifted the pistol to her forehead.

"You said I wasn't human, and that's true. But then neither are you. Not anymore."

"Shut up," she told him. She gripped the pistol in both hands so it wouldn't shake so much.

"You're a shifter now," he told her, as if he hadn't heard her. "Not a human. What you need, I think, is to find Monty. Be a pack with him. That'll fix you up."

"Powell wants to kill me, too," she said.

Dzo laughed. "Oh, come on. Really? You really believed him when he said that?" He scratched at his swollen gut. "No way. He was mad, sure, because you kind of, you know, betrayed him."

"Yes," she said. "I did that."

"But the way he looks at you, man! The way he talks to you. I've been living with him for a long time and I never heard him say more than a dozen words at a stretch. Then you come around and the guy just won't shut up. He needs to be in a pack,

237

too. It's a real shame. I thought the two of you were really going to make it together. Oh well. Hey, I don't know much about guns or nothing. But it looks like your safety is still on."

She yanked the pistol away from her face. Stared at it.

"It's that little catch there. Just switch it to the left," he said, helpfully.

"Dzo," she said, and couldn't think of what to say next.

"You want me to do it for you?"

"Dzo. I don't want to die."

"Then maybe you should leave the safety on." He shrugged.

"I just don't want to be alone." She laid the gun gently on the floor. And then she covered her face in her hands and moaned. Long and loud. Her body shook with it, with the realization. That she did not want to die. That she wanted to survive. "I've made so many mistakes. But I want to live."

It hurt. It hurt a lot. Her body was rejecting her old humanity. Her belief that all this was temporary, or that maybe there was a cure. She was accepting that she had changed, that she was a lycanthrope now. She was accepting what that meant.

It meant, for one thing, that she needed to apologize to Powell. Explain herself to him. Convince him not to kill her. Because the only way she was going to live—and that was what she wanted, it was definitely what she wanted—was with his help.

It might also mean she would have to fight. Bobby and the Pickersgills weren't going to be pleased when she failed to kill herself like she'd been told. They might try to lock her up again. They might try to kill her. She would have to defend herself.

Most assuredly, though, it meant she had to get out of the tower.

"Well," Dzo said, looking slightly uncomfortable, "I guess that's settled, so I'll just be going." He started to stand up.

"Hold on, Dzo," she said. "Can we get out of here? Go

someplace else and talk there? Pretty much anyplace—anyplace at all—will do." He must have come in through the trapdoor, she thought, since there was no other way in. Which meant the door had to be open. She scrabbled over to the trap and yanked on the latch—and nearly pulled her arm out of joint. It was locked up as tight as ever. She pulled again just for form's sake, but nothing had changed.

She turned to look at Dzo. He just shrugged.

How had he gotten in?

Suddenly she realized she was naked and she grabbed for her sweater. Dzo didn't turn away or blush or anything. "This—this means nothing to you, does it?" she asked. She pulled it on anyway. "You don't care if I'm naked."

"Gosh, do you mean if I care what kind of clothes you wear or if you're in your altogether?"

She nodded.

"Well, to be honest, not as such." He scratched his belly. The question seemed to make him much more uncomfortable than her nudity. "I mean, I barely have time to notice what color your skins are. Humans kind of all run together in my head. They're like mayflies, eh? Here for a second and then they're gone. I like you shape-shifters better 'cause you last a little longer, but, well, still and all."

She nodded again, understanding none of that.

Maybe she could worry about it later. "Dzo, you got in here somehow. I'm sure that if I asked you how I wouldn't understand the answer."

"Dove through the water. I'm a pretty strong swimmer."

"See what I mean?" she said. "Can—I—dive through the water?" she asked. "To get out of here?" Whatever it meant, whatever weird new fucked-up action it might entail, she knew she would do it. Anything to get out of the tower.

239

His face opened up as he considered her question. "Well," he said, finally, "no."

"Okay."

"No, you see, because the water I'm talking about, it isn't water like you're used to. It's everywhere all at once, kinda, and I don't think you know how to swim like that."

"Right," she agreed.

"Now, as for teaching you, that's been done before, but that's a long time since. Like back when all the stories were still true."

"I have no idea what you're talking about," she said, defeated. She slumped back against the wall of the fire tower and closed her eyes.

"But that's not to say there's no way out for you. Why, I can see a pretty good way right now," he told her.

"You can." It wasn't a question. Because she didn't expect an answer, at least not one that made sense.

"Yeah, sure," he told her. "You just open up one of these windows and jump out."

part four

post stadium

fotty-six

"**I**t's at least thirty meters down," Chey said, looking out into the darkness. She had one shutter propped open, but the moon was down (of course it was, she thought, otherwise she'd be in her wolf form) and she couldn't see anything beyond the branches of the nearest trees. She couldn't, for instance, see the ground below her. She thought if she could see how far the drop was she might be more afraid than she was already. In the pitch dark it might be possible to climb up on the sill and jump out. The idea still made her stark raving terrified. "That would kill me."

"No, it wouldn't." Dzo leaned out and looked down. "You're a shifter, remember? It's just going to hurt like a bitch."

Chey licked her chapped lips. "I'm not sure if I can do that. I'm afraid."

Dzo shrugged mightily. "You asked if I knew a way out of here. You're looking at it. Don't blame me if you wimp out."

"You're not human. I don't think you're alive, really. You're more like a ghost or a spirit. Can you even feel pain? Have you ever felt pain?"

Dzo tilted his head and shoulders from side to side. It was a distinctly ambivalent gesture. "Why, sure I have," he said, finally. "Sorta. Actually, no, I guess I haven't."

"Well, it's not fun. That's pretty much the definition of pain. It's the opposite of fun. Maybe I should just take my chances and stay here." And blow my head off with my one silver bullet, she thought. "I mean, even if I did survive the fall, even if I recovered from the broken bones and punctured lungs and blood loss and everything, then I'd still be down there. In these woods, with Bobby wanting me dead. At least up here I'm safe from him."

"Until he comes back for you and finds you didn't kill yourself like he wanted," Dzo pointed out.

"Yeah. How long is it until moonrise?" she asked Dzo.

"No clue," he told her. She stared at him and he shrugged. "You think I got some kind of built-in moon schedule in my head or something? Listen, you want to know where the nearest body of water is, and how deep it is, and what's at the bottom, then I'm your guy. But why do you care?"

"Because when I jump out this window, when I land down there and I break my neck, I'll be in incredible pain until the next time I change. I'd like to spend as little time as possible like that. The perfect time would be to jump just a couple of seconds before I change." She stared at him again.

"Sorry," he said.

She nodded and grabbed all the things she had to her name. The two magazines, the slices of greasy ham, and the pistol. She made sure the safety was on and jammed it in her pocket.

"If I land on my head, and my brains splat all over the ground," she said, "I still won't die. Will I?"

"Don't know," Dzo admitted.

Chey frowned and went to the shutter. It was so easy not to

jump. It was so easy to waste more time. But what if she changed in the next second? What if she had to wait for another night, another day to pass?

And what if she jumped—and there were still hours to go?

"Okay," she said. "I'm going to do it." But then she just stood there. Her legs were frozen in place. "Can you help me?"

"Yeah, definitely," Dzo said. He came up behind her and picked her up as if she were made of paper. Then he tossed her out into the wind, even as she began to scream at him, to beg him not to. She looked back and saw the side of the fire tower, saw Dzo silhouetted in the window, barely illuminated by starlight. His mask was down.

She fell.

The cold darkness around her felt like an illimitable gulf of space. She felt for a particle of time as if she were floating in the depths of interstellar space.

A moment later she collided with the ground so hard she felt like a squashed bug, like a stain on the forest floor.

The pain was unimaginable. Her skin hurt everywhere and she felt bones poking her, fragments of bone sticking in her guts. Her breath sputtered inside her, full of blood—she must have punctured a lung. She could see nothing, could feel nothing but her own insides squirming out through a break in her skin.

She tried to get a hand underneath her, tried to rise. Blood gushed from her mouth and she fell back, her torn cheek grating on the rocks.

The moon—she begged the moon to rise—the moon had to come. It had to come soon. The moon. It would heal her. It had to come. Soon.

Then she felt a hand slip into hers. It was smooth and small, almost feminine. It was a stranger's hand, but she was past caring. The tiny fragment of comfort she took from that human touch

245

was something, a drop of water on a parched tongue. It didn't hurt—that was the main thing.

Who was it? Who could it possibly be? Or was someone even there—maybe, could it just be a hallucination, her brain trying desperately to find some comfort for her, making things up when nothing real presented itself? She could wonder, but she had no way of answering. Her eyes couldn't focus, couldn't make out anything. No one spoke to her—or if they did, she couldn't hear it.

Her breath hitched in her damaged lungs and stopped and she panicked for a second, but the hand just closed tighter around hers and she calmed down, literally felt herself settling down and then, with a noise like a balloon popping, air sagged out of her.

Whose hand was it?

In the end it didn't matter.

She lay there broken on the ground for forty-seven minutes. She had no way of measuring that time—to her it felt like hundreds of hours. It would have felt like an eternity if not for that hand in hers.

Then silver light came like a grace upon her, a divine breath of mercy.

Confused, her head still buzzing and unclear, the wolf rose on strong legs and howled for her newfound freedom.

fortγ-seven

Like fungus after a rain the white tubes stuck up out of the earth around the tower. They stank of men. They stank of timber wolves, and of silver. The wolf moved around one of them, uncomprehending. She studied it, inspected it with nose and ears and eyes. She licked the outside of it and felt it thrumming, felt the tension inside of it like the fear in a field mouse's belly. She licked the edge, tasted oil there, tasted wolves. Timber wolves—not her pack. Not even her nation.

Still—

She snuffled around the edge of the pipe. It was no mere curiosity that drove her, nor was it the tantalizing smell. This was a man-made thing, and therefore, she hated it. Hated it, hated it, hated it. That was the law, the iron margin of her existence. She hated it, without further reason or meaning except that it was touched by human hands, that it was part of their world. Yet it didn't move or offer any resistance. So she took her time.

The top was open and dark. She looked inside, but her eyes weren't her strongest sense. She put a paw up on the edge.

Then she twisted around it and sank her sharp teeth into the

247

yielding, cracking whiteness of it, dug in deep and then yanked backward with the powerful muscles in her neck.

The pipe slid up out of the ground with a noise like thunder. Something fast moved past her cheek, flew into the darkness. She cast the pipe away from her and danced backward, her ears stinging with the noise it had made.

Her mouth snapped open and her tongue came out, tasting the air.

What was that, was that, was that, what was that?

Someone was playing a joke on her. She snarled and slashed the air in rage. Humans—humans had put this thing here, just to distract her perhaps. Or maybe they had a darker purpose.

Humans. The humans had imprisoned her. They'd tried to break her, tried to destroy her mind. Maybe they'd succeeded, a little.

Now she was free. She didn't know how that happened. But she knew she wanted their blood in vengeance.

She could smell them in the air. Their perfumes clung to the tree trunks, their sweat dotted the ground. She ran through the woods following that track, looking to show them, to show them, to show them who they were dealing with.

She found their camp. The wolf howled and tore into a bedroll with her teeth. She slapped at the kerosene lanterns and tore at the tents. The stink of humanity was everywhere, everywhere, all around her. They had been there. They had been so close! How had they gotten so close to her?

She would destroy them. They had harmed her—they had—they had—they had done something, she wasn't clear on what but something—they had imprisoned her. She recalled her starved howling. She could remember pain.

She would tear them apart. She would find their throats and—

They were gone. The remains of their fire still warmed the earth, but they were gone. They had headed out, toward where the sun had set. She could sense their path like an arrow of as-yet-unspilled blood painted across the forest floor. Blood that belonged to her. Her blood, her blood, her blood to lap up, her blood by right. Her blood.

On bounding legs she ran, following that trail. Through dawn and most of the day, she ran.

Her paws splashed across water, her tongue lapped at the reindeer moss and the lichens on the bare rocks. Above her the trees seemed to part, to lean away from her path. The moon, a narrow crescent like the blade of a knife, anointed her fur and her eyes as she streaked over tree roots and broken ground. She came to a shallow pond and didn't even slow down, the freezing cold water scattering into round droplets on her guard hairs, her feet down and touching slimy rocks, fish scattering from the thousand small impacts of her running. She ran for hours, and did not tire, because there was blood at the end of the trail. Her blood to claim.

She could feel them ahead of her. The one who had chained her—yes, it was coming back to her, now. She had trouble telling them apart, but she knew there was one, one in particular. He was ahead. The male human, the one who had locked her away. He was there, and with her tongue flapping in the corner of her mouth she could taste him and then, and then, and then—

A human warbled in the trees, a high-pitched fear sound. Her blood pumped cold in her veins with blood joy. The human was nearby, very close, nearby. It wasn't the human she wanted, not the male that had locked her up. But this one would most certainly do for a start. She spun around, her paws slipping on pinecones and fallen needles. Her ears twitched, triangulating his position. She remembered when she had been taught to hunt and she dropped to the ground, her belly cold on the surface, her joints bent, poised like a spider's legs are poised just before the strike.

The human moved through the trees, blundering like a bear. Making so much noise she nearly cringed. His stink was so complex—metal wood leather wool body odor meat breath urine human urine human spoor. It flashed in the chill air like an abstract painting, a wild disarray of smells.

He called to her, but she did not answer. He crept closer. He was big, big for a human, bigger than her. His bones were long and she could hear his joints rolling. She could smell his skin. She could smell his blood.

He called again. He knew she was there, knew she was lying in wait for him. Her lips drew back over her massive teeth. *Fine,* she thought. *Fine, fine, fine. Let him know.* Let him see her with those cold human eyes. Let him smell and taste and touch her. She would not move. Not until, not until it was, not until it was—time.

She stood up on all four legs at once, raised the saddle of fur between her shoulders like a battle standard. He was within snapping range, close enough to touch her with his human hands. He had a piece of metal and he brought it up, metal and wood and oil and, and, and yes, she smelled silver and it banged in the air, exploded in the dark just like the white pipe back at the tower. She knew there was danger in that sound, knew it carried her death. She felt silver glide across her skin, felt silver filings get lost in her fur and they burned and she howled, but the silver didn't break her skin.

The silver was gone. It had not pierced her. Had not killed her.

Now it was her turn.

forty-eight

She swung around, her massive mouth wide open, and pulled the human into her jaws. His weapon fell to the ground and he screamed and her blood sang. She closed her jaw like a vise and twisted and pulled and tore and his leg bones snapped inside her head. She could hear them thrum against her upper palate. She could taste his blood on her tongue.

His body surged with pain and fear and it made her rejoice. She shook in convulsions as she tore at his flesh, as she swallowed chunks of him. He rattled and wailed and fell away from her and part of him tore free. His leg tore open in her mouth, and he toppled backward like a felled tree. She gulped down his blood and meat and lunged forward for the rest of him. Bloodlust scattered her senses—all she knew was to press forward, to press the attack. She did not see his arm come around, would not have guessed he had any strength left, and when his closed fist smashed into the top of her head, crushing her sensitive ears, she yelped and dropped to her side.

Light swirled in her eyes. Her mouth was full of nothing, full of air, of air—her paws beat at the carpet of pine needles and dead leaves. What had happened? How had—how had he hurt—how had—

He pushed away from her, scuttling into the darkness like a pill bug, his hands pushing at the snow and the rocks. She shook herself, trying to throw off the dullness, the ringing numbness in her head. When she recovered he was not there. She cast about, threw her forelegs down and touched the earth with her muzzle, sniffing for him. He couldn't have gotten far. She knew she'd wounded him badly.

She took a step forward, another, another. She smelled water and breeze, cold air like the trailing hem of a ghost's gown flapping in space. Another step and—no. She stood on a precipice looking down at a sunken stream bed. Far below her, down a raw slope of disturbed earth, he had crashed to the bottom of the trickling water. He was down there moaning and bleeding and still alive.

The need to kill filled her up. Her hackles lifted and a growl grew in her throat. Yet it was over. There was no way for her to get down that sharp slope. She was no human with fingers and toes to grab at the descent.

No matter. He couldn't live long. She'd given him a death wound, and it was only a matter of time before blood loss finished him off. She turned around a few times and settled to her belly, to listen to his screams and wait.

The moon sank behind the trees and caught her yawning. And then—

Chey came to sobbing, her body cold and damp. She remembered blood, but whose, and how it had been shed, was lost to her. She lay on the edge of a riverbank maybe five meters high, a carved-out shore of mud and tree roots. She looked over the edge—and then she shrieked in horror.

Her wolf had killed a man. There could be no doubt about

it, this time. She could see his bent and twisted corpse down there. It was Frank Pickersgill, and his blood stained the water. Naked and shivering, she stared down at her own handiwork.

Frank Pickersgill. She had not hated the man, though she'd been afraid of him. He'd never shown her anything but kindness. And she had killed him. Her stomach rumbled and she realized she must have—must have—

"Lady," he croaked up at her.

Oh, God, he was still alive. Chey stepped forward onto the sloping bank and clods of dirt tumbled away from her foot, pattered down across him. She hurried down as quickly as she could manage, grabbing at exposed roots and bits of rock, sliding down as much as she climbed. She was covered in mud and dead leaves by the time she reached bottom, by the time she knelt by him in the frigid water.

"Lady," he sighed, and she heard his breath come weakly in and out of him, dripping, almost gently, from his lungs.

"Don't try to move," she insisted.

"Lady, they see you," he protested. "They're gonna kill you."

She searched him for wounds. Found most of his left leg gone. She started to vomit but forced herself to stop. "You're going to make it," she promised him, because it sounded like something she was supposed to say. She tore at his pant leg and found raw meat underneath. Blood trickled out of dozens of small wounds. Teeth marks.

Chey put the guilt aside. This was what she'd chosen, wasn't it? To be a monster. To accept that she was a monster. This was what monsters did.

The wolf had felt no guilt. Just as Powell's wolf had felt no guilt when it devoured her father. Just as Powell's wolf had felt no guilt when it had tried to kill her, up in the tree. When it had scratched her.

253

"We got our orders. If you come down from that tower, we gotta shoot on sight. Figured you should know that."

She pressed down on the raw tissues of his leg, tried to stanch the bleeding. She had no idea how much blood he'd lost already. "Don't talk. Does talking hurt?" she asked.

"Shit," he laughed. Weakly. "Everything hurts. Gimme my pack, willya? I'm gonna die."

"Not necessarily," she said.

"Nice." He smiled at her. His eyes weren't tracking, just staring straight ahead of him. Was that a bad sign? "You're a nice lady. I want you to know I ain't sore. I know this wasn't personal and I'm sorry they're going to kill you. My pack?"

She looked up and saw a leather satchel lying near his head. She grabbed it with her free hand and pushed it into his arms. He opened the flap and reached inside.

He wasn't going to die. She knew it, understood it. He wasn't going to die. But he was going to change.

"The moon will rise in a while," she said. How many hours would it be? If he died of blood loss first—but no. He would make it until the moon rose. "Do you understand what's going to happen to you?"

"I heard the story from Fenech, yeah. It's like rabies or somethin'. You get bit and you become one yourself. Lady, you get out of here. You head east. Get as far from . . . Get away from Port Radium, and maybe you'll make it. Don't look, now."

"What?" she asked.

He drew a pistol from his pack and it wavered as it moved around between them. She reared back, thinking he was going to kill her. Instead he pushed the muzzle of the gun into his mouth and fired.

"Jesus!" she shrieked, the noise lost in the gunshot. She fell backward into the water, her hands back to catch her.

forty-nine

She forced herself to look at Frank Pickersgill's body. It was awful. She got up and stumbled away from him, staggered down the creek bed.

Forced herself to go back again.

She'd made her choice. She'd known, when she jumped out of the tower, that she was letting the wolf out as well as herself. She'd known what it was capable of, better than anyone.

Bobby, Balfour, the Pickersgills—they wanted her dead. They had accepted what she'd become and they were acting accordingly. She had to do the same.

She had to start thinking like a fighter. Like someone who was going to survive this, no matter what. If she was going to live long enough to get back to Powell, to explain herself to him, there were things she was going to have to do. Things she was going to have to learn to live with.

She managed to climb up on the far bank, a gentler slope. She rolled in the dead leaves and mud there and just breathed for a while, and thought of nothing. Then she went back to the body.

His coat was stained with blood in a couple of places. She pulled it off of his arms anyway and struggled into it. He'd been a giant of a man and she was an average-sized woman. The coat sagged across her, dangled from her arms and across her knees. It was still warm. She shuddered, but she didn't take it off. It was better than being naked in that trackless wilderness.

She rifled his pack. It felt like sacrilege. Evil, pure evil.

No.

It was the smart thing to do.

Her conscience stayed mostly quiet as she searched through his things. She found a packet of ketchup chips, which she ate with one hand while searching with the other. She found a mickey bottle of bourbon, which she put aside for maybe later. Though surely drinking a dead man's liquor was enough to bring down heavenly wrath on her, if anything was. She found a box of silver shotgun shells and she took one cartridge out and held it in her hand. She unraveled the red paper wrapper and picked one of the spherical pellets out. It was perfectly smooth, but it felt like a piece of broken glass rubbed against her fingers. Blood welled in the whorls of her fingertips and she threw the pellet back into the pack.

She reached up and touched her shoulder, then craned her head around and tried to look. There were distinct scratches there, ugly red marks that looked infected. They could only have been made by silver—so Frank Pickersgill had shot at her first, before she had attacked him. He had drawn first blood.

That helped, a little.

There was a map in the pack. A good one, with contour lines and lumber roads drawn in fine gray ink. She found the fire tower. Powell's cabin wasn't shown, but she found the tiny lake where Bobby had landed his helicopter. She had no idea where she was—she was near a little stream, but there were hundreds of those on the map. She could be anywhere. Giving up, she looked for Port Radium, wherever that was, and then she found it.

Frank Pickersgill had said she should stay away from Port Radium. That had to be where Bobby had gone. And Bobby would be following Powell. It was where she had to go, if she was going to finish this. If she was going to survive.

Port Radium was on the eastern shore of Great Bear Lake, a body of water so big it filled the left-hand side of the map. There was something about its location that seemed odd to her. She studied it and turned the map around and wondered why it should seem familiar. She hardly knew this part of the world at all. Then she remembered. It was the same place she'd seen on maps before, the only town anywhere near Powell's cabin. She'd always seen it before referred to as Echo Bay. Maybe they'd changed the name—"Port Radium" hardly sounded like a place anyone would want to visit.

At the bottom of the pack she found a satellite cell phone. Just like the one she'd used to summon Bobby and screw up everything. Bobby. What a fool she'd been, to—

No, she wasn't going to think that way. She'd been used. Taken advantage of.

Now Bobby had ordered the Western Prairie guys to shoot her on sight. He wanted to kill her. Just like Powell. All the important men in her life wanted her dead.

Well—except for one.

Not really knowing why, she placed a call. She had trouble remembering the number, but after a couple of false starts she got it. She pressed the phone against her ear and listened to clicks and static for a couple of seconds, and then the phone began to ring. Then it clicked and answered.

"Hello," the phone told her. "You've reached the Bolton's

Valley Horse Ranch. We're most likely out riding fences right now, but if you press one, you can—"

She pressed one and shoved the phone back to her ear. She could barely hear the beep on the other end. Then she spoke, as quickly as she could.

"Uncle Bannerman, this is Cheyenne. I wanted to let you know what's happening to me. I've been . . . changed." She closed her eyes. Let herself feel human for a moment. Was that what she was doing? Saying good-bye to the only human being she still loved? Or saying good-bye to the little girl she'd been, the little girl who was still human? "There's no cure. There's nothing anyone can do. But you should know that Bobby—Fenech—sent me up here expecting me to be killed. You were right; he wasn't trustworthy. I guess . . . I guess that's all I wanted to say. I'm going to a place called Port Radium. I'm probably going to get killed there, but if I don't, I think I'll be alright. I thought you'd want to know that."

She didn't know what else to say. What else she could say. She ended the call and shoved the phone in a pocket of Frank Pickersgill's jacket. Then she sat down and for a while just tried not to fall apart.

She took Frank's boots. He had three pairs of dry socks in his pack, and if she wore them all at once the boots almost fit her. For once, at least, her feet were warm.

fifty

That night Chey walked through the forest with the fatal-ism of the truly damned. Her feet hurt, blistered by the loose boots, and her body trembled with cold, hunger, and fatigue. None of it mattered. If she had thoughts in her head they were dark, earthy thoughts that crumbled like clods of dirt when she tried to grab at them. The landscape changed around her as she hiked, but she barely noticed as the trees grew thinner and shorter. The world got wetter, too, became a realm of swampy half-frozen muskegs where the tree roots dipped like bent pipes into dark water. Once she had to ford an actual river, a ribbon of brown water deep enough in the middle that she was forced to swim across its width. The chilly dip woke her up a little—enough to see the dead forest beyond the further bank.

The trees over there stood white as bones, pointing at random angles at the cold stars above. They bore neither leaves nor needles and their branches stuck out like broken ribs or were missing altogether.

The ground at her feet was caked with ash. There must have been a forest fire here recently, she thought. Every step stirred up more of the powdery gray debris. What had happened? Surely the Western Prairie guys hadn't been foolish enough to throw a lit cigarette butt into the underbrush. Maybe lightning had struck nearby. She knew that after a forest fire the smaller plant species—grasses, mosses, shrubs—came back quickly, but she could find nothing green anywhere.

She trudged into the dead forest and soon found herself in a place as desolate as the back of the moon. No owls hooted in the darkness and no wildflowers grew up from the ash to tremble in the breeze. She saw very few insects—beetles, mostly, their wingcases snapping open as she approached, their greasy-looking wings convulsing in the air to zip them away from her on long curved paths. She touched the white trunks of the dead trees as she passed by and their wood was dry and rough as if they were half petrified.

She still didn't know exactly where she was. She had headed west from the stream where Frank Pickersgill died, figuring that no matter how badly lost she got, her wolf would find the way when the moon rose again.

In time the trees grew thinner on the ground, and thinner still, until she was no longer in a forest at all but in a sandy flatland punctuated here and there by the occasional dead stump. Streams rolled across bare rock and through drifts of shallow snow, as far as her eyes could see. After the myopia of the forest she felt like she could see to the very edge of the world. The starlight painted the ground white and the water black and the world seemed striped and piebald between the two. On the horizon she saw what could have been the ocean—an endless wrinkled mass of water. It had to be the shore of Great Bear Lake.

She pressed on.

The sun rose while she was still human. Its warmth on her back and shoulders filled her up, made her skin tingle, eased the soreness in her joints, even as it painted the vast open ground with yellow light. It felt good. She knew it wouldn't last.

"Dzo," she said, as if he could hear her. She thought maybe he could.

She heard a splash behind her and saw him clamber up out of a black pond. His furs streamed with water, but by the time he reached her he was dry. He tipped his mask back onto the top of his head. "Uh, yeah?" he asked, as if he'd been with her the whole time. She still had no idea what he really was, but she understood he was a lot more at home in this weird land than she would ever be.

"Dzo," she said, "is it much farther?"

"Yeah," he said. "But your wolf can make it today." His face screwed up in bewilderment. "You scared or something?"

She nodded. "Yes, I am."

"Humans seem to get scared a lot. When animals get scared, sometimes they just freeze. You know? Their muscles lock up and they can't move. You ever try that?"

"That won't work for me. Dzo—I killed a guy. Kind of. I don't know what that makes me."

"A predator?" He sat down on the ground and rubbed his hands together. "I'm not really the guy you ought to be asking these questions."

She nodded. "I know. The funny thing is I'm not as scared of getting killed as I am of talking to Powell again. But you wouldn't understand that."

He raised his hands in weak apology. "Maybe you'll get killed before you get that far," he offered.

"Yeah." She started walking again. "Thanks, Dzo," she said.

"My pleasure. Listen," he called after her, "this is as far as I can go. They poisoned the water out there and I can't follow you now. If you do see Powell, will you give him a message for me?"

"Sure," she said, turning around.

"Tell him I have his boots in my truck. In case he's looking for 'em."

Chey smiled. It felt wrong on her face, but she liked it all the same. "I'll do that."

An hour after the sun rose, the moon followed.

fifty-one

The wolf didn't understand why the breath in her lungs felt rank and bitter. She did not understand why her skin crawled as she closed on her goal. She barely cared. The human stench was full upon her and a few toxins weren't about to stop her.

She trotted out to the top of a sand esker, a long, low bar of sand atop slickrock that had been deposited by glaciers when true dire wolves still roamed the earth. She wanted to howl in jubilation and anticipation of the bloodshed to come, but she didn't want to alert her prey to her presence just yet.

Her eyes were not sufficiently keen to see the buildings a half kilometer from where she stood. She could make out some square outlines—unnaturally square, humanly square. She could not see the red and green pigments that painted the tops of the waters all around, but she could smell the heavy metals floating in great swirls like oil slicks there.

She could not feel the radiation that leaked upward like darkness from the very ground she stood on. She could not in any case have understood that the very land here was cursed with uranium, with radon gas, with the vast deposits of pitchblende and raw radium that gave the place its old name.

But she could tell the place was cursed.

Cursed, she panted, *cursed, cursed.* Cursed forever. She would have chosen another place if it had been up to her. Any other place. But she was a predator and she followed her prey. If they went to ground in tainted earth she would wallow in poison to get to them.

And they were nearby, she knew it. Even over the bitter wind, over the stinks of heavy metals and broken ore and disturbed earth and rusted metal and decayed plaster and crumbled concrete, she could smell the humans. *The* human. The one who had chained her and tried to drive her mad.

As the sun began to set she picked her way down from the esker and into Port Radium, and it was there she yelped and whined, for the change came too soon.

Chey cursed and spat at the pain in her limbs. Her arms and legs were sore and stiff. She rose slowly and saw that the world had changed while she was gone.

She was standing, for one thing, on a road.

Not just a logging path or an animal track. A real, paved road. Long broken slabs of concrete led off to the horizon in either direction. In places they had cracked and rotted away, and in the gaps some grayish weeds had poked up, and the uneasy soil of the Arctic had bucked and shifted the concrete around until it looked half like crushed rock. Nature was busy reclaiming the abandoned road. But it was still a road.

Chey covered her breasts with her arms. She had become accustomed to waking up naked in an uninhabited forest, where the nearest voyeurs were hundreds of kilometers away. But now she was effectively in a town—and she was completely lacking in clothing.

She hurried off the road and between a pair of giant steel cargo containers, one rust red, one a faded and streaky blue. She ducked inside the blue one and listened to her footfalls echo alarmingly. She had to be in Port Radium, she decided. Her wolf must have reached the fabled town.

Peeking around the edge of the container, she saw buildings off to the west, long industrial sheds with fallen-in roofs and decaying walls. She saw dozens of smokestacks like cyclopean chess pieces on a board of upturned soil. Nearer than the buildings she saw a forlorn bulldozer, its blade gnawed by rust, its black leather seat turned into a nest for some absent bird.

She got the message. Port Radium it might have been, but Port Radium had long since stopped being anywhere. There would be no people here other than those she'd come to confront. At least she had that.

Moving as quickly as she could, she ducked out of her cargo container and scrambled up a slope of loose dirt and fist-sized rocks. The nearest building looked like an aircraft hangar, an enormous structure of corrugated tin. Wind and rain had bored holes in it until she could see the setting sun right through its metal walls. She found a door, or rather the frame where a door might once have been, and slipped inside.

Orange light fell in dusty beams to make burning spotlights on the floor. Overhead a massive skeleton of iron girders remained partially intact. At the far end of the enclosed space stood a conical pile of rubble, bright brown and steep-sided. A dump truck stood by the pile, its bed tilted upward as if it had been abandoned in the middle of depositing a new load.

Closer to her a small portion of the building had been enclosed to make office space. The wide windows were broken and smeared, but she could see desks inside and lockers—maybe there would be clothes hanging up inside that she could use. She went to the office door and pulled up on the latch, half-expecting it to be rusted shut. Half-expecting that she would need her extra-normal strength to open it. Instead the door almost flew open and she staggered backward, nearly losing her balance. It felt almost as if the door had been kicked open.

In fact, it had. Bruce Pickersgill stood in the door frame, stupid mustache, fur collar, and all. He held his twin pistols at arm's length, one barrel trained on her forehead, the other on her heart.

He had orders to shoot on sight. Chey closed her eyes and prepared to accept the inevitable.

He didn't fire.

fifty-two

Chey's feet padded effortlessly across the broken ground, while behind her Pickersgill stumbled and cursed with every bump or irregularity of the stony earth.

Bobby's helicopter stood motionless in the air, maybe half a kilometer away, maybe seventy meters up. The bubble cockpit was turned her way—was he watching her, was he watching Pickersgill march her across a field of broken stones? Was he wondering why she wasn't dead yet? Maybe he wasn't even inside. Maybe it was just Lester up there.

"Okay, head over to that utility pole," Pickersgill said from behind her. He wasn't taking a lot of chances—she had to keep her hands straight up in the air or he would jab her in the back with one of his pistols.

The field had been a parking lot once, she thought. It was relatively flat and it was interrupted here and there only by ten-meter-tall light poles, each crowned with a pair of long-broken Klieg lights. The poles were as thick as her arm and made of some metal that hadn't corroded over the years.

"Listen," Chey asked, "could I get a coat or a blanket or something? I'm freezing like this."

He tossed her a pair of moth-eaten, grease-stained coveralls and she struggled into them. They were meant for a larger person than herself, but she was glad just not to be naked anymore. "I appreciate it," she said. "Can we talk for a second? I'd like to—"

He didn't let her finish. "Turn around and grab the pole behind you with both hands," Pickersgill said.

She did as she was told. The metal was freezing cold and plenty sturdy, though she could feel that the pole was hollow. Nothing more complex than a pipe sticking out of the ground with a few wires running through. Pickersgill moved around behind her and clicked one end of a pair of handcuffs to her left wrist. She could feel him fumbling around behind her with the second cuff—he had to do it one-handed, since he kept a pistol in the crook of her neck the whole time.

"It ain't silver, but tensile steel's got to be worth something," he told her. He clicked the second cuff shut and came back around to face her. He had one pistol in his hand, the other in its holster.

"You're not going to kill me?" Chey asked.

"Not yet, no. We still need to catch your alpha. He's smarter than your average canid, obviously. That's the only reason it's taken us so long to catch him. He's still prone to the weaknesses of his kind, however. What we call, in the business, taxic behaviors. Instincts. For instance, he won't abandon his mate."

"I'm not his mate," Chey said. "He wants to kill me."

Pickersgill shrugged. "One lure is as good as another in this case. When he hears you, he'll come."

Chey frowned. "Are you sure?"

"When we had you up in that fire tower, howling like a bitch on heat, his exotic half couldn't keep away. Every night he came closer, and once we even got a couple of shots off at him. If he had kept that up we would have had him. He must have figured as much. After that his human half just up and ran off and came here, far enough away that he wouldn't be tempted by your vocalizations." He scratched at his mustache. "Took us a while to track him. He's real good at moving quiet up here. But now we got the two of you in one place, this should be dead easy."

"You think if he hears me howling here he'll come to investigate," she said.

"You got it. As soon as the moon comes up you'll start in to howling and he'll show himself. Then we'll finish this contract and we can all go home. Except for the two of you, of course."

"And your brother," Chey said. Taunting Pickersgill was probably a mistake, but she couldn't stop herself.

"Yes. We haven't heard from Frank in a bit. I suppose you had something to do with that?"

Chey sighed. Guilt squished around in her stomach as if she'd eaten tainted food. "I killed him, I guess. My wolf did. I'm a predator now, it seems."

Pickersgill scratched his mustache again. She wondered if he had fleas. "Well, yes, I suppose you are," he said, finally. "Which means I'm a better predator. I'm smarter than you and I've got better weapons. So I guess I win."

She didn't have anything to say to that.

Pickersgill took a phone out of his pocket with his left hand and dialed a number. The pistol in his right hand drooped until it wasn't pointing directly at her, but he didn't holster it. He was pretty smart, she had to give him that. He'd thought this through better than she had.

Well, Chey had never been very good at making plans. She'd pretty much followed her gut her whole life. And now it was going to get her killed.

No.

Her wolf wouldn't accept that. It wouldn't accept death so easily.

There had to be something she could do. She stared out at the broken plain of the parking lot, at heaps of stones and broken chunks of asphalt. The helicopter was moving away, headed toward the far side of the town. Soon it was gone behind rust-stained walls and mounds of dark soil, lost in a purpling sky that was about to turn into darkness.

Her mind turned over and over, trying to decide what to do next. If Pickersgill would just step closer she could kick him. Maybe get her legs around his neck and snap his spine. She could spit in his eyes and when he went to wipe them clean she could kick the gun right out of his hand. Then she could bring her knee up into his chin hard enough to knock him out.

What she would do then, still handcuffed to the light pole, she had no idea. But it was worth a try.

"Hey," she said.

Pickersgill looked up.

"Your brother told me something right before he died."

"Yeah?" he asked.

"Yeah. If you come over here I'll whisper it in your ear."

He grinned at her. "Nice try." He actually took a step back.

Okay, she thought to herself. Time for plan B.

She tried flexing her arms, tensing against the chain that held her hands cuffed together. She could feel how solid the metal was. She was stronger than any normal human being, but she didn't think she could break that chain. In fact, she was sure of it. She pulled anyway. The muscles in her arms tensed and burned and the steel held. She grunted and gritted her teeth and pulled harder. The cuffs dug into her wrists and scraped at her skin like dull knives. Sweat broke out on her forehead.

The chain held.

"I didn't think so," Pickersgill said. He gave himself a good long scratch and let his pistol arm hang loose at his side. "Just relax, okay? It's a long time until moonrise. You don't want to dislocate your shoulders."

She stared right into his eyes and pulled and yanked with every muscle fiber in her body. She felt the blood pounding in her head, felt the bones of her arms flex and start to fracture. She pulled harder. The chain didn't give.

Instead the light pole behind her did. As she heaved forward the chain put pressure on the hollow pole and it crimped, slamming forward across her shoulders. The pole flicked forward and the twin light fixtures at its top slapped against the ground, shattering what little glass was left in them. Chey was thrown sideways by the toppling pole, her wrists screaming with abrasions. Feeling like an idiot, she looked over at Pickersgill.

He didn't look back. The collapsing light pole had connected with the space between his shoulder and his neck. Maybe it had broken his spine, or maybe it had just given him a concussion. Either way, he lay sprawled across the broken stones, his eyes wide open but seeing nothing.

Chey kicked and kicked at the pole until it broke off at the crimp and clattered to the ground. She pulled down on the cuffs until they came loose from the pole. She struggled and bent and twisted until her hands were in front of her. Then she ran over to check Pickersgill's neck. She couldn't find a pulse.

Behind her she heard someone clapping, very slowly. She looked up and was not surprised to find Powell standing not ten meters away.

fifty-three

Night had officially fallen. The stars were out, thick in the heavens, and they gave enough light for the two of them to see each other but not much more. The moon had not yet risen, so they were still human.

Powell wore a pair of coveralls much like her own—she guessed he, too, had been forced to scrounge for clothing since he'd been in Port Radium. He didn't have Dzo around to follow after him in a rusty pickup truck anymore.

He had an ugly scar across his forehead and cheek. Either he'd been injured since his last change or he'd had a near miss with a silver bullet. His icy green eyes were quiet—she couldn't quite gauge what he was thinking. Or what he was planning.

She wondered if he'd given as much thought to this confrontation as she had.

"Hi," she said, moving toward him as sedately as she could manage. "Powell. Listen. There's something I have to tell you, something I—"

"Save it," he said.

Then he leapt right at her, his head down, his arms wide. He grabbed her around the midsection and knocked her off her feet. She went skidding along a rough section of asphalt and her head bounced off a broken stone. Light erupted behind her eyes and she couldn't seem to breathe.

He was on top of her, a piece of rubble in his hands as big as her head. He brought it up high, clearly intending to use it to smash her face in. She lunged upward with her knees and he flew off of her. Rolling onto all fours, she looked over and saw him doing the same.

"Just give me a second," she called. "Just let me—"

"No more lies," he said.

Together they jumped to their feet, their arms in front of them. They wheeled around each other like sumo wrestlers. Chey had been trained in unarmed combat by the U.S. military. She knew how to hold her own. But Powell had had a century to learn how to fight. He rushed her and she dodged, but he must have expected it—he turned in mid-swing and grabbed her around the waist, twisted up underneath and slammed her to the ground. The wind went out of her, but she managed to kick out with her legs and hit him in the ankle, toppling him to the ground, too. They both rolled over, panting for breath. Then he looked up and met her gaze.

Could he kill her? Did he even want to?

"Please," she begged. "Just let me explain."

For a second they just stared at each other. Then he reached out and grabbed the chain that held her hands together. She cried out as he yanked, hard, and dragged her across the stones, but she couldn't get her feet underneath her, couldn't twist out of his grip.

He dragged her inside the big corrugated tin building. The darkness inside was nearly complete. He pulled her a ways farther, then dragged her up and off the ground. Both of his hands grabbed at her flesh and then she was airborne, hurtling over the poured concrete floor. She hit hard enough to make spit fly out of her mouth.

"So you're just going to kill me? You won't even talk to me first?" she shouted. She couldn't see him at all in the shadows.

"I never want to kill anybody," he said. "It just sort of happens." He was moving around, circling her. She thought of her training. She needed to move, too. She needed to get a wall at her back. "I'm sorry that I killed your father, but believe me, I did what I could to prevent it. You should understand that by now."

"Maybe I do," she said. "Maybe better than you think."

He didn't bother to reply.

She could feel him nearby, but she couldn't determine where he was. She scrabbled up to her feet and started moving toward the wall ahead of her.

She felt his body heat a moment before he scooped her up and threw her back into the dark. She landed badly with an arm underneath her, crushed by her own weight. She cried out in pain.

"You done yet?" he asked. He was close, but not close enough to hit. "Why can't you just go away and leave me alone? I never wanted any of this. I just want to survive the mess you've made for me."

"I know," she said. "And I'm sorry. You have to see my side, though. You killed—you killed my father. I had a right to . . . to something. But things have changed. I've changed. And I know, now, that I can't do this alone. Like it or not, you're the only one who understands me right now. Who knows what I'm going through. And those assholes out there want me dead, too. We're on the same side. Aren't we?" She crawled forward through the gloom. Maybe this time he'd actually heard her. Understood that she didn't come here to fight.

But he hit her hard, then, hard enough to pick her up and carry her, screaming, across the floor. They smashed into the wall and through it. The corroded tin collapsed under their combined weight and she saw stars, real stars as they rolled back out into the parking lot. Her shoulder gave way with a popping noise—if it wasn't broken it still hurt like a bastard. He pushed her away and staggered into the night. She knew better than to think he was done with her.

fifty-four

The pain curled her inward on herself. It made her want to scream. She forced the pain down, away from her, and rose to her feet. If not for the strength her wolf shared with her she knew she would be unconscious, maybe even dead already.

She spun around in a circle, looking for Powell. Looking for any sign of movement—a flash in the darkness, a dull glint. There was nothing.

"Talk," he said. "You want to talk to me. Fine. Talk."

But she couldn't think of what to say. So instead she looked at Port Radium.

It lay beneath her, spread out at the bottom of a long, rolling hill. What few structures remained intact had collapsed roofs or had tumbled down to fall in on themselves. There had been dozens, maybe a hundred hangars and warehouses and who knew what else, once, but the vast majority of the buildings had been burned to the ground. The roads remained, long dark ribbons sectioning the land into parcels. Long poles of stripped wood had been pounded into the earth at every crossroads and intersection. She knew what they were for—when the snow came, as it would early this far north, that would be the only way for anyone to know where a building's foundation lay. There were streetlights as well, in some places, but the metal poles had sunk and listed as the permafrost beneath them shifted over the years until they stood at angles like the trees of the drunken forest.

Abandoned—no, more than that. There was a pall over the remains of the town, nothing visible or even tangible, really, but there was a wrongness about it. Chey felt like waves of regret and desolation were rolling up out of the ruins. Maybe they were haunted. A ghost town, in more ways than one.

Between Chey and the ghost town's near edge glimmered the black mirror of a pond, a big oval pool of water. A heap of twisted metal and broken rock stood in the center of the pond like a gigantic cairn. She recognized a few outlines, of dump trucks and backhoes and cranes, but most of the metal had softened and lost its shape to rust and wind until it became a single agglomeration of bent girders and decaying engines. Hundreds of tons of forgotten equipment, left to soften like compost over a span of millennia. She could only imagine how toxic the water must be with runoff from the dead machinery. "Jesus," she said, astounded despite herself. After spending the last few weeks in the utter natural serenity of the forest this man-made ruin startled her. "What was this place?"

Powell answered her from the shadows. "It was a mining town, once." She didn't turn or give any sign she'd heard him. She didn't want to move. She didn't want him to hit her again—her shoulder still hurt from the last time. "The rocks here are some of the oldest on Earth and they're full of radium, cobalt, and chromium. It also contained one of the biggest silver lodes ever discovered."

"And you thought it would be a nice place to hide out," she said, quietly. "Why was it abandoned if it was so lucrative?"

"This is what you wanted to discuss?" he asked. The scorn in his voice made her spine shiver.

She couldn't find the right words, though. The words that would explain what she'd done to him. "Just humor me," she said, bargaining for time to find the words.

He growled in frustration. But then he answered her question. "It was too expensive to mine the silver profitably. It cost more to dig it up and ship it back to civilization than it was worth."

"So everybody just left."

"Not quite," Powell told her. His voice came from over to her left—she was sure of it. She had to be ready, in case he attacked her again. She could feel his anger like heat on her back. But so far he was still talking. "They found something else here, too. This is where the Americans got the uranium for their first A-bombs."

She gasped in spite of herself. "Really?"

"They hired the local Dene Indians to carry it out of here in burlap sacks. They've always claimed they didn't know how dangerous the stuff was, but an entire generation of Dene men died young here. You see those dark mounds down there?" he asked, and she nodded—there were piles of dark earth almost everywhere, sticking up from the empty ground like mammoth anthills.

"Those are pitchblende tailings, what's left of what they dug out of the ground after they refined the uranium ore. Every couple of years someone from the government comes out here to measure how radioactive they still are."

"Radioactive. This place is radioactive," she said, and cold sweat burst in pinpricks under her hair.

"I didn't think your friends would follow me here." He was closer now, she could tell by following his voice. "I figured they had to know how dangerous it was. Maybe you can tell them. Maybe they'll leave, then."

"Bobby wouldn't listen to me now," she said. "He doesn't think I'm human anymore. And he's right, isn't he? That's what I wanted to tell you. That I understand now, what we are. I've . . . accepted it." She turned, her hands up, ready to reach for his. He was so close she could smell his skin—she could smell his wolf.

She expected him to lunge forward and knock her down. He didn't. She overbalanced and had to stagger to keep from falling. When she'd straightened again, wary, too stiff, he raised a hand toward her and she swung to block his punch. He wasn't punching, though. He had a square black pistol in his hand. He must have gone back to Pickersgill's corpse and recovered one of the man's guns.

"Powell," she had time to say. "Please. Don't do that. Don't you understand? I know why you came here. I know why you've spent your life away from other human beings. I know I have to do the same thing, now. But I can't do it alone. You're my only chance, if I want to survive. I have to learn from you."

"I killed your father," he said. "How could you ever forgive me for that?"

"I . . . can't," she said. "But that's not the point, that—"

"I'd be an utter fool to trust you," he said. "Do you think I'm a fool? Get the hell out of here, Chey. Run away and don't come back."

"Without you I won't make it," she told him. "I can't survive up here alone."

He turned around and started to walk away. He gave her one last glance—not so much a look of sympathy as curiosity, as if he expected her to say something or do something to make him stop.

"Powell," she said, "I need you."

It wasn't enough. He kept walking and soon the darkness swallowed him whole.

fifty-five

For a long time she just wondered what to do next. It had seemed so simple, back in the fire tower. She would find Powell, convince him that they needed each other. Then they would run off into the horizon together. Find some way to survive, together.

Without him she was doomed to an eternity alone. Trying her best to do what he had done, to get as far away from people as she could so she didn't end up killing them. It seemed like the worst possible fate she could imagine. Was it really so much better than taking the way out Bobby wanted for her, one quick silver bullet to the head?

She was supposed to have died on the Yellowhead Highway. Lycanthrope kills two in bloody road rampage, no survivors— that was one way it was supposed to have played out. She had thought many times that she might have, well, actually, preferred it. The guilt of surviving her father's death, the blankness and trauma and fear and depression and unhappiness that followed, the sleeplessness that had defined her life—none of those things would have had to happen. If she died now, if somebody killed her twelve years after the fact, things would still balance out. In their own bad way. Chey knew she understood very little about the universe, but she knew that things coming to a bad end was not unheard of. That sometimes happy endings were too much to ask for.

Lycanthrope kills two.

No.

She didn't like that ending. She had worked so hard. Sometimes without focus, sometimes to no point, but she had worked hard. She had jumped out of a fire tower and survived the fall. She had convinced her uncle to do something he hated. She had tattooed a wolf's paw on her breast to steal some of Powell's strength.

No, she wouldn't stop now. She wouldn't die.

She ran out to where Pickersgill still lay dead in the parking lot. She searched his pockets, and found the handcuff key and spent a long frustrating while figuring out how to unlock the cuffs. With them off she felt minutely better. More free, at least. She dropped them to the ground and stood up, chafing at her wrists where they'd been abraded when Powell dragged her into the warehouse.

Before she could plan her next move she heard the helicopter coming toward her. Almost certainly coming around to look for what had happened to Bruce. Its chopping noise was almost deafening in the perfect silence of that dead place. It circled the warehouse a couple of times, then slowed to a stop in midair and just hovered there for a while.

Then, slowly, as if feeling its way down through the night, the helicopter sank through the air. Coming down for a landing.

"Shit," she said, and dashed inside the corroded warehouse. Pressing her back up against a wall, she peered out into the darkness, wondering what she would do if Bobby found her there.

He would try to kill her if he saw her. He wouldn't hesitate. Her only chance would be to strike first. But would she really be able to kill him?

You're a monster, she told herself. That's what monsters do.

She found it hard to convince herself.

So far she'd killed two men, the Pickersgill brothers. The first time it had been her wolf who did the dirty work. The second time she'd just been trying to get free of the light post.

It occurred to her she might feel a little more confident with a weapon in her hand. She cast about, looking for anything, and found a short length of rusted rebar. It would make an adequate club. Then she crouched down in the shadows and waited.

The helicopter blew dust high up into the air as it settled gently to the ground. Its door popped open and Bobby jumped out. He rushed over to Pickersgill's corpse and bent low over it.

Chey was faster than he was. She could run out there right now while his back was turned and lay Bobby's skull open before he could even turn around, she thought. That would solve some problems. It would make her free.

Then she saw the gun in his hand. No doubt it was full of silver bullets. If she made more noise than she thought, if she tripped on her way toward him, if she gave him even the slightest moment to realize she was there—he could turn and shoot her.

She shifted her grip on the iron bar and tried to think of what to do.

Then he turned and looked right at her and her blood froze.

In a second he would raise his gun. He would aim at her and fire. Her muscles tensed and she got ready to pounce. She would have one chance, maybe, one fragment of a moment to jump before he fired. Her skin itched with the need to move, to leap—

—except before she could make the move, he turned around again and walked back to the helicopter. Climbed in and made an impatient gesture. The aircraft lifted off the ground again and flew off.

He hadn't seen her at all. He'd looked into the warehouse, but in the dark his human eyes hadn't seen her.

Chey let out a long desperate exhalation. That had been too close.

She couldn't stay in the warehouse, she knew. It wasn't far enough from Pickersgill's body. Bobby may not have been willing to check the place out himself, but he might send Balfour to do it. Balfour, who was the scariest of the three brothers, the "shootist."

If she was going to survive she had to find another place to hide. She looked down at Port Radium and saw the pond full of castoff machines corroding away in their polluted bath. Down there, certainly, there would be something.

Chey raced down the hill as quickly as she could manage. At one point her feet went out from under her and she rolled part of the way, dust and mud flecking her face, getting in her mouth, gravel pattering through her hair, stinging her eyes, but then she was up again, moving again. She splashed out into water that felt all wrong, thicker, stranger than water. Muck bloomed in great rolling clouds wherever she disturbed the surface and a bad saline stink came up to make her choke, a disused, decayed smell, wholly inorganic and asphyxiating. She coughed up bloody phlegm and spat it into the ripples around her legs. She pressed on.

fifty-six

Up near the top of the junk heap was what looked like a school bus. Most of its windows were still intact. If she could get inside of it she could hide, for a while at least. Of course, getting up there wasn't going to be easy, but that actually made it even more desirable as a refuge. As hard as it would be for her to climb up there, it would be next to impossible for a human being.

Directly ahead of her lay the enormous crumpled bulk of a tunnel borer, a big round machine with a toothed maw on one end. It must have been used to dig out the mines, back in the day, and she didn't doubt it had been great at cutting through solid rock. Its teeth were blunted by age and shiny with erosion now. A length of massive chain, each link as thick across as her thigh, lay draped over its cab. She grabbed onto the chain and pulled herself up, out of the polluted mud, climbing the links like a ladder. She dragged herself up on top of the borer and then stumbled across the side of a tailing heap, a pile of fist-sized rocks that crumbled under her touch.

There, ahead, she saw where a pile of metal rods had rusted

together into a thick stalk that jutted out from the side of the pile. The individual rods were no thicker than her thumb. She could swing up on top of the pile and then the school bus would be easy to get to.

She grabbed one of the rods and pulled on it. It gave, but just a little. She worried it might snap off in her hand. She looked down and saw that her footing was ridiculously bad. She had one foot on the loose tailings, the other on a flap of rusted metal that probably wouldn't support her weight.

It didn't matter. She had more important things to worry about than falling in the lake. Chey leaned out as far as she could and then jumped, swinging on the rod, all of her mass conspiring with gravity to pull down hard, to shear off a length of metal.

The rod held. She brought her feet up to get them on top of the pile, but missed.

Chey screamed a curse and swung back, got one foot on the tailings again. The skin of her palms screamed in agony where they held the rod. She paused a moment, but just a moment, and then shifted her grip on the rod.

As she readied herself for another swing she heard a flat snapping sound. Dust exploded next to her cheek, one of the rocks on the tailing heap spontaneously turning into gravel. Or maybe not so spontaneously.

Another snap, like a robot coughing, and something whizzed by her ear. Something hard and metallic. A silver bullet.

She turned in slow motion, unable to hurry anymore, and saw a human figure standing on the shore, holding a hunting rifle. Taking his time, he raised the rifle to his eye and sighted on her. She barely had time to jump before he fired a third bullet at her.

It could only be Tony Balfour shooting at her.

286

It didn't make a lot of sense. Silver bullets would be useless in a rifle. They would be too inaccurate. Bobby had been quite clear on that fact. Balfour had already put three bullets close to her head. He wasn't having any trouble with accuracy. Was he using normal lead bullets? But why?

He smiled. She could see his teeth by starlight. He switched the rifle over to the crook of his arm and then took a long knife out of a scabbard on his belt. The blade almost glowed in the darkness and she knew it was made of silver.

She understood. He wanted to shoot her with lead bullets not to kill her but just to stop her in her tracks. If he blew her head open with the rifle it wouldn't technically kill her—but it would leave her unable to run away. You need a functional medulla oblongata to be able to run. She imagined herself spread-eagled on the scrap heap, her blood leaking out on the rusty machinery, her eyes unable to focus, her mouth unable to close. In her mind's eye she saw drool leaking from one slack lip. Then she saw him climb up carefully, taking all the time he wanted, the knife ready in his hand.

Would she feel it as he stabbed her to death? Would she be aware even then? Would he do it quickly, one jab into her chest, or would he take his time?

He gave her a jaunty little wave and came toward her.

Down on the shore he stepped gingerly, almost delicately, into the dark water. The mud surged around his boots and he winced almost comically, but he didn't stop. One leg in, then the other, wading in hip deep. Then he stopped and looked up at her. He switched the rifle back into his hands and watched her expectantly.

She realized then that she hadn't moved a centimeter since he'd stopped firing. She needed to get up, she needed to run. Why didn't he fire?

He took his eye off the rifle's sights and lifted one hand. He flicked his fingers dismissively, telling her to move on. He wanted to see her run, she realized. He wanted to chase her because he would enjoy her death more that way.

Adrenaline surged in her blood and made her go. She didn't worry about her footing, just jumped across the pile of tailings and leapt onto the tires of an overturned truck. She got her hands down, grabbed for anything that presented itself, and threw herself around the side of the pile, toward the shadows, toward the toxic junk.

Behind her a bullet blew out one of the truck's tires and it deflated with a sagging, sighing sound. She flinched and missed a handhold. Her body rolled forward and she slid, her feet unable to grip the loose tailings beneath her. She was falling, sliding, falling in slow motion down the side of the heap. Suddenly she did care if she fell into the water. She would be slower down there, unable to run. Her hands flew out and she grabbed at a side mirror on the upside-down truck, a long rectangular shadow with splinters of broken glass winking at her. Her feet flew free and she was hanging by her arms in empty space. Her weaker left arm twitched as it tried to hold up her weight. The fingers uncurled and she swung like a pendulum by her right hand, and that arm felt pretty weak, too.

She couldn't hear him coming for her, but she knew he wouldn't be long behind.

fifty-seven

Her arm grew tired with alarming quickness. It wouldn't hold her weight for long. She looked down and saw a three-meter drop to muck and probably submerged rocks. Her feet kicked wildly, looking for purchase that just wasn't there. They knocked and hit against the side of the overturned truck. Maybe—maybe if she could get them inside the driver's window, which she saw was rolled down—maybe then she could—

The truck rumbled as if it were coming back to life. She heard clattering footfalls above her and knew that Balfour had climbed up on top of the dead vehicle. He stopped suddenly as the truck dipped forward. It had been dumped unceremoniously on the heap with no effort given to finding balance or stability. Now, disturbed after a long rest of many winters, it rocked in its bed.

With a creaking, tearing sound, as of metal being pulled to pieces, it lurched a few centimeters forward. The motion was enough to send Chey swinging. She clutched hard to the side mirror but knew she had only seconds before she would have to let go. Already her palm and all the joints of her fingers burned. Her left hand flailed to find something to hold onto.

One last effort. It was all she had in her. She brought her legs up as if she were on a trapeze and swung, hard, for the window of the truck. Her feet went through into darkness and then the lower half of her body followed. Her hand let go without warning and she nearly fell, but she braced herself with her legs and slithered inside the truck's cab like a mouse disappearing into a hole.

The truck moaned and slid forward again, dipped forward a millimeter at a time, with rocks and bits of debris pattering away with every grudging incremental motion. Then it stopped. Was Balfour still on top of it, clutching on for dear life? She was sure he must be.

The inside of the cab was almost warm compared to the outside world. The windshield remained intact except for one long diagonal crack, and it cut off the frigid breeze, at least. As a result, though, the air inside was close and it stank of mildew. There had been leather on the truck's seats once, but it had succumbed entirely to rot. Now Chey, lying on the ceiling of the cab, looked up into sharp-edged springs that poked down at her like coiled snakes ready to strike. The steering wheel, cracked and peeling, and the gearshift and controls looked all wrong from where she lay, but she didn't have time to think about it. She lay there gasping for breath with her mouth wide open, trying not to make too much noise.

She could not have gotten up at that moment, could not have moved from that spot, even if Balfour had climbed in beside her with his rifle and his silver knife.

Slowly she recovered herself. Very slowly. The truck had stopped moving—perhaps it had settled down into something approaching equilibrium. She heard a footstep from above her, a clattering noise. Balfour must have been wearing steel-toed boots. That first step sounded almost hesitant, as if he weren't sure of his footing. Then he clambered forward, moving steadily closer to her. She somehow found the energy to hold her breath. She heard him step almost directly above her—and then stop.

Then nothing happened. Her lungs complained. She let the breath out and still nothing happened. He must not have seen where she'd gone. He must be looking around up there, trying to follow her trail. He would not be able to see her, even if he were standing outside the cab looking in—the darkness where she lay was almost absolute.

She waited, and listened. And finally she heard the footsteps moving away.

Slowly Chey let herself relax, let her body shift into a more comfortable position inside the truck's cab. Finally she let herself exhale the breath she'd been holding.

Instantly Balfour surged forward. He must have been waiting for her to give herself away—waiting in ambush. His footfalls clattered on the underside of the truck and then he was climbing down the grill, using the bars there like a ladder. His feet swung into view through the windshield and then his legs. He dropped to the tailing pile in front of the truck, his whole body silhouetted in the windshield. Then he lifted a flashlight and switched it on and pointed the beam inside the cab. The light blinded Chey and she raised her hands to fend it off.

He drew a pistol from a pocket of his jacket. She had no way of knowing if the bullets inside were silver or lead—it didn't matter. He had her. She couldn't get out of the cab, not quickly enough to get away from him.

fifty-eight

"**O**kay," Balfour said. His voice matched him perfectly. Gruff, but not too low.

"Okay what?" she asked.

He gestured with the gun for her to climb out of the truck. Chey studied his face. There was no smile there anymore. He'd had his fun, and he'd won his game. Now he was just going to finish her off so he could collect on his contract. It was over.

Chey lifted herself from the ceiling of the cab with her arms and legs. Then with a sudden inspiration she threw herself forward, against the windshield. She didn't weigh all that much and she had little strength left to add to her momentum, but it was enough.

The truck screamed as metal tore apart from metal. Welds popped, rivets shot out like bullets. The whole massive multiton body of the truck scraped forward. Broken rock tailings rolled away, out from under all that mass, and the truck jumped forward as if it were moving on rails. Balfour's eyes went wide and he fired through the windshield. Chey couldn't see where the bullet had gone. A second later the truck rumbled forward, gaining speed, and smacked right into him. He was carried forward as the vehicle tilted down and fell into the water with a noisy splash and one extended bass note of metal folding in on itself.

The windshield had become the floor. Chey lay sprawled across it, groaning with pain. The fall had hurt, but not in such a way that it mattered—not in any way that could kill her. She rubbed her forehead and then opened her eyes.

Under the water, Balfour looked right back at her, lit up by the beam of his flashlight. His cap was gone and his sparse hair floated in the silver bubbles that streamed out of his mouth. She couldn't tell if he was alive or dead. His eyes were wide, very wide.

Then he slammed on the windshield with the flats of his hands, slapped at the glass as his mouth opened and toxic water poured in. Chey screamed as she saw the muscles of his face constrict, as he drowned while she watched. He was trapped under the weight of the truck, unable to get out from under. His muscles went slack—his hands drifted away—and finally, after far too long, his eyes lost their focus.

She made no move to save him.

Frigid water gurgled in through the bullet hole in the windshield and through the open window. It leaked around her body, soaked her clothes. The saline stink of the muck filled what little air there was in the cab. Chey jumped up, away from the touch of the water, and pushed her way back out through the open side window, just before the water surged over the sill of the window and filled the cab.

In the water she kicked and flailed and struggled to get clear. Making all the noise in the world, she scrambled out onto the shore and lay gasping on the bank, in pain, half-frozen, and knowing she wasn't done yet. Bobby was still out there. She needed to get up. She needed to run.

For some reason her arm hurt. She couldn't remember landing

on it when the truck hit the water. She thought she should take a look at it, maybe.

In a second, she promised herself. She stared up at the stars. In a second she would start again, she would get up and get moving. In just a second.

Above her the aurora borealis flickered and snapped like a windswept curtain. It was so beautiful. Green coruscations like waterfalls of pure light dazzled overhead. It was hard to look away. She didn't want to.

She had to—but she could give herself a second, she thought. Just a second to look, to see one last beautiful thing. In a second, she would—

Her arm really hurt. The pain was acid, eating away at her. It was poison rushing through her blood. It was—it was—

She managed to look down and saw blood welling from a wound in her bicep, staining her coveralls black in the darkness. A small, perfectly round hole had been punched right through the cloth.

Oh no, she thought. No. Balfour had fired at her right before he died. She'd thought the bullet had gone wild. It couldn't have hit her—she would have felt it. Wouldn't she have felt it? Unless shock and horror had flooded her bloodstream with adrenaline to the point she couldn't feel anything.

That was a gunshot wound, alright. And he'd fired it from a pistol. Which meant the bullet might be silver. If it was—if it was she had to do something; she had to—had to—she was so tired—she would have to dig it out, God it hurt, she had to—

Then Chey passed out.

The silver bullet in her arm was sapping her strength. She'd already pushed herself past her limits, and now she had nothing left to fight off the poison. Her body couldn't go another minute—it was just that simple.

She did not wake when the sun rose and warmed her chilled body. She did not wake hours later, when the moon came up too, and silver light transformed her.

Silver, silver, silver inside, silver.

The wolf stood up and panted into the wind.

Silver. Silver, silver, silver. The wolf knew exactly what was wrong. She felt weak, weaker than she ever had before. She felt sick, and thoughts of food made her sicker. She felt hot and cold at once, and she knew she was dying. There was silver in her leg—how had it gotten there? She couldn't even begin to imagine.

She lifted her hurt leg and grabbed it with her jaws. Pull it off. Bite it out and spit it in the poison water where it belongs. She had done as much before, to get out of chains.

Her teeth sank through her fur and then she was yelping and rolling on the ground, rolling her forehead along the hard ground, her eyes squinted tightly shut. Pain! Her teeth had touched the silver and her whole skull had erupted in pain, in agony. Her nerves sang a high thready note that buzzed in her ears and in her brains. She rolled and shook herself and warbled out a kind of muted scream until the pain had lessened a little, until she could think again.

She couldn't bite off the leg. She couldn't bite out the silver. Every fiber of her being cried out for relief, for comfort, but she had none to provide.

Silver, silver, silver, silver inside her, silver, poison silver!

She ran in circles. She ran in random directions as if she could get away from the pain. She tilted her head back and howled, howled and howled, yelped, mewled, roared. None of it helped. She heard the echo of an answer, a callback, from far away and she knew the other wolf must be nearby. Maybe—maybe he could help her. But would he? He had tried to kill her, hadn't he?

It didn't matter. He was the only possible source of help. She ran toward him and howled and followed his answering howls. They would meet. They would join together again. They would meet like packmates and he would help her. He would do something, something, something for her.

Before she'd even smelled him, though, a buzzing roar chopped up the night, chopped it to pieces. The human flying thing. The wolf could not conceive of what a helicopter was, but she knew what it was carrying—her death. She watched, her ears flicking back, as it came up over the far side of the junk heap and turned to head right for her.

The wolf ran.

fifty-nine

*S*ilver. *Silver silver.*

Silver in her body. Silver in the moon. Silver bullets that smacked the ground and whined away into darkness.

She ran—*silver. Silver silver silver.* Silver everywhere, she could smell it in the air. The only thing she was afraid of.

The wolf was very much afraid.

The wolf was terrified.

The wolf ran.

Silver. It came down like evil rain from the helicopter, bullets blasting away at the earth in the rhythm of her panting thoughts, of her laboring heart.

Silver silver silver silver silver.

She dashed around the side of the pond, her paws splashing in horrible water thick with toxic runoff. The helicopter bobbed and twisted on its rotor and came after her. She ran so slowly—her body ready to give out. Still the bullets came down, invisible rays that would cut through her. Cut her to pieces.

In the distance the other wolf howled. He was closer, much closer. Still too far to help.

She ran. Bullets tore up the ground to her left, to her right. The spitting gun up there could not seem to hit anything it aimed at, but she knew she had just been lucky so far. One of those bullets would hit her, eventually. And then she would die.

Silver cut the soil ahead of her. She wheeled and turned and ran right back toward the helicopter, as if she could charge it, as if she could leap high enough to get her claws in its metal belly. She snarled with joy as the helicopter actually bobbed in the air, rolling from side to side as if afraid of her. There were humans inside it, she knew. It was a man-made thing and there were humans, humans, humans inside. She could smell the blood inside them, smell the sweat on their skin. She even recognized the particular stink of one, the one, the one who had chained her. Oh, how she longed for the feel of his throat between her massive teeth.

A bullet came so close it kicked up shards of rock that got in her eye like dust. She shook her head and feinted to the left, then darted to the right.

A good move—the helicopter swung around wildly to follow her, wobbling, nearly turning on its side. But she was growing weaker. She couldn't run much farther.

He howled, so close now she could hear him running. What could he do? Would he give his life for hers, take the bullet meant for her skull? She doubted it. He had wanted to kill her, kill her, kill her—she'd been so wrong about him, this male— he was not her enemy. He was the only one who could help her. He was—he should be—her mate. She longed for him, crooned out a long lonely howl for him, for a moment forgetting to look where she was going—

Silver passed right through her front left paw.

She yelped in surprise, then yowled in pain. Her blood made a footprint on the ground. She was panting for breath already and this new wound made her curl, made her curl inside her belly, made her want to lie down, to surrender, to die. But those were men up there, humans, and she would not stop for them. She would never stand down for humans.

A hill ahead of her. It would be a hard climb, even if she were at full strength. It would slow her down. But there were buildings up there, big, square, unnatural buildings men had built, and their shadows blocked out the stars. If she could run between them, if she could, if she could, she was tiring already, if she could get between the buildings, into their shadows, the helicopter could not follow. She dug in with her hind legs and pushed, leapt, jumped up the slope.

Silver silver silver silver silver silver silver silver silver silver silver— it did not stop, shafts of moonlight falling all around her, shafts of silver moonlight frozen, hardened and made cruel, made deadly. The ground beneath her churned with the soft impacts as the bullets crashed around her.

There—the top of the slope, the crest, the summit, she could see it. She pushed and pushed and shoved herself through the air, leapt like a salmon leaping upstream. Ahead of her the buildings stood, wrong and square, her only possible salvation. She dashed down a side street and silver silver silver behind her, silver, she had no energy left, she could not run, she could only cower, *silver silver silver.*

A bullet passed within inches of her spine. It lodged in her liver and she felt her body surge with a new wave of poison. She screamed, screamed in horror and pain and rolled, rolled on her side and kept rolling, slid into a shadow, rolled into darkness. A bullet pranged off the metal side of a building just above her head.

Silver inside her, silver, silver inside her, silver in her guts, silver in her leg. She could not take another step. The pain was just too

299

great. She collapsed in a heap, then strained, pushed, lifted herself onto her feet. She gathered up her breath and gave voice to one last howl, a cry of a dying being, a plaintive, one-note symphony.

Above her the helicopter sank through the cold air, its noise so big, so loud, so big. Silver, once, banged off the building face, even closer to her this time. Silver again. Bang. The helicopter dropped farther, dropped to the level of the building's roof. There was nothing she could do but watch her death come for her.

Then he, the other wolf, leapt from the roof of the building and got his claws in the plastic bubble of the helicopter. His body swung like a pendulum, loose and muscular, as the helicopter rolled and dipped and turned. His weight pulled it around, dragged it through the air. He was shaken free almost instantly, his body thrown through the air, but not before he had overbalanced the helicopter on its rotor, made it list to one side.

The tip of the rotor kissed the corrugated tin wall of the building with a high-pitched shriek. In that contest neither side could win—the wall peeled open as if by the effect of a giant can opener, while the composite resin of the rotor splintered and snapped. The helicopter slewed around on a wide arc, suddenly off-center of its own angular momentum. As if a giant had thrown it like a discus, it swerved through the air, out of control, until it smashed into the side of another building. Then it just dropped like a rock. Sounds of tearing metal, of crumpling plastic, and of human screams followed. There was a flicker of light and then fire lit up Port Radium for the first time in decades as the helicopter's fuel caught, all at once. It didn't burn for long.

sixty

He came for her, the other wolf. She had seen him fall through the air, and though she had not heard him smack into the ground she knew he must have been hurt when he landed. He did favor one hind leg—maybe the other had broken on impact. He did not mewl or whine as he slinked through the shadows, his muzzle twitching as he sniffed for her.

When he found her she was barely conscious. Her breath came in and out, in and out, shallow draughts of air wheezing in and out, in and out of her lungs. It was not even panting, but the labored breathing of one about to die.

She had silver inside her. She was poisoned and she was done for. He did not waste time greeting her, but fell upon her at once with a vicious snarl. With his powerful jaws he tore at her, pulled her apart. He ripped open her guts and they spilled with a rank smell across the broken road surface. He tore off her leg and threw it into the darkness like so much poisoned meat.

The pain was intense, but she could not complain or fight him off. She lacked the energy to even raise her head. He tore and bit and ripped her apart and she could only experience it passively, as if from some remove.

Somehow she knew that he wasn't killing her.

That he was saving her.

When he was done, when all the silver was torn out of her body and cast away from her, she breathed a little easier, and then she sank into a fitful sleep. He stood watch over her throughout the night, occasionally howling as the moon rode its arc across the night sky. Occasionally he would lick her face, her ears, to wake her up, to keep her from fading out of existence altogether. Once when he could not wake her he grabbed her by the back of the neck and shook her violently until her eyes cracked open and her tongue leapt from her mouth and she croaked out a whine of outrage.

When the moon sank behind the buildings of Port Radium, she was glad for it. For the first time ever the wolf was glad for the change.

Chey woke curled in a ball, naked, cold, hungry, and in massive amounts of pain, but she was alive. She lifted her left arm and saw there was no blood there. Nor was there any bullet wound. She touched herself all over, felt her smooth skin and found it unbroken.

Her head pounded, but she rolled up to a sitting posture. She had no idea what had happened during the night. She knew somehow, though, that Bobby was dead. The exact circumstances eluded her, but she was sure of it.

"Here," Powell said, and he threw her a blanket. He'd been standing behind her the whole time. He was wrapped in a blanket himself and he sat down next to her, close enough that his

302

body heat warmed her a little. She snuggled closer to him and pulled his arm around her shoulders.

He seemed surprised when she pulled him close. "You forgiven me or something?" he asked.

"Never," she told him, honestly.

"But things have changed between us."

She shrugged her shoulders. That wasn't good enough, though. "Yes," she said. "I want to stay with you. I don't want to be alone anymore."

"Fair enough," he said.

The sun was halfway up the sky when they moved again. They'd both heard a sound, a familiar and unwanted sound. The noise a helicopter makes as it cuts up the air. Together, pulling their blankets close around themselves, they jumped up and moved around the side of the abandoned hangar, keeping to the shadows.

A big double-rotor helicopter passed over the buildings of Port Radium. Chey recognized the symbol painted on its underbelly, a red maple leaf inside a blue circle. She also had a feeling she knew who was inside.

Before Powell could stop her she ran out into the parking lot and waved her arms at the helicopter. The pilot brought it around and then dropped to a soft landing twenty meters away. A hatch opened on its side and soldiers in blue-gray uniforms jumped out. Behind them came a man in a dark blue suit. It looked like a uniform, but it wasn't. The man was retired and he wasn't even Canadian.

Chey couldn't hear anything over the noise of the rotors. Uncle Bannerman gestured at the soldiers and they all stood back. Then he dashed over toward her, only stopping when she held her hands out, warning him to keep his distance. "Listen," she said, "I'm okay. Everything's okay. But I'm going to change in a little while." She could feel the moon trembling on the horizon. In fifteen minutes, maybe less, it would rise. She didn't know if the soldiers standing in formation by the helicopter had silver bullets. She didn't want to find out. "You have to go now."

He stared right into her eyes. The way he always had. Then he glanced sideways at Powell, who was lingering in the shadowy entrance of the hangar building. Bannerman studied Powell for a second and then looked back at her.

"Is he . . . ?" Bannerman asked.

The lycanthrope who ate my brother, your father. She could see the words in her uncle's eyes.

"Yes," she said.

"I have equipment with me. I can keep you safe. I can keep you from hurting anyone," he told her. It was a question.

She could guess what kind of equipment he meant. Chains. Cages. Maybe he wanted to take her back to his ranch in Colorado, where he could lock her in a shed every time the moon came up.

That wasn't acceptable to her. It would never be acceptable. She was a werewolf, and she needed to be free. If he locked her up she would go insane.

"I'm going with him," she said. Powell took a step forward, but she waved him back. "We'll go where there aren't any people."

There was a lot more to be said—Bannerman clearly wanted to argue with her—but she had no more time. She was going to change any minute.

"I don't know what happened to Fenech," he said, finally, "but I doubt the Canadians will just leave you alone." It was a warning—not a threat, not an attempt to make her change her mind. She thanked him with a nod.

Three minutes later the helicopter was in the air and headed south.

A moment later the moon rose, and two wolves headed north.

acknowledgements

A much shorter and less polished version of this book appeared online in 2006. I'd like to thank everyone who read and commented on that version—your thoughts helped make this version so much better. I'd especially like to thank briangc, who suggested the title, which is often the hardest part of writing a book. Regarding the current incarnation of the book, I'd like to thank Russell Galen and Carrie Thornton, who saw it with fresh eyes and decided it had potential, and Julian Pavia, who did such an excellent job editing it. Jay Sones and all the great people at Three Rivers Press deserve thanks for their tireless work. As always I would be remiss if I did not thank Alex Lencicki and my very patient wife, Elisabeth Sher.

Watch out for David Wellington's next werewolf novel,
coming soon from Piatkus:

RAVAGED

Be careful what you search for. You just might find it . . .

When a strange wolf slashed Cheyenne Clark's ankle to the bone,
her old life ended, and she became the very monster that haunted her
nightmares for years. Worse, the only one who can understand what
Chey has become is Powell, the man – or wolf – who's doomed
her to this fate.

They vow to find the release to the curse, yet as the line between
human and beast blurs, so too does the distinction between hunter
and hunted. Because someone is on the trail of Powell and Chey,
determined to get revenge – someone as deadly and as fierce
as they are . . .

978-0-7499-5243-3

Other Piatkus titles available now:

THE HARROWING

Baird College's Mendenhall echoes with the footsteps of students heading home for Thanksgiving break and Robin Stone, who won't be going home, swears she can feel the creepy, hundred-year-old residence hall breathe a sigh of relief for its long-awaited solitude. As a massive storm approaches, four other lonely students reveal themselves to Robin: Patrick, a handsome jock; Lisa, a manipulative tease; Cain, a brooding musician; and Martin, a scholarly eccentric. Each has forsaken a long weekend at home for their own secret reasons.

The five unlikely companions establish a tentative rapport, but they soon become aware of another presence disturbing the building's ominous silence. Are they the victims of an elaborate prank, or is the energy evidence of something genuine – something intent on using them for its own terrifying ends?

978-0-7499-4158-1

THROUGH
VIOLET EYES

In a world where the dead can testify against the living,
someone is getting away with murder.

To every generation a select few souls are born with violet-
coloured eyes – and the ability to channel the dead. Both rare and
precious, and rigidly controlled by a society that craves their
services, these Violets perform a number of different social duties.

But now the Violets themselves have become the target of a brutal
serial murderer – a murderer who has learned how to mask his or
her identity even from the victims. Can FBI agent Dan Atwater,
aided by Violet Natalie Lindstrom, uncover the criminal in time?
Or will more of Natalie's race be dispatched to the realm that has
haunted them all since childhood?

978-0-7499-4127-7

Other bestselling titles available by mail: